EAT THE EVIDENCE

EAT THE EVIDENCE

A Journey Through the Dark Boroughs of a Pedophilic Cannibal's Mind

Part One

John C. Espy

KARNAC

First published in 2014 by
Karnac Books Ltd
118 Finchley Road
London NW3 5HT

British Library Cataloguing in Publication Data

A C.I.P. for this book is available from the British Library

ISBN-13: 978-1-78220-033-8

Typeset by V Publishing Solutions Pvt Ltd., Chennai, India

Printed in Great Britain

www.karnacbooks.com

For Treasa Glinnwater

"I'm just a kid magnet"
—Personal communication,
Nathaneal Benjamin Levi Bar Jonah to the author,
Cascade County Detention Center, February 2002

"So we boiled my son, and did eat him: and I said unto her on
the next day, Give thy son, that we may eat him"
—King James Version, 2 Kings 6:29

ACKNOWLEDGEMENTS

This book was culled from hundreds of hours of interviews with Nathaneal Bar Jonah and dozens of others who either knew or were involved with him in some way. A deep appreciation and thank you is extended to Brandt Light, then Prosecuting Attorney of Cascade County, Montana and currently the Attorney General, Criminal Division for the State of Montana, for his invaluable assistance and availability. Special Agent James Wilson of the FBI gave many hours of his time to discuss aspects of the case. A special thank you is extended to the lead investigator on the Bar Jonah case, John Cameron, without whose assistance this book could not have been written. Mr. Cameron was willing to give unselfishly of his time and to provide additional "footwork" in a case that has long been closed. It was Cameron's dedication that ultimately kept Bar Jonah off of the streets. Detective Tim Theisen was also integral in the investigation and ultimate apprehension of Bar Jonah and also provided invaluable assistance during the last phases of this project. Detective William Bellusci also gave many hours of his time to the author. B. J. Spamer, forensic analyst with the University of North Texas Center for Human Identification, made arrangements for the retesting of bone fragments and offered guidance on matters related to DNA analysis. A deep appreciation is expressed to Rachel Howard, for her willingness to grant the author many hours of her time to be interviewed for this book. This was the first time that Ms. Howard has been willing to publicly discuss matters related to the disappearance of her son Zachary. Mystery writer John Herrmann was a continual source of richness and friendship, always available to offer suggestions, criticism, and encouragement.

There were countless others who, because of the subject matter and fear of self-incrimination, have chosen to remain nameless. These individuals offered extensive insights and information into the background and character of Bar Jonah, Doc Bauman and other pedophiles. Many of these individuals were practicing pedophiles themselves. Extensive public record criminal background information was also examined regarding Doc Bauman. Emmy award winning film maker, Melanie Perkins was instrumental in providing critical pieces of historical information regarding associates of Bar Jonah. Extensive material was also culled from the public record regarding this case.

A deep and everlasting "Thank you" and loving appreciation is expressed to my wife, psychotherapist, poet, and photographer, Treasa Glinnwater, who planted the seed that germinated into this book. Treasa's belief in this project and her support has been unwavering. This book could not only have not been done without her but is dedicated to her. Treasa also interviewed Bar Jonah. That interview turned out to be pivotal. It was during the interview with Treasa that Bar Jonah first acknowledged having any understanding of coding. It was *the* ground-breaking interview that resulted in Bar Jonah making countless revelations to the author during subsequent interviews. Bar Jonah adamantly stated that our conversations, outside of what was needed for the court related evaluation, could not be used or revealed to anyone, in any way until after his death. He said that he only had one fear and that was not being able to get into Heaven. Bar Jonah believed that he was doing the work of God, *"But*, one could never be absolutely sure," he said. Bar Jonah was a serial pedophile and by all accounts a serial murderer. His heinous reign began when he was but a small child and ended when he was finally arrested for the last time in December 1999. However, his impact on the lives of others outside of the prison did not end there. This is the first biography that has been written about a serial pedophile. My desire in writing this biography was to not only take the reader inside the inner world of a serial pedophile but also to allow the reader to *experience* someone as pathologically primitive as Bar Jonah from *within*. For many, this will be very disturbing and difficult to read and will most likely be a criticism of the book. However, it is imperative for the reader to understand that pedophiles live for *only* one purpose and that is to manifest their pedophilia. *Everything* that the pedophile does is to find a way to express this profoundly primitive psychological state of being. Inherent in the world of the pedophile is the aspect of lying, deception, and manipulation; they are the life's blood of his inner and interpersonal world and are manifest through a primitive psychological mechanism called *projective identification*.

It is critical for parents and law enforcement to conceptualize how a pedophile lives and functions within their world. It is also critical to understand that pedophiles do not live in isolation. They find and interrelate with each other through a sophisticated network of interpersonal subterranean psychopathy. Children are rarely chosen at random. Rather, the pedophile trolls for a child that "fits" his primitive pathological desires. He then grooms the child. The grooming involves, if you will, tenderizing children psychologically, opening them up, discovering their vulnerabilities, and then exploiting them. Even when it appears that children have been taken randomly, it is rarely the case. They have usually been marked well before their abduction or assault ever occurs. To understand who the serial pedophile is, is to understand how he lures a victim into his psychological lair, uncoils and strikes. Finally, an acknowledgement needs to be made of the many victims of Bar Jonah whose lives were irreconcilably altered by his heinousness.

CHAPTER ONE

Beginnings

There was something about the suppleness of a youthful neck that Bar Jonah never lost his taste for, even with the bigger boys, whose thick neck veins would pop out when they began to realize what was happening to them. And those suddenly startled eyes. It was, he said, the closest thing he had ever known to the sensual. Even more than eating. Those first moments of wrapping his egg-shaped fingers around the throat of a child. The feeling of a neck beginning to give way in his hands. His fingers so strong, the neck so breakable. Then, he would lose control. The brutal jarring and his guttural grunting as he violently threw their heads back and forth seemed to be what his victims remembered most. There were some that would also remember his smell.

Bar Jonah liked to break his victims. To create a fissure in their being that would last a lifetime so that when the thin-membrane scar of the crevasse was ruptured, the hydra would re-emerge and consume them once again from the inside out. At least with one victim however, he not only broke him, he also ate him.

He graduated to ropes and tape as he continued to refine his ways. It was less work, he would say. The older he got, the lazier he became, preferring that his victims came to him. Bar Jonah believed that he was a partisan of God, one who was set forth on a campaign to punish those children who enticed good men to commit evil. He was precocious in his savagery, beginning early in his youth to condition his hands to the feel of a child's neck.

* * *

It would eventually become known as a place of peace. Until then, many battles between warring Indian factions were waged along the banks of Lake Chargoggagoggmanchaugga-goggchaubunagungamaugg. It is rumored that there are many skulls buried in the lakebed. There are some who think that Bar Jonah may have tossed a few skulls into the great lake too.

Even at a young age, Bar Jonah could rhythmically recite the entire name of "Lake Char-gogg/a-gogg/man-chaugg/a-gogg/chau-bun/a-gun/ga-maugg" without taking a breath or missing a syllable. Most of the locals just call it Lake Webster. The lake was but a short walk from where Bar Jonah spent his early years. Webster, Massachusetts was not unlike most New England towns in the 1950s: tidy neighborhoods, morning coffee klatches where housewives got together and gossiped about the neighbor who couldn't make it that day, backyard cook-outs, and silent butlers filled with the burnt-out ends of smoky days. The husbands worked mainly in factories or construction and did projects in their garages on the weekends. Old growth trees shaded the streets and friendly competition among neighbors was an expected way of life. Resentment-laden questions wrapped in a cheerful mistrust abounded for the neighbors who had the money to afford a new car every year.

The Phillip and Tyra Brown family lived in a gabled, white frame house in Bonnett Acres, around a slight bend in the road. There was a driveway on the right side and a tall, white slat fence around the back yard that bordered the steep hill behind the house. If you went high enough over the hill, you could fall off the other side right down into Lake Webster. In the back of the house was the garage. Phillip's tools took up a lot of room, so there really wasn't any place to put the car. He had a well-pounded workbench in the back and quarter-inch plywood nailed to the 2 × 4 girders with ten-penny nails. Phillip's hammers, screwdrivers, channel-lock pliers, dikes, and wrenches fit just right into the wire loops that he had fashioned from bent coat-hangers. When he got some more money, he always said he was going to hang some gypsum lath too.

Beside the driveway were tall hedges that gave the Browns some sense of privacy. On the other side, lawns intersected so the question always came up about whose yard belonged to whom. The DuPonts lived right next door to the Browns. Phillip constantly complained about how trashy their yard was and how their seven boys ran wild throughout the neighborhood. It wasn't long after old man DuPont put in a swimming pool that Phillip insisted on having one too. But the DuPonts never kept their pool up. Phillip was constantly leaning over the hedge and yelling at old man DuPont to clean up the damn thick green water that was stinkin' up his back yard.

If you went out the Browns' front door and walked across the street, you would walk right smack dab into Connecticut. The state line ran straight down the middle of the road. All the kids thought it was pretty funny and would play a game jumping from one state to the other.

Turning right out the Browns' door and walking about a hundred yards up a little hill would take you to the woods. Scoot your feet down a little embankment and you could take a dip in that part of the lake. Sitting along the bank, imagining they were part of the polished Chris Craft promenade, was what every man on the street dreamed about. It was a declaration to all that you had made it. Phillip Brown had no boat.

The blessed event

At age forty-one, Tyra Brown started bleeding and expelled a zygotish looking thing, thinking she must have miscarried. A few weeks later, Tyra went to her doctor and said she was still feeling like she did when she was pregnant with her other two kids, even though she thought she had lost the baby.

In those days, pregnancy was determined by doing what became known as the rabbit test. When a woman is pregnant, she excretes a hormone in the urine called human chlorionic gonadotropin. A urine sample was taken and injected into the nape of the neck of a New Zealand white rabbit. A few days later, the rabbit's neck was broken, its abdomen cut open and its fallopian tubes examined. If the fallopian tubes were puffy and swollen, the woman was pregnant. Even though *all* the rabbits died as part of the test, it became a cliché to say "the rabbit died," meaning, you're pregnant. In Tyra's case, the rabbit died. She was still pregnant.

At the end of Tyra's first trimester, another driver slammed into the back of her car while she was sitting at a red light. She had to be in a neck brace the last six months of her pregnancy. Tyra said she didn't know if there was any damage to the fetus but her doctor assured her everything was okay. The doctor told Tyra he could hear a strong heartbeat when he put the cold bell of the double-tube stethoscope to her swelling belly. Around the end of the fifth month, Tyra was concerned because the baby wasn't moving much. Her other kids had moved around a lot more. Every baby was different, her doctor said.

* * *

In the early morning hours of February 15, 1957, at Fairlawn Hospital in Wooster, Massachusetts, 8.5 pound David Paul Brown, who on March 22, 1984 changed his name to Nathaneal Benjamin Levi Bar Jonah, was born. Dr. Baker told Tyra the baby was twisted around a bit as he was coming down the birth canal. But once they got him turned around the right way, he came out as smooth as a whistle. There were no problems at birth, other than it took him a bit to start breathing. A few swats to his bottom and he pinked right up.

Tyra said he developed normally, for the most part, with the exception that he was insatiable and *always* had to be eating. The baby also slept for a lot longer than her other two kids, Tyra noticed. When he was awake, he cried all day long. There was almost no way to console him, leaving Tyra confused and often feeling helpless and frustrated. The only way to calm him down him was to feed him.

Tears would stream down Tyra's face once Bar Jonah started teething, as he chewed on her nipples when he nursed. Trying to pull him off only made him bite harder. When Tyra picked up her son, he would stiffly arch his body backwards and toss his head to one side. She said it felt like he was trying to snap himself right out of her arms. With his voracious appetite, he quickly gained so much weight that he became difficult to carry around. In many ways he seemed more comfortable when he wasn't being touched, evidently preferring to be left alone except to be fed or diapered. Tyra said that she could never describe him as an active baby.

People always seemed to be commenting on his stubby little hands and feet. Photographs of Bar Jonah as an infant show a fat, flabby baby with little muscle tone. Tyra said Phillip was also bothered by how small Bar Jonah's penis and testicles were. Somehow it was a personal affront to Phillip and made him angry. He called Bar Jonah's testicles, "BB nuts." Bar Jonah always seemed to have bruises that popped up out of nowhere on his arms and legs. His mother began to find them when he got old enough to move around in his crib. At night Tyra would put Bar Jonah in the middle of the crib, padding the sides with soft rolled-up baby blankets.

* * *

5

When excessive spinal fluid builds up inside the skull, it causes what is known as hydrocephaly. It is especially dangerous to an infant's fragile developing brain. When this happens, the brain becomes too crowded inside the skull. As the fluid continually builds up, it causes the brain to contort from its natural shape, impeding its ability to grow and develop normally. It also causes the head to enlarge to accommodate the excess fluid. In the 1950s, people with hydrocephaly were called water heads. Early photographs of Bar Jonah show a baby with characteristics of a water head. At three weeks old, his head was enormous-looking, swollen, and bulbous, making him appear older than he was.

When Bar Jonah was about six months old, he came down with a fever. It lasted four days, spiraling upwards to 106°. On the third day, Tyra took him to the hospital where they were able to cool Bar Jonah down by bathing him in a corrugated steel tub filled with ice water. In the 1950s, high fevers weren't thought to be that much of a problem either. Unless there was some immediate indication that something had gone wrong, everything was assumed to be okay. "He'll outgrow it" was the common reassuring cliché given by physicians. We now know this is frequently not the case. High fevers are one of the main culprits of early brain damage in infants. The longer a fever lasts, the greater the possibility of permanent injury. After his fever lessened, the doctors assured Phillip and Tyra that he would be fine.

One afternoon, a few weeks after the fever, Tyra was looking into Bar Jonah's almond shaped eyes. For a moment she thought something was wrong with her vision. She took him over to the window where the light was better. Sure enough, one of his blue eyes had turned brown. In Greek mythology, chimeras were thought to be fire-breathing monsters with a lion's head, a goat's body, and a serpent's tail. One thing we do know is that different color eyes are one of the first signs of chimerism, and that something went awry in the womb. If an

6

expectant mother is pregnant with twins and one miscarries, the whole fetus is usually expelled. In rare cases, not all of the fetal tissue passes out of the mother. Instead, some of the aborted tissue gets absorbed *into* the other fetus. This is known as chimerism. There are no predictors of how this will impact the developing fetus. Even more of a mystery is what happens if leftover brain tissue from one fetus is absorbed into the brain tissue of the remaining fetus. Because this is almost completely unexplored, no one knows how this will affect the developing child. There is speculation that an inflammatory response may occur in the brain, resulting in ongoing brain damage. A question would always remain as to whether or not Bar Jonah manifested any traits consistent with chimerism. He may well have manifested a neurological inflammatory response consistent with chimerism, which would contribute to a more comprehensive understanding of Bar Jonah's many anomalies.

About six months after the high fever, Tyra's problems with Bar Jonah dramatically got worse. He would pull away even more, making it more difficult to soothe and comfort him. Bar Jonah went from being difficult to almost impossible. Screaming tantrums became a regular part of his daily routine.

Tyra was an attractive woman, about four foot eight, narrow of lip, and strong of jaw. In one photograph, she is dressed in a light print dress that shows her small waist and full bodice. She is wearing rhinestone glasses that magnify her deep-set tired eyes. She is not smiling. Tyra is standing stiffly, her shoulders back and her knees locked tight. She looks somewhat disheartened in the photograph. She said she didn't remember the picture or when it was taken, but she did say she it was after Bar Jonah was born.

Tyra was the easy-going, understanding parent while Phillip, according to Tyra, was more of the stubborn disciplinarian and difficult to get along with. In the family photo album, Phillip looks hardened and detached, his shoulders rolled forward with long arms, big hands, aloof eyes. Phillip was an aircraft mechanic, who at five foot seven would struggle to reach parts taller men could easily to get to. In private moments, Phillip used to complain to Tyra how inadequate it made him feel, when the other mechanics would poke fun of him. Early in Bar Jonah's life, Phillip moved his family to Lantana, Florida to work for McDonnell Douglas Aviation. The family was in Florida about six years, before they moved back to Massachusetts where Phillip took a job as a heavy equipment mechanic for a local construction firm. It was in Lantana where Bar Jonah, at barely seven years old, would first try to strangle one of his playmates.

Bar Jonah, later in his life, would cast Phillip Brown as one of the main villains responsible for the heinous crimes he committed. Claims of being beaten by Phillip, with a thick black strap of leather that he called a Garrett belt, was one of the few things that Bar Jonah ever told the truth about. There were many times Tyra would stop Phillip from beating Bar Jonah with the belt or his fists. Phillip seemed to hate Bar Jonah right from the beginning. He told Tyra shortly before he died that he always knew Bar Jonah was queer. How he had been able to bear it all those years, he just didn't know. Phillip said he knew the other men at work talked about how his son was queer. The idea that Bar Jonah was "that way" was so distasteful to Phillip that he would hock and spit whenever he thought about it.

Phillip and Tyra Brown's other two children were Robert and Lois. According to Tyra, they were easy children who never got into any more trouble than other kids their age. When Lois and her mother would later reminisce about Lois's misadventures, they were light-hearted stories told with affectionate smiles and good memories. When recalling Bar Jonah, however, Lois's face would flush and her eyes would suddenly take on a weather-worn look, as she cast them heavily toward the ground.

CHAPTER TWO

The morass of childhood

Bar Jonah started stealing from Bob almost as soon as he could walk. Bob said that Bar Jonah also began telling far-fetched lies from the moment he was able to string sentences together. He would regularly steal his brother's Davy Crockett card collection and his prized cat-eye marbles. Sometimes he'd stuff the marbles in his mouth, and walk around the house with his cheeks bulging. When he was caught, he would lie as he muttered through the wet marbles rolling around in his mouth, "Bi bibbent dake dem."

Bob said even early on, he didn't have any interest in cultivating a relationship with Bar Jonah. He didn't believe he would have been able to, even if he had tried. Bar Jonah was incredibly lazy, having no interest in bathing or cleaning up his room; even for a little kid, he stunk. Lois, however, did play with her little brother, dressing him up in girls' clothes, saying how much she longed to be a mother. She said she had no memory of ever having even one conversation of substance with Bar Jonah. Lois recalled there was never an ebb and flow to their interactions. He was only interested in himself and never in anyone else, unless he thought he could get something out of it. Even as a kid, she said, he was good at feigning concern and interest in order to convince someone he was not only harmless but also blameless.

At five, Bar Jonah began to have toothaches, severe toothaches. Sometimes he would cry for hours. The pain in his jaws was debilitating. Tyra and Phillip continually took him to the dentist. The dentist said his teeth were rotting out of his head. He had little if any enamel coating. His teeth were abscessing at an alarming rate. The massive amounts of sugar he ate only added to the rate of the decay. But sugar was not the culprit. Tyra had taken a medication during her pregnancy that inhibited the production of enamel. By the time his permanent teeth began to come in at seven, he had only half of his baby teeth left. He chewed his food with calloused gums. Several times the dentist had to lance his gums so his permanent teeth would be able to break through.

Bar Jonah said it was a late summer afternoon when the boxer, whose ears weren't clipped, showed up in his back yard. He was just barely into his sixth year, playing by the back fence near the pile of brush that despite promising Tyra, Phillip never seemed to get around to picking up. Phillip, looking out the screen door, saw the long eared boxer run wildly into the yard. Before Phillip could get to Bar Jonah, the dog was already viciously attacking him. The dog, foaming at the mouth, knocked Bar Jonah down, biting him on his hands and back. Phillip grabbed a shovel leaning against the back of the house and beat the dog in the head. It tried to attack Phillip too, but he was able to keep it away with the shovel before it took off running out the gate. Phillip yelled for Tyra who came running around the side of the house. They cleaned Bar Jonah's wounds, put him in the car and drove to the hospital. Tyra reported the dog to the police once they arrived at the ER. It had also attacked a couple of other neighbor kids earlier that day, the cops said when she called. When one of the police officers cornered the dog it attacked him too before he could shoot it.

In 1963 the hyperimmune antirabies serum was commonly used to treat rabies exposure though it was known to have neurological side effects that could potentially cause damage to the frontal lobes. The alternative however was certain death. The ER physician vigorously scrubbed Bar Jonah's wounds, cutting off stray bits of torn skin before he sutured him up. For two weeks Bar Jonah had to have daily injections of antirabies serum into his abdomen. He had to go back on the tenth and twentieth day for his last two shots. Tyra said he was a tough boy though and didn't cry once.

* * *

At six, he began picking his skin. It would usually start with a sore or a cut. Bar Jonah would pick and pick and pick until the sore was festering. If he didn't have a sore he would find a loose piece of skin and pick it until it bled, sucking on the blood, telling Tyra how much he liked the salty taste. But it was always better if there was a scab that he could pull off and eat. Bar Jonah said Tyra even tried putting tape on his fingers or make him wear cotton work gloves, but he'd just pull them off. His teachers at Webster Elementary School called Tyra over and over again telling her she had to do something about her son; picking his open sores was upsetting the other children. When Tyra took Bar Jonah to the doctor, he said there was really nothing medicine had to offer. He was just a difficult boy with a nervous habit.

Many years later the guards at Montana State Prison also complained about Bar Jonah picking the blemishes on his face, rolling the skin around between his fingertips and then popping the little balls of flesh into his mouth. Even to the guards, who had seen just about everything, there was something unreal about, not just the act, but also the intense pleasure Bar

Jonah seemed to take when he rolled the scab remnant around in his mouth. One guard said it looked like he was having sex.

Mary

In late July 1964, right before the Browns moved back to Massachusetts, Mary, their five-year-old neighbor, came over to play with Bar Jonah. He had told Mary that he got a Ouija board for his birthday. It could predict the future, he said. Tyra answered the door to Mary's soft little knock and told her that Bar Jonah was down in the basement. A short time later Tyra heard a commotion. As she went down the stairs, she saw Bar Jonah. Tyra said his head "looked like a cherry getting ready to pop." His hands were wrapped around Mary's throat, violently shaking and choking her. Tyra screamed at Bar Jonah. Bar Jonah said she "screamed seven times." He finally uncurled his hands from around the little girl's throat, sat down on the floor and started screaming that he hadn't done anything. Mary had grabbed *his* hands and put them around her throat, Bar Jonah said. She made him choke her. Tyra later called the child's mother to see if Mary was okay, and to apologize for what Bar Jonah had done. Mary's mother told Tyra her son was sick; if he was a dog they'd put him down, she said. She also told Tyra her daughter would never be allowed around Bar Jonah again. If Tyra didn't keep Bar Jonah away from her child, she'd call the cops.

One strange boy

Phillip and Tyra would often lie awake, talking long into the night, trying to figure out how to control Bar Jonah's developing proclivities for violence, lying, and stealing. Tyra thought it would be best if she became Bar Jonah's chauffeur and constant tender. When Bar Jonah incessantly demanded to be taken where he wanted to go immediately, Tyra mostly agreed.

She said she figured if she didn't take him, he'd find some way of getting there anyway, so she thought it best if she just gave in to his demands. Phillip became increasingly more distant, wanting even less to do with his son.

Bar Jonah threw temper tantrums sometimes lasting hours if his demands for candy were not immediately met. He constantly stole food, be it candy, cakes, or pie. It wasn't that the family did not have enough. Bar Jonah, by his own admission, said they always had a well-stocked pantry. He declared, "I just love to eat, I can't get enough food, I'm always hungry."

Apples, apples, apples, there *had* to be apples all over the house. Bar Jonah was obsessed with apples. Walking through the house Tyra would find apple cores sitting on top of the television, tossed in a plant pot, or tucked under his pillow. When Tyra took Bar Jonah with her grocery shopping he would come out of the store with his pockets stuffed full of apples that he had stolen. It was a constant job trying to stop him from stealing. When she confronted him, he denied not only stealing them, but even having them in his obviously bulging pockets. Tyra would march him back into the market and try to make him tell the clerk that he had taken them. Tyra said he never *once* admitted that he took anything. He would toss the apples on the checkout counter, smirk, and calmly say, "I didn't put 'um in my pockets, I don't know how they got there. She's lying." Tyra described a time, when Bar Jonah ran out of a grocery store screaming, flailing his arms in the air, after she made him return the apples he had taken. He then squatted down beside cars in the store parking lot and watched for Tyra's feet as she walked around, calling his name. She spent more than two hours looking for him. Later, laughing about this incident, Bar Jonah said he always liked to be one step ahead of mother; "It was good practice."

Sometime in early spring, 1965, Bar Jonah sat down to dinner with his family and as always he heaped his plate high with roast beef, mashed potatoes, gravy, and fresh green beans.

Somewhere in the middle of his second helping, he suddenly pushed his chair back from the table, and asked if he could be excused. Phillip nodded yes, and took a deep drag on his cigarette in between bites of dinner. Bar Jonah got up, went over to the telephone stand, picked up the Boston phone book, and went to his room. The family was puzzled, but not surprised at his odd behavior. Later that evening Tyra went to check on him. Bar Jonah was sprawled across the bed, phone book open, writing lists of names page by page. Beginning with the As, he didn't stop until he copied eight thousand names onto sheets of thin white onion skin typing paper. Shortly after he made the list, he began writing letters to as many of the names on the list as he could. The letters were brief. They were out-of-the-blue requests for any boys of the families to become his pen pal. He received a few responses, but more important, Tyra received numerous calls from parents saying how peculiar it was to receive a random letter from someone they didn't know, trying to solicit their children as pen pals. This was the first time Bar Jonah made what might be termed an attempt at collecting, through the thinly-veiled illusion of connecting. This was a pattern Bar Jonah would repeat over and over again throughout his life.

Later that year, Tyra picked up Bar Jonah from school to take him with her to Sears, to shop for curtains for her newly remodeled kitchen. Bar Jonah liked to go places with his mother, so it took little convincing to get him to go. He also liked to take off at the first opportunity to escape from his mother's meddlesome eyes. As Tyra was looking at the curtains, Bar Jonah slipped away.

A few minutes later, Tyra heard her name being paged over the store intercom, "Would Mrs. Brown come to plumbing immediately … *please*." As Tyra began walking across the store looking for plumbing she said she felt a sense of dread. When she turned a corner, a wall of display toilets came into view.

Sitting on one of the toilets, with his pants around his ankles, was Bar Jonah grunting loudly, having a bowel movement. He looked up, grinned, and demanded she get him some toilet paper loudly yelling "So I can wipe my butt." Tyra was mortified. She grabbed Bar Jonah, pulled him off the toilet and dragged him wailing and screaming to the ladies' room.

The store manager met them as they came out of the bathroom. He told her to never bring him back into the store. Tyra pulled a defiantly laughing Bar Jonah through the store to the car. Phillip's attitude about what happened was one of resignation. He said, "We're going to have real problems with that boy; you mark my word. He's not right in the head." Phillip told Tyra he was going to give Bar Jonah the whipping he deserved, but she said that wasn't the way to handle it. Phillip and Tyra talked to Bar Jonah about what had happened, trying to understand why an eight-year-old boy would do something so offensive and outrageous. His only response was that he had to poop. If they didn't want people to use the toilets, they shouldn't have put them out there. Tyra said she and Phillip walked away bewildered. She also believed that Bar Jonah was the reason Phillip became so sullen and brooding later in his life because he felt so helpless. Phillip and Tyra talked to their pastor, who counseled them to get Bar Jonah involved in the congregation and let God have his way with the youngster. Tyra had regularly taken Bar Jonah to the Assembly of God church but now saw a need to get him involved in youth groups and more of the church's activities for kids. Bar Jonah didn't resist and became a regular at Sunday school. It didn't take long for it to become apparent that he wasn't like the other kids in his class. Bar Jonah quickly began concocting his own interpretations of Bible stories and arguing with the Sunday school teachers, insisting that *only* his interpretations were right. One teacher told Tyra he thought Bar Jonah somehow believed that he was put on earth by God to do something

15

special, something only Bar Jonah knew and would not talk to anyone about.

My best friend Kevin

Ten-year-old Bar Jonah and his eight-year-old friend Kevin Labret were playing in the woods that ran along Lake Webster, when suddenly eight boys leapt from the bushes. Bar Jonah said the oldest boy was about twelve. He was a lot bigger than Bar Jonah. It was the twelve year old who grabbed Bar Jonah and shoved him to his knees while several of the other boys jumped on top of him and held him down so he couldn't get away. The older boy walked up to Bar Jonah dropped his pants and shoved his penis into Bar Jonah's mouth. The other boys took Kevin, ripped his clothes off and tied him between two trees. Then they began pouring gasoline over Kevin's naked body. One of the boys pulled out a pack of matches and began striking them. As the matches ignited they threw them on Kevin's gas covered torso, burning him terribly, causing him excruciating pain. Bar Jonah said he could hear the "sizzle" each time a lighted match struck Kevin's helpless body. The other boys by now had ripped Bar Jonah's pants off and were forcing sticks and a broom handle into his rectum, while the older boy was continuing to force him to suck his penis.

Bar Jonah, in excruciating pain, looked over and saw Kevin fighting for his life. He began biting the penis of the older boy. The boy screamed and begged for Bar Jonah to let go. Bar Jonah in a show of courage and brute strength broke free of his captors and began kicking and beating them. He was bleeding terribly from his rectum, as he ran over to the boys burning Kevin and began beating them with a large stick he picked up from the forest floor. The boys, realizing Bar Jonah was more powerful than they had imagined, made a quick escape deep into the dense brush. Bar Jonah took out his pocketknife and cut Kevin free. He cleaned Kevin's burned skin with his own shirt and cared for him before they began their trek home. Bar Jonah was an Eagle Scout and had earned a merit badge in first aid. The two boys agreed to never talk about the incident with anyone.

The horrific circumstances he described would have been psychologically devastating to a child. The forced oral sex and rape with sticks and a broom handle would have had severe medical implications. Any young boy who suffered the injuries Bar Jonah described would have required immediate emergency medical attention and possibly reparative surgery. When Tyra was asked about the circumstances surrounding the event, she said bluntly "It *never* happened; he made it up." She first heard about it when he was twenty-two and went to Bridgewater State Hospital. Tyra said she believed that Bar Jonah "heard the story from one of the other inmates." "He was certainly *never* an Eagle Scout and his father would *never* let him have a pocketknife." Bar Jonah repeated this lie to unsuspecting sympathetic others until the day he died. He always told the stories of his life as an expert monologist— highly theatrical in his delivery and making the events rise to the level of a Greek tragedy, with the very forces of nature and the gods united against him for some unknown reason.

Kids will be kids

The kids in the neighborhood hated Bar Jonah. Kids will tease each other mercilessly about anything they see as different about the other. Once the teasing is done and the hurt feelings are soothed, the same kids are back playing together. However, Bar Jonah was so provocative in his interactions with other kids that they wanted nothing to do with him. And, if they had an opportunity to exploit his vulnerabilities, they would do so. Bar Jonah's school bus rides were notorious for being torturous for everyone. With Bar Jonah it was not what he said but how he said it that was so disturbing. When the other kids would say nasty cutting remarks to each other they would typically do so with empty vibrato. However Bar Jonah would stand close to someone and whisper a threat so only that person could hear. The threats were usually not directed at the kids themselves but at their siblings or even their parents. When the kids would report Bar Jonah to the bus driver, or his teachers when it happened at school, he would swear "on a stack of Bibles," that he had said nothing. One afternoon on the bus, Bar Jonah sat down beside one of the girls, leaned over and told her that he wanted her to do his arithmetic homework for him. She looked at him and told him, no, he should do it himself. Bar Jonah leaned in close and whispered into her ear, that if she didn't do what he wanted, he was going to break into her house in the middle of the night, cut up her mother and father and throw them into the lake. The girl started crying and went and told the bus driver. When the driver asked Bar Jonah about what he had said, he gave a mirthless grin and said that the girl was lying to get him into trouble. Bar Jonah then pulled his completed arithmetic homework out of his blue cloth three-ring binder and handed it to the bus driver to prove she was a liar.

All seven of the DuPont boys despised Bar Jonah. They thought he was a sissy and took every opportunity to torture and humiliate him. A large peach tree sat in the yard across the street from Bar Jonah and the DuPonts. The fruit the tree bore wasn't the soft, sweet, succulent peaches that are plucked from a tree and enjoyed on a summer day. These peaches were made for throwing, not eating. The DuPont boys would regularly hide with pocketfuls of peaches, waiting for Bar Jonah to come outside. When he did the DuPont boys would surround Bar Jonah and pelt him with the hard fruit. Bar Jonah would take off running. He could get a burst of energy going and take off pretty fast. But because of his weight he couldn't keep it up for long. Soon Bar Jonah would run out of steam and be overtaken by the DuPonts who would pepper him with dozens of hard peaches. Tyra used to complain to Mrs. DuPont who would reply that she had seven boys, what did Tyra expect her to do, she couldn't watch them all the time! Bar Jonah would just have to toughen up. During the summer, he would regularly have small round black and blue marks dotting the soft white fat folds on his back.

Noir

Much to Tyra's dismay, when Bar Jonah turned ten he became obsessed with horror films. *Dracula Has Risen from the Grave* (Francis, 1968) was his favorite. He claimed to have seen the film more than 100 times. Although the number was wildly exaggerated it was clear he had seen it enough times to be able to quote line for line dialogue from the film. Bar Jonah said he loved the part where Count Dracula was awakened from the dead by the blood of the Monsignor. He said Dracula, along with Christ, were his only heroes. Bar Jonah would frequently rattle off lines from either horror films or scripture. To the chagrin of his youth minister, Bar Jonah would sometimes confuse scripture with the dialogue from Dracula.

It was also about this time when he also became obsessed with wearing baseball caps. He cared nothing about baseball, but he always wore a cap. He preferred the kind with a long wide bill, which prevented others from seeing his eyes. Bar Jonah said when strangers approached he would peer out from underneath the duck bill on his cap and say in the voice of Dracula "I *vant* to drink your blood," snickering at the odd looks people would give him.

The Texas Chain Saw Massacre (Hooper, 1974) became another favorite. Bar Jonah was seventeen when the movie came out and no longer had to rely on Tyra to drive him around. He said he went to every showing at the local theater. When the serial killer in the movie decapitates his terrified victims, Bar Jonah would laugh hysterically. "I thought it was funny. They told me I was making a scene and I had to leave the theater; I told them to shut up and leave me alone."

Filleted

On the morning of Bar Jonah's twelfth birthday, it was cold and snowing heavily. Bar Jonah told his mother he wanted to go sledding. Tyra said he should wait until the weather calmed down a bit before he went outside. Bar Jonah went into his room, put on his coveralls, heavy coat, and winter hat and snuck out the side door into the blowing snowstorm. The driveway he liked to sled on sloped down toward the garage door. Pooled water at the bottom created a frozen moat. Before he started sledding, Bar Jonah scooted down the driveway on his butt, opened the garage door about a foot and peered under the door. He didn't push the door back down, leaving the sharp sheet metal edge of the door exposed. He walked back up the driveway, sat down on his sled and pushed off. His weight was not distributed evenly and the sled began to wobble as it raced down the icy driveway. Bar Jonah thought he would be able to stop the sled when his feet slammed against the partially opened garage door. But his sled hit the ice moat and his right thigh got caught on the bent metal corner of the door. The razor-sharp edge ripped a ten-inch piece of thigh muscle off of Bar Jonah's leg. He began to bleed profusely.

Phillip had gone looking for his son and saw the accident right as it happened. He ran to Bar Jonah, screaming for someone to call an ambulance. The snow was covered in blood from a large piece of his leg muscle hanging from the corner of his sled. Phillip took off his belt and applied a tourniquet around his son's leg. A short time later an ambulance rushed Bar Jonah to the hospital. At the hospital, Bar Jonah screamed at the emergency room physicians not to cut off his underwear because "My mother will kill me if you cut off my undershorts."

The ER staff was amazed at the amount of rectus femoris muscle tissue the door ripped from Bar Jonah's leg. They were even more amazed at Bar Jonah's curiosity about his wound and his complete lack of any expression of pain. As the doctors tried to suture his leg Bar Jonah kept sticking his fingers into the gash pulling the muscle tissue back. One doctor commented in his medical notes that he wouldn't stop caressing the whiteness of his femur. He told one doctor he thought it was pretty neat seeing the flap of meat hanging on the edge of sled. Bar Jonah lay on the ER gurney and loudly sang *In the Name of Jesus All Things Are Possible* (Wesley, 1749) the entire time his leg was being sutured. Bar Jonah spent a total of five weeks in the hospital having skin grafts and physical therapy.

During his stay the nurses bartered with each other in order not to have to care for him, saying he was a "spooky" little kid. At one point his doctor went to the nursing supervisor; the nurses were avoiding changing the dressing on his wound, he said, because they felt so ill at ease in his presence. Bar Jonah would ask the nurses personal questions about their children and seemed only interested if they had boys. One nurse innocently told him she had a small son a few years younger than him. He politely told the nurse to bring her son in to spend time with him. She said when she walked out of his room she felt like he wasn't asking her, so much as ordering her. The nurse thought Bar Jonah wasn't interested in having a playmate. What he wanted was to cause someone else pain. At the time the nurse thought there was something wrong with her for having such a crazy thought. But all the nurses were saying the same kind of things. It wasn't until they began to talk among themselves that they realized that Bar Jonah was trying to pry into their private lives to collect *any* kind of information that he might be able to use to exploit them. Once he was able to get into a wheelchair, Bar Jonah would regularly sneak out of his room and roll into the rooms of other patients, interrogating them about their medical conditions and wanting to see their surgical scars. The nurses said they talked about having a celebratory "we survived" party when Bar Jonah was discharged. They hoped never to see him again.

CHAPTER THREE

Bobby

On a January afternoon, right before Bar Jonah turned thirteen, he decided to go sledding again. This time with Bobby Patterson, the six-year-old neighbor boy who lived in the ranch house right across the street. Bobby was slightly built and by all accounts one of the smartest kids in the neighborhood. He didn't know Bar Jonah very well. Mainly he'd see him get off of the school bus in the afternoon, walk down the street to his house, go inside, and close the door behind him. Bobby rarely saw Bar Jonah come back outside. One of the kids in the neighborhood even said he thought Bar Jonah was a vampire and didn't like to be outside when the sun was out. Sometimes Bobby would look out his living room window and see the DuPont boys hitting Bar Jonah with peaches because the peach tree sat in the small field right beside Bobby's house.

Even at six, Bobby noticed how big Bar Jonah was. You just couldn't ignore him. He was so fat that he stood out from all of the other kids in the neighborhood. Bar Jonah's skin was doughy and pale. At 200 pounds, he had a broad box of a chest. The fat on his belly was so badly behaved that it constantly quivered when he walked.

Bobby was surprised that day when Bar Jonah knocked at his door and politely asked his mother if Bobby could go sledding with him. Bobby didn't know Bar Jonah even knew his name. They had never played together before. But Bobby was excited that one of the bigger boys wanted to go sledding with him. Bobby's mother got him dressed in heavy lined pants, a red-checkered flannel shirt, and rubber boots. Before Bobby left, his mother pulled up the hood on his blue wool coat and tugged at the string tie, making the hood nice and snug so his ears wouldn't get cold while he was sledding. Bar Jonah told Bobby the best place to go sledding was Cemetery Hill. He knew the way, "Just follow me," Bar Jonah said. They turned left out of Bobby's yard and walked down to the end of the street and turned left again. A little ways down was a whitewashed, split rail fence that outlined the cemetery, where hand-hewed lichen-iced tombstones pushed up through a blanket of white snow. Bar Jonah and Bobby pulled their sleds down an icy path and then trudged them up to the top of Cemetery Hill.

When they got to the top, Bar Jonah quickly took his sled and disappeared into a clump of white witch hazel trees, saying that he had to go pee. Then Bobby heard Bar Jonah call out for him. Bobby went into the cluster of trees looking for Bar Jonah and found him sitting atop his sled. When Bobby got close enough, Bar Jonah reached out and grabbed Bobby, jerking him down onto the sled. He then pushed Bobby onto his back and sat on top of him, using his weight to pin Bobby against his Radio Flyer. Bar Jonah unzipped his pants, pulled them down to his ankles, grabbed Bobby by the hair and forced his penis into his mouth. Bobby tried, with no success, to resist. In a few seconds, Bar Jonah ejaculated in Bobby's mouth and then he pushed him backwards, where Bobby fell crying into the snow. As Bobby lay on the ground, he was frantically grabbing handfuls of snow and shoving them into his mouth. Bar Jonah smiled, as he sat on his sled and enjoyed the scene of Bobby spitting and spitting and spitting. No matter how much snow he ate, Bobby couldn't seem to get rid of the bitter taste in his mouth. His lips were beginning to chafe and turn red from the cold of the wet snow. When Bar Jonah stood to pull up his pants, Bobby saw for the first time, the freshly-cooked rhubarb-looking scar on Bar Jonah's right leg. Over the years, that image would haunt Bobby when the incident crept its way back into his memory. After Bar Jonah had zipped up his pants, he told Bobby he was never to tell anybody about what had happened. Bar Jonah squatted down and said Bobby should wipe his nose on his coat sleeve and stop sniveling. Bobby took his arm and made a wide swipe underneath his nose. When he pulled his arm away from under his nose, he was able to escape, for just a moment, in the silvery snot, glistening on his coat sleeve in the bright snow-reflected sunlight.

Moonlight drive

Shortly after Bar Jonah turned fifteen, Phillip awoke suddenly about 1 a.m. to someone starting the family car. He looked out the window to see the family car being backed out of the driveway. Phillip rubbed his eyes trying to make himself more awake than he was and pulled on a pair of pants. He opened the bedroom door and walked down the hallway to check Bar Jonah's room. He knocked, to no answer, opened the door and found Bar Jonah's bed empty. Phillip jerked open the front door and started out on foot. After he walked a short ways, what appeared to be tail lights situated at an odd angle began to come into view. As Phillip got closer to the red lights he saw his car had been driven off the road and crashed into a split rail fence. Steam was hissing from under the hood, curling upward against a faint mist hanging in the night sky. Bar Jonah was leaning cockily against the driver's side door.

As Phillip approached him, Bar Jonah yelled, "Dad, look what someone did to the car. I heard them stealing the car and took off chasing them down the street. They rammed the car into the fence. I screamed at them and they got afraid of me, jumped out of the car and took off running into the field. Do you want me to go after them"? Phillip confronted his son's lie. Bar Jonah steadfastly denied any responsibility in the theft or the accident. Phillip Brown looked at Bar Jonah and said, "Son, you aren't in trouble, if you just tell me the truth." "Really son, just tell me the truth, that's all I'm asking you to do."

In 2001, when Bar Jonah was interviewed in prison, he said about the incident, "I got there before my dad because I was on the track team … I could run fast even though I had a weight problem. I heard someone start the car because I was awake. I guess my dad left the keys in the car. I took off after them when they took the car. I was screaming at them all the way down the street. Then the car ran over the curb like they didn't know how to drive or something, then they hit the fence. I yelled at them to stay put, when they got out of the car and took off running through the field. So I just stood there waiting for my dad. When he got there he started accusing me of taking the car; I was the one that almost caught the guys who stole it. I tried to tell him how I tried to catch the guys but he wouldn't listen to me. My dad told my mom I was the one who took the car. He tried to turn my mom against me all the time." Bar Jonah was never on the track team.

In 1972, when he entered Bay Path Vocational High School, in Carlton, Massachusetts, Bar Jonah was even more outside of the mainstream. He weighed more than 375 pounds and his attitude was one of profound entitlement. His grades were below average at best. One of his high school teachers said, "You felt like he was getting you to do things you really didn't want to do." Several of his classmates described him as odd and being uncomfortable with him. They said he didn't walk down the halls like the other kids. He would saunter, swinging his arms wide, taking up as much room as possible, never speaking to anyone. Sometimes Bar Jonah would settle his eyes on one of his classmates and hold them in his gaze like they couldn't get away. Prison guards later experienced him the same way.

Jimmy and Tommy: almost

Two boys were riding their bicycles down Bar Jonah's street. He could hear them coming, the playing cards in their spokes gave them away. Jimmy's tenth birthday had just been a few days earlier. He loved showing off his new gold bike as he proudly sat atop the black and yellow speckled banana seat. Tommy, his best friend, had his tenth birthday last year, so he'd been riding bikes a lot longer. He also knew about the cemetery at the end of the street. He said it was a neat place to go and see what was written on the tombstones about the dead people.

Bar Jonah had seen Jimmy and Tommy around the neighborhood before. He never talked to them but he knew who they were. When they were almost to his house, Bar Jonah started yelling for Jimmy and Tommy to ride over to the curb. He asked them where they were going. Jimmy excitedly said they were going up to the cemetery to read the tombstones. Tommy sat on his bike not saying anything. He didn't know the fat kid. He didn't want to talk to him. Bar Jonah said he knew what tombstones had the best stuff on them; he would show them. He started walking toward the cemetery, telling them to follow him. Jimmy and Tommy started slowly peddling behind him, their spoke cards ticking quieter now. Tommy got up beside Jimmy and yelled that he heard his mother calling him to come home. Jimmy thought that was stupid, they lived too far away for him to hear his mom calling. Tommy said, come on we gotta go *now*, or I'll get in trouble. He pulled in front of Jimmy, cutting him off and making him turn his bike around. Jimmy twisted the fork of his bike and reluctantly followed his best friend.

Bar Jonah looked back and frustratedly saw Jimmy and Tommy peddling away. He called out to them a couple of times but they couldn't hear him because of how fast their spoke cards were clicking. Much later in Bar Jonah's life, he said that he had been watching the boys for several weeks around the neighborhood, right after he got his temporary driving permit. When Tyra took Bar Jonah out to practice driving, he kept an eye out for the two boys because they were always together. He guessed they were pals. Bar Jonah said he had planned to murder the boys that day and bury them in the cemetery with the other bodies, but Tommy messed up his plans.

Mrs. DuPont's boys: almost

A week after Tommy foiled Bar Jonah's plans, Mrs. DuPont opened her front door and found two envelopes lying on the doorstep. The names of two of her sons were printed in heavy black pencil on the front of the envelopes. Mrs. DuPont stooped down, picked them up and took them inside. She thought that her sons were probably being invited to a birthday party in the neighborhood. It seemed unusual that the invitations were left on the doorstep rather than having put them in the mailbox. The boys who were playing in their bedrooms looked up and saw their mother holding a couple of envelopes in her hand. "Look boys, someone is inviting you to a party," Mrs. DuPont said. Her eight-year-old son reached out and took the letter addressed to him. His little brother didn't seem interested and sat watching his older brother tear open his envelope. Mrs. DuPont saw her son staring at the letter, seemingly trying to figure out what it said. She reached down, took the letter from his hand, saying "Let me help you." When she looked at the letter, Mrs. DuPont tried to make sense of not only what it was, but also what it said. However, when she read the message, cold chills ran up her spine. Pasted onto the sheet of white paper were colored letters that had been cut out of magazines and newspapers. The message read:

> Meet me in the Bakers Grove cemetery at 6 p.m. and something good will happen to you. I will give you $20 apiece and don't tell your mother and father about it.

The note was signed by Bar Jonah.

Mrs. DuPont had heard tales around the neighborhood that Bar Jonah was an odd boy. But even though he lived right next door, she hadn't had much contact with him. Mrs. DuPont took the letters and walked over to Tyra's. Bar Jonah heard the knock at the door. When he answered, Mrs. DuPont told him to get his mother. Bar Jonah said she wasn't at home. A few seconds later, Mrs. DuPont heard Tyra yell, "Who is it?" Bar Jonah yelled back that it was a salesman and he had sent him away. Mrs. DuPont yelled through the screen door that she needed to talk to Tyra right away. Bar Jonah pushed his way out the door, shoving past Mrs. DuPont. A few minutes later Tyra appeared at the door apologizing for being clad in her flour-covered apron. Mrs. DuPont showed the letters to Tyra. Tyra said she didn't know what she was going to do with the boy and she would tell him not to do it anymore. Mrs. DuPont told Tyra to keep him away from her boys or there would be trouble.

When Bar Jonah later told of the event, he said that since Tommy had messed up his plans to kill him and Jimmy, he guessed he still had the urge to murder a couple of kids. The DuPonts had a lot of kids, Bar Jonah said, they wouldn't miss a couple of them. They didn't have a lot of money, it would make it easier on the family not to have so many mouths to feed. They'd jump at a chance to get $20. Bar Jonah had just seen a movie about a kidnapping. In the movie, the kidnapper made the ransom note out of letters that were cut out from magazines. He thought that was a good way to tell the DuPonts that something good would happen to them if they met him at the cemetery. Once the boys got to the cemetery, Bar Jonah said he was going to choke them to death back under a bunch of thorn trees. Then he was going to cut them up.

CHAPTER FOUR

Ascension to the throne

On a summer morning seventeen-year-old Bar Jonah and his mother came home from church. Tyra went into the kitchen to begin preparing lunch, while Bar Jonah went into the living room to wake his father who was sleeping on the couch. Bar Jonah shook his father's shoulder. With a dull thud, Phillip Brown rolled off of the couch, onto the floor, dead. Bar Jonah said at that moment, "I became the man of the family." When Tyra came into the room, he told her Phillip was dead. Bar Jonah immediately called the fire station. All the guys at the firehouse knew him because he was a volunteer fireman. They were there in minutes. Bar Jonah helped the emergency crew put his father on a stretcher and load him into the back of the ambulance. He then began helping his distraught mother, taking her by the arm, putting her into the car. He had to drive at 80 mph to keep up with the ambulance.

Bar Jonah was surprised to find Lois already at the hospital. He didn't know how she'd got there before him. But Lois, out of the blue, went crazy. She ran toward Bar Jonah and began choking him. Bar Jonah slapped her hard across the face to keep her from strangling him. Tyra was screaming at Lois and

31

pulling at her hands to stop her from killing her brother. The scene was chaotic. While Lois was trying to strangle Bar Jonah, the doctor came out and said they had done everything they could. Phillip Brown was dead. Tyra broke down. Lois took off running insanely through the hospital. Bar Jonah sat his mother down and told her to stay put. He didn't want to have to chase two people through the hospital. He then went from room to room looking for Lois. Finally after at least an hour of searching, Bar Jonah saw her shoes sticking out from under a drawn curtain in a patient's room. Lois was sitting crying, pressing her back against the concrete wall. The old woman in the bed above seemed to be in some kind of coma. Bar Jonah spent the next hour comforting Lois, before she would get up and go back to the ER to be with Tyra.

Tyra, however, remembered the day that her husband died differently. After she and Bar Jonah came home from church she heard Bar Jonah screaming. Tyra went into the living room and saw Phillip lying on the floor. She said she knew he was dead because his head was almost black. Bar Jonah was screaming hysterically. He called the fire department but Tyra took the phone away from him because he wasn't making sense to the dispatcher. The men at the firehouse *did* know Bar Jonah because the chief had called Tyra and told her to keep him away from the firehouse. He was a constant pest, the chief said. Bar Jonah insisted on driving to the hospital but several times almost ran into the back of the ambulance. Lois trying to choke Bar Jonah was utter nonsense, Tyra said, it never happened. When Lois heard about Bar Jonah's recollection of the day her father died, she looked down heavily and said, "I don't even know what to say; all of this is just so bizarre."

* * *

Phillip Brown's funeral was held at the Don Luther Funeral Home in Webster, Massachusetts. Mr. Luther was said to be a staid man who showed little emotion. But he was known to be good with the families grieving over the loss of their loved ones. While family and friends were viewing Phillip's remains, Bar Jonah was following Mr. Luther around the funeral home, asking him if he could see the embalming room. He wanted to know the particulars of how they had prepared his father's corpse. Bar Jonah had even called the funeral home the night before the viewing to see if he could help embalm his father. He badgered the undertaker demanding to know how to keep a dead body from smelling if you don't bury it right away, how cold do you have to keep it, how long can you keep it for before it starts to get "stale." Mr. Luther finally went to Tyra and told her she had to keep Bar Jonah under control. If Bar Jonah wouldn't behave himself he would have to leave the viewing. Tyra tried her best, but he continually kept trying to sneak off and go down to the embalming area. He had to be escorted back upstairs over and over again during the viewing. He never cried, she recalled, he just stood there touching Phillip, lifting his hands, trying to look in his mouth. It was as if Phillip wasn't his father but some kind of specimen.

Tyra was thankful when the service was over, not just because of the grief of suddenly losing her husband, but also for getting Bar Jonah out of the funeral home.

Little blond-headed boy

In late March 1975, about a year and a half after Phillip Brown died, Bar Jonah dropped his mother off at work because he wanted to drive her car to school. There was going to be a big pep rally and he wanted to get to school early to show his school spirit.

On the other side of town, a blond-headed eight year old decided that morning he wanted to be a big boy and walk to school alone. His mother struggled with his sudden burst of independence but reluctantly agreed as long as he stayed on the sidewalk, followed the exact path they had taken each and every day, and not talk to strangers. The little boy proudly left home with a kiss and hug from his mother, who watched him walk down the sidewalk heading off toward school.

A few minutes after the child left home he turned right, onto the main road where his school came into view. The little boy proudly bustled along, his metal lunch box chinking and swinging by his side.

Suddenly a white station wagon pulled up onto the sidewalk. A big guy in a blue police jacket with a gold sheriff's badge pinned to the pocket jumped out of the car, and identified himself as a policeman. He told the boy that his mother had been hurt and to come with him right away. The policeman opened the door for the now distraught little boy and ordered him into the front seat. He then reached over and pulled the seat belt tight around the child's waist. Bar Jonah took a look around, got back into the car and drove away.

A neighborhood busybody looked out her window as the fat man, dressed like a police clown sped away. She picked up the phone and called the police who sent an officer out to begin searching for the child.

Bar Jonah drove past the school where one of the patrol boys reported him to a teacher for driving through the crosswalk when he had his orange flag out. He continued to speed down the busy thoroughfare to a local shopping center parking lot where there were few cars that early in the morning. The child was frightened; the fat policeman was acting funny. Bar Jonah leaned over and told the boy to take his clothes off. The child refused. With one hand, Bar Jonah grabbed the boy around the neck and began choking and shaking him violently until he almost passed out. The child, crying in between gasps, helplessly tried to push Bar Jonah's hand away, as he began to unbutton the boy's pants. Roughly reaching into his underwear, Bar Jonah wrapped his hands around the boy's penis and testicles and began to squeeze so hard that the boy almost lost consciousness. The boy screamed, losing control of his bowels and bladder, shitting and pissing all over himself and Bar Jonah's hand. Bar Jonah became enraged, smearing his soiled hand on the boy's shirt and face. Bar Jonah's other short fat hand was clamped perfectly around the boy's small neck. He squeezed and let go, squeezed and let go, taking the boy to the brink of unconsciousness, then shaking his head violently and bringing him back again and again. Bar Jonah felt the boy start to retch, but tightened his grip around his neck so that the child began to aspirate on his own vomit. Bar Jonah pulled the boy to the edge of the car seat. He momentarily released the pressure on the boy's throat, allowing the child to puke onto the floor of the car. The child's neck and face were bruised and swollen; he had blood coming out of his nose and eyes. As best as he could understand, the boy believed that he was about to die.

A patrol car driving past the parking lot noticed a vehicle, matching the description of the car reported to have been used in a child abduction, parked far away from the few other cars in the parking lot. The officer put on his lights and siren, turned around and pulled into the parking lot, while calling for backup.

Bar Jonah and the child were sitting in the front seat of the car, when the officer jumped from his patrol car, drawing his .38, ordering Bar Jonah out of the vehicle. Bar Jonah rolled down his window, put his hands out and yelled, "Don't hurt me. I didn't do anything, I'm getting out." Several officers arrived on the scene and surrounded Bar Jonah's car. Bar Jonah pushed open the car door and stepped out onto the blacktop. The patrol officers tackled him, shoving him down to the asphalt and handcuffing his arms behind his back. Bar Jonah was screaming that he has done nothing wrong; it was all a mistake, he said.

A female police officer climbed into Bar Jonah's car and began to comfort the hysterical child, assuring him he was safe and that she was a *real* police officer. The boy was taken to Hubbard Surgical Hospital, where he stayed for two days, under the care of Dr. Corrado. His face and neck were still swollen and the sclera of his eyes were still blood-engorged on the day he was released.

Bar Jonah was taken to the Webster, Massachusetts's police station and charged with felony kidnapping, assault and battery, and sexual assault of a minor. He told the police the kid reminded him of some guy who'd sold his mother a car and put sawdust in the transmission, to make it run smoother. At least for a while. Bar Jonah said it was a good thing he gained his composure or he would have killed the kid. Then, taking a moment to think about what he had done, he told the officer that he waited too long. It would have been better if he had just choked the boy to death, dumped him somewhere, and gone on to school. Bar Jonah said he knew his rights and demanded the police call his mother. He was a minor too. "You can't question me without my mother and my lawyer being here." Tyra was called at 2 p.m. She dutifully drove to the police station where Bar Jonah was being held. One of the cops told Tyra that Bar Jonah was the most dangerous person he had ever arrested. It wasn't that he tried to resist or anything, the cop said it was just that there was nothing inside of him. It was as though he wasn't even human. The cop tried to talk to Tyra, telling her Bar Jonah needed to be committed somewhere. He was going to kill someone. Tyra wanted no part of what he was saying. Since Bar Jonah was a juvenile, Tyra requested that he be released into her custody.

He denied knowing anything about the kidnapping or the assault and told Tyra he must have "blacked-out." As the week wore on, Bar Jonah became more despondent. Tyra thought he might be suicidal and decided to put him in the hospital.

* * *

On April 4, 1975, Bar Jonah was hospitalized under the care of psychiatrist, Jesse O. Arnold, MD. Dr. Arnold admitted him to St. Vincent hospital with what he called an episode of a loss of awareness. His episode lasted for three hours. Dr. Arnold was perplexed at what would cause such an odd symptom, particularly for such a long period of time. Bar Jonah claimed he remembered having the boy with him only for a brief amount of time. He said he remembered nothing about kidnapping and sexually assaulting the kid. He certainly didn't remember trying to choke him to death. He did remember the kid pooping and peeing in his mother's car and her being upset.

On the following day, in the late afternoon, as the sun was going down and the day room was losing its light, a young female schizophrenic patient approached Bar Jonah and kissed him on the mouth. He roughly shoved her away and filed a complaint with the hospital accusing the nursing staff of failing to protect him from the "deranged woman." The nursing staff who observed the incident charted that a female patient walked up beside Bar Jonah, leaned over and kissed him on the cheek. He reacted hysterically demanding the patient be put in restraints for sexually assaulting him.

* * *

Metabolic brain imaging in 1975 was all but unheard of. Certainly the few imaging machines that did exist were experimental and maintained by the researchers themselves. It so happened that St. Vincent had one of the few neuroSPECT brain imaging machines in the world. The SPECT (single photon emission computed tomography) sat in a small cable-crowded cubicle, right off of the elevator next to the boiler room in the catacombs of the hospital basement. In 1975, images of the brain were done with an X-ray of the head or possibly an X-ray with air injected into the spine to look at the shape of the ventricles. But a neuroSPECT is different. It doesn't look at the brain structurally like an X-ray, rather it looks at the brain metabolically. In other words it looks at what parts of the brain are working too much, what parts are not working enough, and what parts are working just right.

Dr. Arnold was intrigued by Bar Jonah presenting symptoms and his history. He personally accompanied Bar Jonah to the basement of St. Vincent's, casually talking with him on the elevator ride down.

The neuroSPECT at St. Vincent's did not have an attached table for the research subject to stretch out on. Instead they used a surgical gurney. Bar Jonah groaned pitifully when he raised himself onto the gurney, wanting to make sure Dr. Arnold appreciated his struggle. Dr. Arnold softly umm'd, empathizing with Bar Jonah. Then Dr. Arnold thanked Bar Jonah for his willingness to take so much of his time away from the daily activities on the ward. He would be sure that Bar Jonah's cooperation was noted in the medical record. Dr. Arnold instructed Bar Jonah to put his hands down by his side and contain his belly, as he wheeled him around to the front of the cavernous SPECT.

Bar Jonah's light bluish radial arm vein was barely visible through the thick layer of fat on his left arm, as Dr. Arnold prepared to inject him with the radioisotope, HMPAO. After a bit of probing with the needle, Dr. Arnold was finally able to pull back the plunger and see a trickle of blood being sucked into the barrel of the syringe. Then he slowly pushed the plunger causing the isotope to begin surging its way toward Bar Jonah's brain. Dr. Arnold was curious though that Bar Jonah didn't flinch when he had been poking deep into his arm trying to find a vein.

Dr. Arnold stepped away and took a few minutes to calibrate the machine. He also had to wait for the HMPAO to cross Bar Jonah's blood brain barrier and begin tagging constellations of molecules that the SPECT would then "see" and create an image of his brain. After the SPECT was calibrated, Dr. Arnold smiled at Bar Jonah laying quietly on the gurney and with difficulty rolled him into the SPECT tube. Sixteen minutes later an image of Bar Jonah's brain appeared. It appeared to be "normal."

However, what Dr. Arnold and other neuroSPECT researchers didn't realize at the time was that they were tagging the wrong molecules with the radioisotope. Because of this error, brain scans that were declared to be "normal" were actually three to five standard deviations below the mean, (Hipskind, June 2009). In Bar Jonah's case this meant that the frontal lobes of his brain were barely functioning, creating a condition known as hypofrontality. This meant that Bar Jonah's ability to be able to discern right from wrong in the moment was broken as was his ability to foresee the consequences of his behavior before he did it. But most important, his ability to control his rage toward children was irreparable.

* * *

During the eighteen days Bar Jonah was in the hospital, he did not have another episode of blacking out. He was released with a successful plea agreement and was placed on a year of supervised probation. He visited his probation officer no more than a half a dozen times during that year.

The weeks after he assaulted the eight-year-old boy were busy for Bar Jonah. He was getting ready to graduate from high school, beginning to think about going to college and getting a job for the summer. As part of his plea agreement he was not allowed to have any contact with children and agreed not to break any laws. That was easy, he said. He didn't remember doing anything wrong in the first place.

Little pixie-haired girl

A few days before the pomp and circumstance of Bar Jonah's high school graduation, a pixie-haired, nine-year-old girl was zipping down the sidewalk on her bicycle. She was not far from her house in Hartford, Connecticut. Bar Jonah, again, was dressed as a police officer, in the same blue coat and same shiny gold badge. He pulled up to her and ordered her into his police car, saying, "Your mother has been in a bad accident, she needs you to come right away." The frightened child jumped off her bicycle, not bothering to put her kickstand down. Her bicycle with pink and white handlebar streamers fell onto the sidewalk. Tears began to roll down her face, as she whimpered that she wanted her mommy to be okay. She ran towards Bar Jonah's police car. The blue-jacketed policeman reassured her that he would take her to her mommy. He lifted her into his car and pulled the lap belt so tight around her waist the girl complained to Bar Jonah's now unsympathetic ears. As Bar Jonah pulled away from the curb, he violently swung his right fist into the little girl's face and screamed for her to shut the fuck up. Driving down the road he continued to pummel her face and head. The child suddenly began convulsing, trembling and shaking violently. Then she vomited and wet her pants. Bar Jonah then drove up onto the sidewalk, slammed on the brakes, unbuckled the child's lap belt, and violently threw her out of the car onto the concrete. He then casually drove away enraged that *another* kid had soiled his mother's car. Now he'd have to clean it up before he got back home.

Another car drove up just as Bar Jonah was pulling off of the sidewalk. The driver got the license number of Bar Jonah's car. The little girl was lying on the ground hysterical. Her face was a pulpy mess. One of her bottom teeth was hanging by its nerve across her bloody lip. Her once pretty dress was now covered with blood, vomit, and urine. The little girl was taken to a local hospital where they called her mother. She described her attacker like a trained observer. A short while later the police arrived at Tyra's and arrested Bar Jonah. He complained, as the cops were taking him out the door, about how rough they were being. Bar Jonah said he must have blacked out again. He didn't remember anything. The little girl's mother, fearful of retribution, refused to let her daughter testify. Somehow the assault never got back to Bar Jonah's probation officer. He was released from probation in May 1976. A note was placed in his file about how cooperative he had been.

* * *

Bar Jonah is standing with his arm wrapped around his mother in his high school graduation picture, taken one week after the assault occurred on the nine-year-old girl. The family album bears witness to the illusion of a benign young man, standing in stark contrast to his sixty-year-old mother's tired weather-beaten look of exhaustion. His 5' 7" 375 pound body fills half of the frame. In interviews later in his life, Bar Jonah would assert that he desperately wanted to get away from his mother, whom he both idolized and said dominated his life.

In high school, Bar Jonah had been a member of the camera club. He loved taking pictures of others. He liked to say how he "captured them from afar." He also worked at the school concession stand at home games and was a "helper" in his shop class. Bar Jonah had one date in high school, with a girl whom Bar Jonah later described as "homely and no one else wanted to go out with." But he said Tyra broke off the relationship because she didn't think that she was the girl for him. In 2001, when then forty-four-year-old Bar Jonah was being held on charges of deliberate homicide and kidnapping in Montana, he said, "I still haven't found the right girl, but maybe someday I will, and be able to have kids of my own." Tyra remembered Bar Jonah once taking a girl to his senior prom, but she said she never attempted to break up their relationship, because there wasn't a relationship. After the prom, Tyra said he never saw the girl again.

Stretching his wings

Shortly after high school, Bar Jonah went to work for the O. F. Wanders Company in Norsetown, Massachusetts, as an apprentice furniture restorer. But the job didn't last very long. When one of the workers tried to teach him how to strip and varnish a piece of furniture, he became enraged. He would storm out of the warehouse swinging his arms, pouting, yelling how no one gave him a chance to demonstrate his talents. On the last day he was there, Bar Jonah got pissed off at one of the female workers and forced her into a corner. One of the men in the warehouse saw Bar Jonah and grabbed him by the shoulder, throwing him up against a stack of boxes. The worker screamed at Bar Jonah, pulled his fist back and told him he was going to break his jaw. The woman was afraid she would get into trouble and yelled for the man to let Bar Jonah go. He lowered his fist and stepped back from Bar Jonah. Bar Jonah shoved over some boxes and stormed out of the warehouse. He never came back to work.

* * *

Rarely did Bar Jonah miss Sunday school or worship service. He saw himself as not only deeply religious but also secretly held the belief that he was called upon by God to do His work. Not preaching but something far more important, that *only* Bar Jonah could do to assure his special place in Heaven as one of God's chosen few. In order to better understand how he was to serve God, Bar Jonah decided to go to Bible College. In 1976 he was accepted into the Valley Forge Christian College, affiliated with the Assembly of God Ministries, in Greenlane, Pennsylvania.

At the end of his second month on campus, Bar Jonah was hired by the college as a night watchman for one of the student laboratories. One night while he was on duty, Bar Jonah turned a corner and struck his head on the edge of a jagged piece of metal that was left on a scaffolding cart. It cut a deep two-inch gash over his right eye. Bar Jonah left the building with the cut bleeding profusely and walked back to his dormitory. A short while later, another student walked into the dorm's common bathroom and found Bar Jonah standing in front of a mirror. His face and uniform-shirt were covered in blood. A needle, attached to a long piece of thread, was clinched between Bar Jonah's thumb and forefinger. With the fingers on his other hand, Bar Jonah was squeezing the gash together. The other student said it looked like he had stitched up about half the open wound. Bar Jonah wryly smiled at the reflection of the wary student in the mirror and continued to slowly push the needle through the thick fold of skin above his eye. The student ran screaming out the bathroom door and reported Bar Jonah to the dorm monitor. It took about eight to ten stitches, Bar Jonah said, but it didn't hurt. He didn't feel anything.

The following Sunday morning, Bar Jonah went to church service in blue jeans and a dirty white tee shirt. During the service, the preacher noticed how Bar Jonah was dressed and confronted him from the pulpit. The preacher loudly exclaimed that Bar Jonah was being disrespectful in the House of the Lord. Bar Jonah got up, left the service, and went back to his dorm, where he drew a black and white spotted tie on his soiled tee shirt with a thick black marker. Bar Jonah then went back to the church service, lumbered down the aisle, swinging his arms widely from side-to-side. He sat down in the front pew, directly in front of the preacher. The preacher looked down from the pulpit and saw Bar Jonah staring directly into his eyes. "When the preacher looked at me, he knew I wasn't going to take any crap from him. I didn't have to say a word," Bar Jonah said. "I do things my way, period." The preacher didn't make any further comments on Bar Jonah's attire during the service. After the service, the preacher contacted the college dean and said he thought they had a problem student. Because of the way he came back into church and stared at the preacher, he might even be dangerous. The dean said he thought the student the preacher was talking about was the same one the dorm monitor had complained about earlier. Later that afternoon Bar Jonah was called into the dean's office. The dean wanted to talk with Bar Jonah to see if he was contrite for his irreverent conduct in church and for frightening a fellow student at the dorm. Bar Jonah, clearly irritated, told the dean that the preacher and the student were lying. He had done nothing wrong. They were just trying to get him into trouble, because *they knew* he had a special relationship with God. Everyone on campus talked about it; Bar Jonah was surprised that the dean didn't know. Bar Jonah's accusation that the preacher and the student were lying made the dean think that Bar Jonah might try to get back at them. His grades were poor at best, in fact Bar Jonah would probably be on academic probation for the first semester. The dean told Bar Jonah he would have been able to work with him if his grades were better. At least that would have shown that Bar Jonah had initiative and was a serious student of the Bible. But, given that his grades were so bad and the complaints were so serious, he had no choice but to suspend him. The dean also had the sense that the problems with Bar Jonah were only going to get worse. It was best to get rid of him while he could, before he created any more havoc. Campus security was outside of the dean's door waiting to escort Bar Jonah back to his dorm room. Security stayed with Bar Jonah while he packed up. The dean had made arrangements to get Bar Jonah a bus ticket back to Massachusetts that same day. Bar Jonah said, "The dean just didn't understand me. He just couldn't see how special my relationship with God was, so I left. I don't think they really had much to teach me anyway." Bar Jonah also thought the Devil may have been at work on the campus.

After Bar Jonah left college, he moved back in with Tyra. He was becoming increasingly restless and even more difficult for Tyra to deal with. He now weighed 390 pounds and Tyra said she just couldn't keep him fed. She described him as an eating machine, consuming everything in sight. Tyra encouraged him to get a regular job, but the few menial ones he was able to find at fast food restaurants were short lived because he continued to threaten the other staff. The employees would tell their manager either Bar Jonah had to go or they would. They hated his guts.

Billy and Alan

On Saturday morning, September 24, 1977, Bar Jonah woke up hungry. He usually had his mother Tyra fix him a big breakfast but this morning he said that he had a huge appetite. He wanted double of everything. Bar Jonah sat down at the kitchen table, too excited to talk, except to tell his mother to fix him eggs and toast until he told her to stop. He ate until Tyra thought his belly would pop. Bar Jonah told his mother he needed her green Plymouth Fury that night to meet some friends. He was vague about whom or when, just some friends he said. Tyra thought this was odd because he didn't have any friends. He was antsy, wandering around the house until about noon. He didn't seem to know what to do with himself. But there was so much to do, so many details to take care of.

Bar Jonah went to his bedroom, rummaged around in the back of his closet and found his hunting knife, which he would later admit to stealing from his neighbor's garage. He rolled the knife up in an old pair of boxer shorts. Earlier, Bar Jonah had taken one of Bob's old army duffle bags and hidden it behind some boxes. He pulled it out, shook it open and neatly folded it end over end. An oily rope he had found along the side of the road lay on the floor beside his bed. He picked up the rope and began quickly twisting it between his hand and elbow, making figure eight turns. This way he could just toss the rope and it would unroll easily.

Hanging in between two pair of pants was his favorite dark blue nylon police jacket. He always kept it on a special wooden hanger. Tucked into one of his socks was his most real-istic looking silver police badge. He took it out, clipping it to the police jacket. Bar Jonah closed the closet door and shined a pocket flashlight on the badge. He touched each of the five points on the tin badge, marveling how each one seemed to reflect a sense of power. In the bottom drawer, were two pairs of handcuffs; he didn't have a key. They were real. Standing in the corner was the pop-up canopy he used for his newly minted antique and collectable toy business.

It took several trips, but he finally got everything, just the way he wanted it, packed into the Plymouth. He tucked the knife under the driver's seat just to where the hilt was within easy reach.

Bar Jonah had begun spending a lot of time now going to flea markets. He was talking with antique dealers learning about how to buy and price toys. Mrs. Beverly Dupont (no relation to his neighbor), one of the dealers he became friends with, was teaching him how to price in code. This way you could always have the upper hand when you haggled, she would say. The customer would think they were getting a good deal, when they really weren't. You could haggle away. The more you haggled, the more you pulled the customer in and the more likely they were to walk away with something.

Bev's Flea Market in Auburn was basically a bunch of tents, in an empty lot where people who called themselves antique dealers rented space. Bar Jonah had just rented a space at Bev's. Catering to children was his specialty. He had a couple of plywood shelves stacked on top of cinder blocks, where he displayed toy trucks and guns that he had found at neighborhood sales and flea markets. He specialized in police badges, the more authentic the better. He also considered himself an expert in teddy bears and used to say he was a loveable teddy bear himself.

Helium balloons were strung around the table calling out to children as they passed by. Bar Jonah was always generous with his time, explaining things to little boys, putting his arm around them, pulling them close. He would look right into their eyes. Bar Jonah ignored little girls. It was as though they didn't exist. There was a cardboard sign thumb-tacked to one of the shelves that advertised his new babysitting services. He said he was dedicated to caring for children. Busy parents are always looking for a babysitter, he would explain, since good ones are hard to find.

The evening of Saturday the 24th was going to be a special night. But first Bar Jonah *had* to get his pop-up tent set up. He would not get off work, as relief manager, until about nine. There wouldn't be time after he left work.

Bar Jonah's grey polyester pants swooshed, swooshed, swooshed, in time, as his thick thighs rubbed together as he walked to the car. The light blue shirt separated where the last button was missing, making an upside down "V". His belly rolled over his waist, through the opening. His hair was lightly Brylcreemed back. The fall wind stung Bar Jonah's freshly Aqua Velva'd cheeks.

Driving away from home, he made a series of turns and ended up on Route 20. A little ways down was Bev's. When Bar Jonah got to the antique market, he grabbed the steering wheel to pull himself out of the car. He walked out in the parking lot to get a lay of the land from closer to the street. The line of canopies was a little back from the main road but he still didn't want to take any chances with prying eyes. He liked to say that if someone could stick their nose in your business, they would. One thing for sure, the opening flap of the tent had to be facing away from the main road.

Bar Jonah walked back up the parking lot and unloaded the pop-up, carefully laying each of the aluminum legs out onto the pavement. The tent went together like Tinker-Toys, each piece pushing into spindles that held the whole thing together and made it secure. He then stretched out the canvas canopy which would slip over the frame last. Bar Jonah bent down and pounded long spikes through the rope stays, into the black-top to make sure the tent could withstand being pulled on. He carefully rolled the flap up and tied it with a quick release knot. This way he just had to give the rope a quick tug and the flap would unroll quickly behind him. He had not set up the canopy before, and today the wind was blowing wildly, making it hard for one person to manage the flapping canvas panels. A gray-haired woman who was walking by kindly offered to help. While the elderly woman was tugging on the unruly canvas, Bar Jonah noticed her bent arthritic hands. He reached over, took one of her hands, and told her he would pray that God healed her.

About four, he had everything ready. He had to be at work at five, so he had plenty of time to get over to the Natick Store of Cumberland Farms and put in a few hours as a relief manager.

After his shift ended, he stopped at a convenience store to get some cigarettes before heading over to the White City Theater, in Shrewsbury. Two thirteen-year-old boys, dressed in worn jean jackets and baggy pants, were coming out of the ten o'clock movie. They stepped off of the curb and began walking across the parking lot. There were always boys leaving the late show. Bar Jonah had been here many times before.

He gunned the engine and pulled up beside the boys. When he turned on the inside light, they could see the fat man was a police officer. He rolled down the window and flashed the badge pinned to his jacket. "What are your names," he demanded to know. "Billy" and "Alan," they responded. He ordered them to get into his undercover car, saying he wants to talk to them. As Bar Jonah lectured the boys about how dangerous it is to be out so late alone, his fist suddenly flew off of the steering wheel and bloodied Alan's nose. He demanded to know where they live; he was going to take them home. Alan's nose was bleeding as he was beginning to cry, asking Bar Jonah why he hit him. He hadn't done anything wrong, he said.

Bar Jonah drove around for a while telling the boys to keep their mouths shut. They were becoming annoying, crying, asking over and over again where he was taking them. He pulled off onto a dirt road, stopped the car and grabbed the hunting knife from under the seat. He kept screaming at the boys to put their hands behind their backs. The handcuffs clicked in place; Bar Jonah tightened them around their wrists. He then pulled the green duffel bag from under the seat and ordered Billy get in. "The bag is too small; I can't," said the boy. Bar Jonah said he'd cut Billy's legs off if he didn't. His legs only went so far into the bag. Billy was trying so hard. Bar Jonah was becoming more agitated. He grabbed the bag, tearing it off of Billy's legs, throwing it out the window and onto the side of the road. The boys kept pestering Bar Jonah, wanting to know if he was going to kill them. "No, if you do what I tell you, then no," Bar Jonah said back. They kept asking him to take the cuffs off, they were cutting their wrists. They didn't know that he didn't have a key.

He pulled back onto the main road and drove to Bev's. He hid his car behind the tent and yanked the boys out of the car by their shirt collars. He smiled as the tent flap effortlessly dropped when he pulled the cord.

Bar Jonah pushed the boys to the back of the tent, tying them with the oily rope to the metal sidebars of the canopy frame. If you ever want to see your parents again, take your clothes off, he said. The boys stubbornly refused. He was getting pissed. He untied the boys, and shoved them out the back of the tent and into the back seat of the car. The boys were terrified, trembling, laying on top of each other.

Bar Jonah drove to the old Cemetery Road in Carlton, near the Assembly of God, Royal Rangers Campground. He was enraged. Nothing was going the way it was supposed to; they'd messed up everything.

Alan felt the cool night air on his face as he was grabbed by the hair and pulled out of the car. Bar Jonah's hands encircled his throat, violently shaking his head back and forth, strangling him. The boy recoiled, as Bar Jonah backhanded him across the face, knocking him to the ground. Bar Jonah began kicking him in the ribs. He flicked ashes on him from his cigarette, kicking him again. Bar Jonah, breathing hard, squatted and sat on top of Alan. He took a moment to rest, before he began bouncing up and down on the boy's chest. Alan felt his breath being pushed out of him. Everything began to spin, then there was nothing but black.

Through squinting eyes, Alan saw Bar Jonah get back into the car. He heard Billy screaming as he was being choked. Bar Jonah was trying to break his neck. The car door flew open; he was dragging Billy from the back seat. Alan thought Billy looked like a rag doll. His handcuffed wrists made both arms hang together lifelessly. He opened the trunk lid and rolled Billy across the threshold. Bar Jonah reached into the trunk and shoved the spare tire around, so he could get Billy's feet into the side of the compartment without having to break his ankles. Alan wasn't moving. Billy was now tucked away. Bar Jonah slammed the trunk lid. What the hell should he do with the body in the trunk, Bar Jonah asked himself.

Alan lay still on the ground, knowing Bar Jonah had killed his friend. When he saw Bar Jonah's tail lights getting fainter in the distance he managed to get to his feet. Alan began limping toward the campgrounds. There was a light on in one of the buildings.

George Nickerson, the Assembly of God Youth Director of the Royal Rangers, was surprised to hear someone pounding on his door so late at night. Nickerson turned on the porch light, looked out the small, leaded-crossed window cut into his door and saw the battered boy. He quickly opened the door and helped Alan inside. The boy was talking fast. Nickerson was tending to the boy's injuries, trying to make sense of what he was saying. He began to glance around nervously when Alan said some man had killed his friend and thrown his body into the trunk of his car. Nickerson picked up the phone and called the police. The state police dispatched an officer before Nickerson had hung up the phone.

When State Trooper Bennett arrived at the campgrounds, the handcuffed boy told him a cop made them get into his car and then tried to kill them. He asked Bennett to take off the cuffs. Alan's teeth were clattering as he told the trooper what had happened to him and Billy. His hands were rubbing his red swollen wrists. Alan hysterically said he saw the fat man kill his best friend. An all points bulletin was issued for the green Plymouth Belvedere.

Bar Jonah was driving around trying to get his bearings; he was soaked with sweat. He was beating the steering wheel with his fists, admonishing himself. It was stupid to leave the kid's body just lying beside the road. He should have taken time to kick it into the brush or throw it over the hill. He hadn't been thinking. Slamming on the brakes, he turned the car around.

Officer Sterns, who was called to assist in the hunt for the assailant of a murdered young boy, was not far from the old gravel road leading to the Rangers' campground.

Bar Jonah was drawing hard on his cigarette when he turned back onto Cemetery Road. Officer Sterns, of the Carlton Police Department, saw the car matching the APB. He put on his lights and siren. Bar Jonah floored the car, swerving, throwing gravel, tearing down the narrow road. Officer Sterns stayed close to Bar Jonah, not letting him gain any distance while calling for immediate backup.

At a curve in the road, the cop forced Bar Jonah's car into a clump of thick brush. Sterns got out of his car, shielding himself with the door of his patrol car while drawing his revolver. He screamed for Bar Jonah to get out of the car and fall to the ground. The door opened and Bar Jonah rolled out onto the gravel. As Sterns approached Bar Jonah he heard screaming from inside the trunk. He shoved his knee into Bar Jonah's back and handcuffed him. By now another trooper, Phillip Christiansen, had arrived on the scene and was assisting Sterns. Christiansen reached into Bar Jonah's right pants pocket, and found the keys to the trunk. He slipped the key into the thin slot, lifted the trunk lid and found Billy handcuffed, battered, bruised, and terrified, but alive. It was 12:40 a.m.

Bar Jonah was arrested and taken to the Sturbridge Police Barracks, where he dictated and signed a full confession of the crime that differed from what actually happened. The confession sounded like Bar Jonah was a police officer, giving the report of a crime that someone else had committed. It did not have the tone of an assailant.

On September 24, 1977 Bar Jonah appeared before Judge Gentry, who set a cash bond of $50,000. He was charged with two counts of attempted murder, two counts of kidnapping, impersonating a police officer, and failure to stop. Bar Jonah was transferred to the Worcester House of Correction to await trial. Gentry also ordered for Bar Jonah to be interviewed by psychiatrist Steven Cronin. Cronin would eventually become chief of forensic psychiatry at Bridgewater State Hospital.

Cronin interviewed Bar Jonah on November 12 in preparation for his hearing in December. The interview only lasted thirty minutes. However, in that short time Dr. Cronin saw Bar Jonah for who he was: "He clearly acknowledges that he has trouble controlling his impulses toward young boys. He also acknowledges that two years prior to these charges he was arrested on similar ones. There is no evidence to support the possibility that he enters any type of dissociative state. His view of himself is quite fragmented. Although he lacks the glib, social facility stereotypically associated with psychopaths, there is considerable evidence to suggest a primary diagnosis of psychopathic personality. He has never internalized a set of well-developed moral rules by which he lives. His interactive ability is weak and he does not easily articulate the consequences of his actions. His behavior is quite impulsive. Despite his psychopathic tendencies, his ego function has other features more typically associated with borderline personality. Among these features are his poor defended raw oral aggressive impulses. His characteristic modes of behavior have resulted in a failure to crystallize into a more integrated personality structure. He feels he has shamed his mother. He has also never successfully separated psychologically from early familial objects and longs to remain tied to them forever. His therapy should focus on getting him to experience guilt and to develop a more adaptive conscience."

Susan

In 1974, a ten-year-old girl was riding her bicycle along Masapaug Road. Masapaug was a long road that goes from Shrewsbury straight through to Connecticut. There wasn't a lot of traffic on Masapaug Road but it was bordered with lovely old growth trees and tall shrubs. A bucolic route. As Susan Terry was riding along, singing—she always liked to sing when she rode her bicycle—a car pulled up and forced her to ride her bicycle into the dense brush. No one saw her crash but someone did report seeing a green car pulled off of the side of the road. Another driver reported seeing a fat, unkempt man leaning against the side of a parked car, smoking a cigarette.

Susan's parents were frantic trying to figure out where she was. She only was going out to ride her bike. Susan was never gone for very long. Her father went looking for her: no trace. While he was out looking, Susan's mother called the sheriff.

One of the things a police officer dreads is missing children. Most of the time it turns out that the kid has been distracted and is late getting home. But other times, they simply vanish, never to be heard from again. Then there are those times when they are found and the ending is not good. This was the case with Susan Terry. A driver noticed the rear wheel of a pink bicycle, sticking out from some thick brush, still spinning. He stopped to see, if perhaps, a child was injured. As he pushed back the thicket he found Susan's body. Her arms and feet were bound with white cloth bandage tape, her shorts and panties had been removed. Her face and head were severely beaten and she had been strangled.

Questions

Right before Bar Jonah was transferred from the local jail to the Worcester House of Detention, Officer Stephen Bennett went to interview him. Bennett said Bar Jonah was one of the oddest people he had ever met. During the interview, Bar Jonah talked to Bennett like they were partners out on patrol together. Bar Jonah sat with his arms stretched out over the back of two chairs, his head cocked to one side. His eyes were glaring at Bennett, who questioned him about the kidnapping and attempted murder of the two boys. He acted contrite, saying he must have blacked-out. Even though he wrote a statement about what had happened, he really didn't remember doing it.

As the interview was winding down, Bar Jonah spontaneously brought up Susan Terry. He said, "Yea, she was the girl who was killed with a large rock and bound in tape." Bennett was stunned. Those details hadn't been released. When Bennett confronted Bar Jonah, he hesitated and said, "Well, it was some kind of blunt instrument that killed her."

Bar Jonah had been a student at Bay Path High School at the time Susan Terry was killed. He always used Masapaug Road on his way to and from school where Terry's body was found. It was a nice drive, he said.

Officer Bennett spoke with Chief Denault of the Sturbridge Police Department. The chief told Bennett on the day the girl went missing a heavy set man, fitting Bar Jonah's description, was seen hanging around the area where the child's body was found. The child's panties and dungaree shorts were missing when they found her body covered with some brush. She was bound with white cloth adhesive tape; bandage tape. When Bar Jonah's green Belvedere was searched after the kidnapping, officers found three first aid boxes containing the same kind of bandage tape used in the Terry murder.

As Officer Bennett investigated Bar Jonah's background, he discovered the boys he abducted and assaulted all had short light brown or blond hair. The Terry girl had short blond hair and could easily have been mistaken for a boy.

Bennett asked a district judge to sign a search warrant for the Sutton Apartments in Worcester, where Bar Jonah and Tyra were now living. In the search warrant, Bennett wrote that he was looking for "two inch wide white adhesive tape, one pair of girl's white cotton panties, blue dungarees, shorts with flowered embroidery along the seam and newspaper clips pertaining to the Terry murder".

A clerk from the Sturbridge PD called Tyra to see if she was going to be home. When Tyra answered the phone and learned that the cops wanted to come over and search her apartment, she said she was going to be out for a couple of hours. Could they come then, she asked. The clerk said that she would notify the officers. Two hours later, when the police arrived at the apartment, Tyra was already there. The apartment was spotless, everything just where it should be. The officers were unable to find anything in the apartment linking Bar Jonah to the child's death. One of the cops put his hand on the hood of the green Plymouth; it was still warm. No one asked Tyra where she had been. They didn't bother to search the car either.

CHAPTER FIVE

Just barely guilty

On December 14, 1977, Bar Jonah pled guilty to attempted murder and kidnapping. He was given the maximum sentence of eighteen to twenty years, on all counts. His handwritten confession was read in court:

> *I live at 59 Harley Dr., Worcester, Massachusetts. I was advised of my rights and I have waived those rights and am giving the following statement to Trooper Stephen L. Bennett on September 24, 1977 at approximately 3:05 a.m. at the Sturbridge State Police Barracks.*
>
> *On Friday the 23rd of September 1977 I was in the White City parking lot on Route 9 in Shrewsbury. It was probably between 9:30 and 10:00 p.m. I was going pretty slow through the parking lot. As I was driving out of the lot I saw two boys, about 13 years old, walking up near the exit. I pulled up beside them and stopped the car. I rolled down the passenger side window and flashed my police badge at the boys and ordered them into the car. One of the boys opened the passenger side door and said "What did we do?" He then asked me to give them a ride home. I told them they shouldn't be out so late alone. I pulled out of the parking lot and asked the boys where they lived. They*

told me and I headed in that direction. After we had drove about two miles one of the boys said "You have to go down this way to get to my house, you're going past where you have to turn." I went around the bend and kept driving. The boys then started yelling something about "Where are you taking us?" I pulled into an alley and reached into my blue police jacket and brought out a hunting knife. That shut them up pretty quick. I put the knife down beside me and told them to keep their mouths shut. I told them to lean over and to put their hands behind their backs. I then cuffed them. Then they started whimpering or something like that. I went down some back roads and came out on Route 9 and then took a side road and kept driving around for about two hours. While I was driving the boys were crying and asking stupid questions like "Where are you taking us?", stuff like that. I didn't give them any answers. I went down some more roads and came to Route 290 and took them to Charlton. I pulled up to Bev's Flea Market behind a tent I had put up about four hours before. I opened the car door and helped the kids out of the car. They asked me if I'd take the handcuffs off. I told them I would but I would kill the first one I caught if they ran. I wanted them to think each other's life was dependent on the other. I made them sit down on the grass under the tent. There wasn't anyone around at that time of night and it was a big field so they couldn't run far without me seeing them even if they did take off. But I weigh 375 pounds so it would have been pretty difficult for me to catch them if they really started running. But they were pretty scared so I wasn't too worried about them taking off. Then the bigger of the two started asking me "When are we going home?", and annoying stuff like that. I told them in a little while or so, not really meaning it. Then I looked at one of them and said "If you want to go home bad enough take your clothes off." They said "No." We were under the tent about 10 or 15 minutes, I don't really know for sure. The boys said they were cold. I said if you want to get warmer you have to get into the car. They were told to stand up and put their hands behind their backs. I then rehandcuffed them. I escorted them back to the car and put them in the back seat and put the heat on so they would be comfortable. We drove out onto Route 20 and back onto the road that led to the campground. That's when I decided they could identify me and they would have to die. I stopped the car and made the bigger boy come out and the smaller boy remain in the car. I ordered him to remain put! I took the larger boy into a wooded area and immediately started to strangle him with my hands around his throat. I guess mainly because he could identify me and I wanted to kill him. After a few minutes he went limp. I assumed he was dead. I went back and got the smaller boy out of the car and started strangling him and trying to break his neck with the crook of my arm. He went limp pretty quick. I opened the trunk and shoved him in. I went back into the woods and drug out the bigger boy and shoved him into the trunk also. It was hard work dragging the bigger boy out of the woods and pushing him up over the lip of the trunk. It got me out of breath. I closed the lid of the trunk and drove back out onto Route 20. I was looking for a place to bury the boys when I looked into the rear view mirror and observed that a Massachusetts Highway Patrol car was following me. I kept on driving the speed limit and was looking for a place to turn around without arousing suspicion. Suddenly the MHP officer turned on his lights and I immediately pulled over without incident.

I looked in the rear view mirror and saw the officer get out of the car with his sidearm drawn. He screamed "Get out of the car with your hands up ... now!" I did as I was ordered. When I opened the car door I heard the boys screaming and kicking the inside lid of the trunk. The officer then came running up and shoved me pretty hard against the car and jerked my hands behind my back and handcuffed me. He then shoved me down on my knees and pushed my head into the gravel and told me not to move, which I did not. He reached in and turned the car off, took the keys and opened the trunk. I thought the boys had

been dead. If they were the MHP officer would not have seen the
trunk lid bouncing around and then used that as an excuse to
pull me over. I wouldn't be completing this statement right now
and I would be free and not facing criminal charges. I want it
on the record that the officer yelled and harshly pushed me onto
the gravel roadway and that the boys really dented the trunk lid
of my car. I think I should be compensated for the damage they
caused. I cooperated fully with the MHP officer and how he
treated me was not called for.

Bar Jonah's time would be served in the Massachusetts Correctional Institute, at Walpole. He was subsequently transferred to MCI at Concord where he would spend two years.

In early 1979, Bar Jonah began aggressively petitioning to be transferred to Bridgewater State Hospital in Bridgewater, Massachusetts. This was a far less restrictive environment, plus his friend Wayne was already there. "It's good here," Wayne wrote in one of his letters. "You should get your ass over here." They hadn't known each other on the outside very long, until they each had a run-in with the law and ended up with about the same length sentences. It was also during this time that prison officials began to notice that all of Bar Jonah's letters contained drawings of himself or doodles. In their reports, they commented many times on his artistic ability throughout the fifteen years he would be in prison.

Bar Jonah had heard from the other prisoners at Concord that the staff at Bridgewater were not as jaded. After dozens of letters and countless calls from Tyra advocating for her son, psychiatrist Daniel M. Weiss, on March 6, 1979 recommended that Bar Jonah be sent to BWSH for a full clinical evaluation. The evaluation would be to determine if he met the criteria of a sexually dangerous person, as defined by the state of Massachusetts. On the day he arrived at BWSH Bar Jonah was greeted by his best friend Wayne who ran up, wrapped his arms around him, and asked why it had taken so long for him to get there. BWSH was known in the pedophile community as "graduate school." You could go in as a freshman child molester and come out with a doctorate in pedophilia. It was a place where snakes went to shed their skin.

* * *

In May 1979 Tyra wrote a letter to Dr. Nicholas Groth, Director of Forensic Mental Health for the State of Massachusetts. Tyra was trying to elicit the help of Dr. Groth in securing Bar Jonah's permanent transfer to BWSH. In the letter Tyra complained that each time Bar Jonah had been considered for permanent status, the same member of the review board, who also happened to be black, denied Bar Jonah's request. Tyra pleaded with Dr. Groth to help. Groth wrote back and said he would look into the situation.

At the end of May, a memo was issued by the Superintendent of the Massachusetts Department of Corrections saying that Bar Jonah would be considered for parole in October, 1989. But first he would have to serve a minimum of ten years of his sentence.

On July 30, 1979, psychologists Robert F. Moore and Robert Levy both concurred that Bar Jonah was in fact a predator and a sexually dangerous person. He should remain at BWSH. But because of Dr. Moore's and Dr. Levy's report, Bar Jonah's sentence, of "eighteen to twenty years", was amended by the court to read "from one day to life." Moore and Levy believed that Bar Jonah was in fact so dangerous and intractable, that he should *never* be released from prison. In fact, Levy was instrumental in keeping Bar Jonah behind bars and off of the streets for many years.

On January 19 and 30, 1990, Dr. Liza Brooks, consulting forensic psychologist to the court, said Bar Jonah told her that his attorney was trying to get him released from prison. In his interview with Dr. Brooks, Bar Jonah tried to convince her that he was ready to be discharged. Bar Jonah also said he had a place to stay in Montana with his brother, Bob. He wanted to get out, study journalism, and get a patent on a couple of board games he had designed while in prison. Dr. Brooks thought better of it and wrote that Bar Jonah was *still* a sexually dangerous person, who would, *without question* reoffend should he be released back into the community.

Leonard Bard, PhD, another forensic psychologist, also attempted to evaluate Bar Jonah on January 26 and February 2, 1990. Bar Jonah refused Dr. Bard's request to interview him, saying he didn't need it. It was time for him to get out; he had things to do. Bard however, did do an *in absentia* evaluation, based on Bar Jonah's clinical and administrative records at BWSH. He noted that Bar Jonah was diagnosed as a borderline personality disorder with psychopathic features. It was also noted that Bar Jonah's fantasies were highly bizarre in nature and included an interest in the taste of human flesh, methods of torture, and dissection. His progress at the BWSH was minimal, even though he had been there for thirteen years. Bar Jonah was uncooperative and refused to become involved in most of the treatment opportunities he was offered.

Bar Jonah was enraged that Brooks and Bard did not yield to his efforts to see things his way. He had written his victims letters of apology, at the suggestion of one of the therapists at Bridgewater. He had said he was *sorry*. What more did they want?

Tyra was sixty-one years old when Bar Jonah went to prison in 1977. During the fifteen years he was incarcerated, she drove the more than 180 miles round trip at least once a week to visit him in prison. During her visits he would say the same thing over and over again, mostly demanding that she send him more money or get him this or that. He also expected her to send him food, particularly cookies. He didn't want the crap they served in the commissary. Bar Jonah was also pressing Tyra to do *something* about getting him out.

* * *

When Bar Jonah's attempts to convince Bard and Brooks of his rehabilitation failed, Bar Jonah demanded that Tyra find a Christian psychologist. He would understand the sacrifices that Bar Jonah had made in the service of the Lord and, more important, see that he had been saved. A Christian psychologist would know only the power of God could bring about real change. This would not be cheap. The state would not pay for outside evaluators; if Bar Jonah wanted it, he would have to pay for it. Of course this meant Tyra.

Bar Jonah petitioned the court to permit evaluations to be conducted by outside psychologists who were "not biased against him." It was his right, he would say. In late November, 1990 the court granted his request. Tyra and Bob found two Christian psychologists, Richard Ober, PhD and Eric Sweitzer, PhD, who agreed to conduct the evaluations. Sweitzer's letterhead identified him as being affiliated with the First Congregational Church, in Middleboro. Their fee for doing the evaluation was $5000 apiece. Bob, it was said, wrote the checks. Bar Jonah was ecstatic at the news.

During the interviews with Ober and Sweitzer, Bar Jonah particularly emphasized the gang rape when he was ten, and his heroic actions that saved his best friend Kevin's life. The evaluators were impressed and empathic. Ober seemed to be particularly impressed when Bar Jonah told him that he now "had only heterosexual interests" and in fact had a pen pal fiancée. Ober referred to this as a maturing of Bar Jonah's sexual attitudes. Bar Jonah also denied having any violent fantasies or desires. Ober believed him. Ober also cited an incident that Bar Jonah said occurred on October 2, 1989, where he was stripped, searched, and raped in prison. Bar Jonah said a black prison guard tried to rectally examine him for contraband. Bar Jonah resisted. The guard, angry at his refusal, decided to teach him a lesson, and called eight of his fellow black guards into Bar Jonah's cell. The guards forcibly moved Bar Jonah to another cell. Early in the day the same eight guards had beat to death another inmate in the same cell they moved Bar Jonah to. The mattress in the cell was soaked thick with the dead inmate's congealed blood. Bar Jonah said a "big black buck" forced him onto the mattress, where each of the guards sodomized him one after the other. He was bleeding profusely from his rectum. One of the guards even videotaped the rape. They all walked out of the cell and left him for dead. Bar Jonah didn't know how he had survived. He only remembered waking up in the infirmary.

Ober was deeply disturbed when Bar Jonah recounted this event. He also noted the gang rape by the guards caused Bar Jonah to traumatically remember the rape that took place when he was ten years old.

Bar Jonah said he attempted to take legal action against the guards, but was unsuccessful because he tried to work within the system: "There was a cover up." Ober judged Bar Jonah's response to the rape was "adaptive." He also suggested, "This incident demonstrates his ability to handle stress as a result of perceived sexual trauma and to control his impulses."

As was Bar Jonah's pattern, he lied about being gang-raped by the guards, taking the opportunity to use one lie to give credence to another. Ober concluded his report by stating, "It is the opinion of this evaluator that Mr. Bar Jonah is not at this time likely to victimize others due to his uncontrolled desires." Ober did not administer any psychological test instruments.

As part of Sweitzer's evaluation, he did decide to administer the Minnesota Multiphasic Personality Inventory (MMPI), the Rorschach, and the Thematic Apperception Test (TAT). These psychological tests are used to evaluate personality traits and any underlying abnormal psychopathology. Over the years Bar Jonah had developed an extensive familiarity with all the evaluative instruments, having had them administered many times before, the most recent being just a few months before by Bard and Brooks. Sweitzer concluded from his evaluation that there was no evidence of a "psychotic thinking style" and "no evidence of sadistic or aggressive preoccupation with sexual ideation."

When Sweitzer reviewed Bar Jonah's records he also concluded there was little evidence to support the sexual deviant nature of his offences. In 2000, Cascade County Attorney Brandt Light said that the conclusions reached by Ober and Sweitzer were inconsistent with *reason*, based upon the thousands of pages of contradictory information in his criminal file.

Sweitzer's assertions were completely opposite from Dr. Brooks's just ten months before. Sweitzer also said that since Bar Jonah had not attempted to recidivate while in prison it would seem the "risk for reoccurrence to be minimal." Sweitzer failed to note that there were, however, no young boys in prison.

Sweitzer's conclusions were that Bar Jonah's offenses were not of a sexual nature nor was there strong enough evidence to support such "intent." He was also impressed that Bar Jonah was able to understand that the boys who raped him when he was ten no longer had any control over him. Sweitzer stated, "This awareness appears to eliminate his need for revenge." Sweitzer, like Ober, also cited Bar Jonah's emotional restraint and maturity involving the gang rape by the prison guards.

"Bar Jonah ran his own greeting card business while at BWSH and had created board games, which he intends to patent," Sweitzer continued in his report. Bar Jonah used other inmates as a "trial population" when he tested his games. Like Ober, Sweitzer was impressed at Bar Jonah's heterosexual transformation and his relationship with a woman from Arkansas. Sweitzer noted that Bar Jonah planned to pursue this relationship, as soon as he was released, in a hopeful but cautious manner. He said this suggested a mature awareness of deeper levels of intimacy and commitment. Ober saw Bar Jonah's devout devotion to Jesus as a means Bar Jonah would use to control his impulses. Bar Jonah had not remained isolated and resistant, as the other evaluators had determined. Their judgment was wrong. They had misunderstood Bar Jonah.

Sweitzer then went on to highlight Bar Jonah's plans to move to Great Falls, Montana, with Tyra and Bob. His brother had a place waiting for them. Bar Jonah's "religious faith" would deter him from any further acts of violence as would the support of his church community, Sweitzer stated. Sweitzer failed to note that Bar Jonah had tried to strangle the two boys he was in prison for on the road leading to his church camp. Bar Jonah would unlikely find himself in the same provocative situation which led to his violent behavior, fifteen years ago, Sweitzer concluded. For these reasons Sweitzer judged Bar Jonah being designated a sexually dangerous person was "inappropriate".

Sweitzer and Ober agreed, the continuation of the sexually dangerous person status was not necessary. He should be released without any qualifications or follow-up recommendations.

A liar and his fools

Walter E. Steele made some good friends on July 18, 1969, the night Mary Jo Kopechne died on Chappaquiddick Island in a car driven by Edward Kennedy. It became known as the Dike Bridge Case. Steele was the special prosecutor in Dukes County, Massachusetts at the time Kopechne died. Her death was ruled an accident, even though no autopsy was performed and the circumstances of the case were highly suspicious. Kennedy entered a plea of guilty to leaving the scene of an accident. He received a sentence of two months in jail. Steele recommended suspending the sentence, saying in an interview, "The reputation of the defendant and his family is known to the court and to the world." Kennedy was not even required to serve any meager time on probation. The Kennedy family thanked Steele publicly for his fair-minded approach to justice. Steele, shortly thereafter, enjoyed a meteoric rise to the Bench in Suffolk County, Massachusetts.

On February 12, 1991, Sweitzer and Ober appeared before Judge Steele. Steele agreed with Sweitzer's and Ober's conclusions and ordered the immediate release of Bar Jonah. Bar Jonah was taken back to BSWH and forgotten about until July. He was furious. Judge Steele had released him. Now he was being held captive by the state of Massachusetts. He had rights. He would sue. On Friday morning, June 28, 1991, Phillip DiPaolo, Program Director at Bridgewater, received the amended order mandating the immediate release of Bar Jonah to the "streets."

Bar Jonah demanded to call his mother as soon as the guard told him he was being released. He told the guard to escort him to the pay phone. His collect calls to Tyra would sometimes cost over three hundred dollars a month. This was the last call he would *ever* have to make from prison, he said. "Come and get me; I'm getting out." Tyra was now seventy-five years old.

When he called Tyra, Bar Jonah told her to buy him a new outfit, black polyester pants and a white shirt. "Go get them now," he said. He wanted his shirt starched and ironed before she left home. Tyra arrived at Bridgewater about three. Bar Jonah was waiting in the lobby, beyond the locked steel doors for the first time in fifteen years. He had several boxes piled on top of each other. His Commodore 64 computer that Bob had given him, hundreds of pen-pal letters and books, mostly on mental health law in Massachusetts, made the boxes heavy. He insisted the guards move his belongings to the front. It was the least they could do. They had kidnapped him; they owed him. Tyra had his clothes hung neatly on a hanger, the pressed white shirt draped over the black pants. He was disappointed. He thought they were cheap, saying she should have gone to a better store. With the pants draped over his arm and the white shirt wadded up in a ball, Bar Jonah disappeared into the bathroom, emerging a few minutes later, spiffed up, ready to go back into the world. He was no longer a sexually dangerous person. Bending over to pick up one of the boxes made him flinch. His back hurt. Tyra would have to carry the boxes to the car. Tyra tried several times to pick up the heavy boxes. Several times she dropped them.

One of the guards saw Tyra struggling. Feeling sorry for her, he got a dolly and offered to help. Bar Jonah sat in the front seat and watched the guard and Tyra, in the outside rearview mirror, load the boxes into the car. "Hurry up," he yelled back, "I haven't had dinner yet."

Tyra found a hamburger joint on the way home and filled his belly with three triple cheese hamburgers, three large fries, and a couple of pastries. He washed everything down with four chocolate shakes. It was important that he get his strength back. Prison had been hard on him. He had lost almost 100 pounds on the garbage prison food even with the cookies Tyra brought him once a week. He also wanted to see a dentist. His teeth hurt continually; his mouth was full of rot.

* * *

Monday morning, July 1, Bar Jonah woke up and called the law offices of Day, Berry and Howard. They had been retained by Tyra to represent Bar Jonah's many complaints while he was in prison; he needed their help again. Later that week they filed a suit on behalf of Bar Jonah, against the State of Massachusetts Correction Authority claiming wrongful imprisonment. The state they said had to pay Bar Jonah for the disruption they had caused to his life.

Tyra pushed Bar Jonah to try to find work. He deserved a rest, he told her, he had been locked up for fifteen years and he was going to take it easy for a while. Bar Jonah spent most of his time lying around the house, watching television, eating, and making phone calls. A thousand dollar phone bill surprised Tyra the first month that he was out of Bridgewater. He had to call his pen pals he said. There was also the woman in Arkansas that Sweitzer and Ober talked about in their report. He was talking to her about marriage. He was looking forward to being a father; she had a couple of young boys who needed a dad. There were more than 100 calls throughout the United States he made to other men that he had met as pen pals while in prison. He said they were his buddies, all 300 of them. They wrote letters back and forth, thick letters. Tyra said she thought they exchanged a lot of pictures of their families.

Michael

It was raining in Oxford, Massachusetts on August 9, 1991. Like most humid, drizzly days, if someone is in a car and it is not running, the windows steam up. Mrs. Surprise left about noon to go to the post office, to mail a package to her mother. Her son Michael, a cute, seven-year-old blond-headed boy, was buckled up in the back seat of the car. Oxford was a pretty sleepy little town, no crime to speak of. The paper mostly listed traffic violations as what occupied the court's time.

Michael's mother pulled into the parking lot of the Oxford Post Office, leaned over the front seat, and told Michael she would be right back. Mommy was just going to run into the post office and mail grandma a present, she said to Michael. There was a bit longer of a line than she had expected, so she sat her package down and started talking to one of her neighbors that she happened to run into.

Bar Jonah is out walking. He liked to walk, especially a little bit after noon. Especially now that he was out of prison. The elementary school was close by and he loved the playground right after lunchtime. So many children out, running around, playing tag. Bar Jonah always cut through the post office parking lot and took the footpath through a small clump of trees to get to the school.

As Bar Jonah turns into the parking lot he sees the head of a small boy, barely peeking through the foggy back window of a car. He takes a quick look around, seeing no one. It is raining. Everyone with any sense is inside.

Bar Jonah was breathing faster now. He jerked open the car door, standing for a moment, looking down at Michael Surprise. He had gained some of his weight back now and weighed about 275 pounds with a full black dingy beard and long greasy hair. Bar Jonah's coon skin cap was dripping wet from the rain. Climbing into the back seat of the car he slammed his full weight on top of the little boy. Bar Jonah was grunting, as he pushed against the top of the car shoving his body into the chest of the child. Michael was trying to scream but he couldn't push any air out, his lungs felt like they were going to burst. The little boy could only feel Bar Jonah's soggy shirt clinging to his face; clogging his nose as h desperately tried to breathe.

Michael's mother almost tore the car door off of its hinges. She had come out of the post office and saw a stringy-haired fat man in the back seat of her car. Bar Jonah felt his face being hit. His nose was bleeding. He was screaming that he was not doing anything. "I just needed to get out of the rain," he said. He felt his hair being grabbed as Mrs. Surprise dragged him out of the car, pulling him off her son. Michael took a deep gasp of air. Bar Jonah slipped and fell onto the wet pavement, quickly getting up, running out of the parking lot. Michael's mother undid her son's seat belt. There was blood coming from his nose; he was having trouble breathing. He began to scream.

Michael's mother never found out who called the police, who arrived shortly after Bar Jonah took off running up the street. An ambulance arrived a few minutes later and took Michael to the hospital. He was treated in the emergency room and admitted for observation. The doctor wanted to make sure the boy was stable. Michael clung to his mother, unable to tolerate a man touching him, not even his father who arrived a while later. Mrs. Surprise was so traumatized by what happened she could not identify Bar Jonah. Michael could only describe his assailant's wet shirt. He said the man smelled bad too, like a wet dog.

One of the police officers taking the report recognized the description of Bar Jonah from fifteen years before. Upon checking, the officer discovered Bar Jonah had been released from prison just forty-three days earlier. Ober and Sweitzer were wrong. Several police officers showed up at Tyra's apartment about 3 p.m. and found Bar Jonah sitting in front of the television, eating a bowl of macaroni and cheese. Tyra said he was starving when he got home, insisting that she fix him some lunch. He offered no resistance to the police, saying only he jumped into the car because he was trying to get out of the rain. He didn't understand what all the fuss was. Later at the police station Bar Jonah did pen a handwritten confession indicating his intent to kill Michael.

He was arraigned and released on his own recognizance. Tyra took him home later that evening. He had a big dinner. It had been a long day. The police had not been very nice, he said. Bar Jonah was upset because the court had issued a stay away order. He was told he was not allowed to re-enter the town of Oxford.

Later that night Bar Jonah looked up the address of the Surprises in the phone book: he wanted to visit them. He called a cab and gave the cabby their address. Bar Jonah handed the driver twenty dollars and told him to pull up in front of their house. He lifted himself out of the back seat of the cab and walked halfway up the walkway. Mrs. Surprise heard the cab, looked out the window and saw Bar Jonah staring at her. She quickly turned off all of the lights and called the police. Mr. and Mrs. Surprise grabbed Michael and locked themselves in an upstairs bedroom. Bar Jonah turned, got back into the cab telling the driver to take him home. He had got what he came for.

When the case against Bar Jonah crossed the desk of Oxford Police Chief James Triplett and County District Attorney John Conte they *immediately* referred it to Probation. Sending Bar Jonah back to prison *would not* be a consideration.

The case was assigned to the docket of Judge Milton H. Raphaelson in Dudley District Court. In their conversations with Judge Raphaelson about probation, neither Triplett nor Conte apprised the judge that Bar Jonah had spent fifteen years in prison for attempted murder and kidnapping. Bar Jonah's handwritten confession or his visit to the Surprises was also not brought into the discussion. However, Judge Raphaelson did insist that Bar Jonah undergo a psychiatric evaluation prior to his final adjudication.

Bar Jonah was called to appear before Judge Sarkis Teshoian, twenty-four hours after appearing before Judge Raphaelson. Judge Teshoian was not informed that Bar Jonah had already appeared before Judge Raphaelson. Judge Teshoian said the facts in the case were compelling. Bar Jonah would be charged with assault and battery and entering a motor vehicle with the intent to commit a felony. The judge also handwrote on the docket sheet that Bar Jonah would receive an indefinite sentence, returning him to Concord State Penitentiary not Bridgewater. Immediately before Judge Teshoian was ready to hand down his decision, Conte informed the judge that a plea agreement had already been reached, which recommended Bar Jonah serve two years of probation. Given the county attorney had already arranged a plea, Judge Teshoian abandoned his original decision to return Bar Jonah to prison. He agreed to the plea, again adding that Bar Jonah was to undergo a complete psychiatric evaluation. Bar Jonah readily accepted. Judge Teshoian also was never presented with Bar Jonah's criminal background. He understood Bar Jonah to be a first time offender.

There was one more detail to the plea be worked out. Tyra had approached Bob, who had moved to Montana after he left the Air Force. He had a good job, teaching computer engineering at Maelstrom Air Force Base, in Great Falls. He was well established in his Assembly of God community and had several rental properties, including an apartment building. Tyra wanted Bob to let her and Bar Jonah move into one of his apartments. Tyra made the proposal to Conte to let her take Bar Jonah to Montana. Conte thought it was a good idea. He discussed the plea agreement with Teshoian, who agreed to let Bar Jonah leave the state, but he still had to serve two years on probation. On August 22, 1991, Teshoian handed Bar Jonah his final decision.

If a probationer from one state plans to move to another state, the state they are moving to must agree to accept them for supervision. The process is carried out through the Inter-state Compact Agreement, which manages the relocation of offenders across state lines. Most states will not accept sexual or violent offenders into their state. Why *should* one state take on the problem of another? Before someone is allowed to leave the state where the crime occurred, the agreement through the compact *must* be in place. However in this case, no one both-ered to tell Montana that Bar Jonah was coming.

At sentencing, Judge Teshoian ordered Bar Jonah to report *directly* to Probation when he left his courtroom. It was down on the second floor, the judge said. Bar Jonah nodded but thought better of it after the hearing and simply left the courthouse. Tyra picked him up out front. He told her to drive him home. He wanted to get on the road right away. He also decided to forgo the psychiatric evaluation.

Tyra rented a small trailer that she could pull behind her car on the long drive to Montana. Bar Jonah had lots of toys he had to bring for his antique business that he was excited about starting. He wanted to get it going as soon as he got to Great

Falls. He let Tyra have a little space in the back of the trailer for her clothes and a few keepsakes. They left for Montana a week after he was sentenced. He did not receive any calls from Probation before they left.

CHAPTER SIX

Montana bound

Bar Jonah and Tyra departed early in the morning, August 29. Heading west, the sun wasn't going to be in their eyes. That morning Bar Jonah said he had a headache so Tyra would have to drive. Once they got on the road, Bar Jonah insisted they go to Montana by way of Arkansas, to meet the woman that he was going to marry. Bar Jonah and Tyra began to head south, instead of due west. The trip was long.

Tyra could only drive about five hours a day before she became exhausted. She was seventy-five. Bar Jonah complained a lot about the heat and feeling cramped in the car. He wanted to stop at every quick food place they passed. They also had to make frequent stops at rest areas, where he could sit for a while and watch the kids run around, while their parents took a break from driving. Sometimes he would try to help the parents out by offering to play with their children. He loved kids, he would tell them.

Along the way there were signs off I-75, pointing to old drive-in movie theaters that had been turned into flea markets. Bar Jonah insisted on stopping at every one, packing any remaining cranny in the car with toy guns and small metal cars. Sometimes he would give them away to the kids he met at rest areas along the way. One mother hugged him, praising his generosity and kindness, he said. He said it was just the Christian thing to do.

Tyra liked to be checked into a motel before they sat down for dinner, preferring to go back to their room afterwards and call it a night. Bar Jonah liked to go out walking. He would be gone for hours. She never knew where he went. He would get in late and be hard to get going the next morning.

Short-lived love

It took a week before they pulled up to the 1965, cream colored, New Moon mobile home, just outside of Little Rock. One of Bar Jonah's cellmates at Bridgewater had told him he knew a good woman who was looking for a good man; someone to help her raise her two boys. Bar Jonah started writing her right away: he had been looking for a woman to settle down with. They fast became pen pals, writing every week for a couple of years. Sandy was about ten years older than Bar Jonah and had two boys, eight and ten. He told her in his letters that was his favorite age for kids, saying they have such impressionable minds and imaginations.

Sandy looked haggard. She'd had a hard life. A couple of marriages that had lasted too long with difficult men, both of them drinkers, she said. Her hair was a dry red, pulled back in a tight ponytail. There were lots of freckles that were accented by gin blossomed cheeks. She was about five foot three and had a belly that looked unruly in her polyester stretch pants, seemingly always trying to go in a different direction than where Sandy was going. Her constrained laughter always sounded wet with tears. Sandy's first vision of Bar Jonah was not what she had imagined. She had only seen old torn pictures he had mailed her from prison. But somehow they had not captured his weight, the droop of his jowls, or his smell. He had lost about 150 pounds in prison. But since being released, he had gained back almost 100 pounds. He was again over 300 pounds.

Almost immediately he began to talk about marriage. Bar Jonah said he didn't want to go on to Montana, he had decided to stay in Arkansas. They would move in together right away. But, they would have separate bedrooms. He didn't believe in sex before marriage; it was against his religion. She said her trailer was too small. There was no spare bedroom. That's okay, he said, the boys' room is where he would sleep.

Bar Jonah stood up and walked into her sons' room, looked at the bunk beds, and declared, "The bottom one will be mine." Sandy was dumbstruck. Bar Jonah told Sandy to change the sheets. He needed to take a nap after coming so far. He was exhausted. A few minutes after Sandy changed the sheets, she smelled cigarette smoke coming from her boys' room. She went in to find Bar Jonah sitting on the bottom bunk, in his underwear, smoking a cigarette. Sandy told Bar Jonah that if he wanted to smoke, to please go outside. She didn't want him smoking inside the trailer, especially in her boys' room. Bar Jonah took one last drag, snuffed out the cigarette on the metal bedpost, and slipped the rest of the unburned butt back into his cigarette pack. Sandy guessed that a lot of Bar Jonah's sensibilities had been washed away in prison. Before Sandy left the room, she glanced down and noticed the massive scar on Bar Jonah's right leg. He hadn't told Sandy anything about having a scar, especially one that took up most of his upper thigh. She found it repulsive. When Sandy walked back out to the living room, she found Tyra asleep on the couch. Sandy took a crocheted comforter off of the back of couch and draped it over Tyra. Sandy was sure Tyra was exhausted after driving the entire way.

Sandy's boys were complaining they couldn't go into their room. They didn't like their mother's new boyfriend. He smelled bad. More important, they didn't want him sleeping in their beds. A couple of hours later, Bar Jonah stretched awake to the smell of pot roast. He came out of the bedroom rubbing his eyes. Tyra had briefly stirred and offered to help Sandy fix dinner. Sandy said no, just rest.

Bar Jonah piled his plate high with meat and mashed potatoes; he hadn't had a home-cooked, sit-down meal in a week. Sandy hadn't noticed before dinner how bad his teeth were. As he ate, she said Bar Jonah looked like a cow chewing cud. Bar Jonah told Sandy he wanted a big spoon to eat dinner with. You can't take big bites with forks, he said, and Bar Jonah liked to take big bites. The dried crusty saliva that always seemed to be caked at the corners of Bar Jonah's mouth also bothered Sandy. How was she ever going to kiss him, she wondered.

Later that night Sandy tried to explain to Bar Jonah that she had needs. It had been a long time since she had been loved. He would have no part of it. Sex was not an option until after they were married. He had saved himself all these years. He wouldn't discuss it until they got married. Sandy said she considered herself a good Christian woman. There was nothing wrong with sex as long as it was an expression of love. Bar Jonah told her it wasn't for her to decide. He said he liked the bed in the boys' room; it was even big enough for the younger boy to sleep with him. It would be a good way for them to get to know each other.

Tyra had not seen Bar Jonah interact with anyone other than Lois's family since he was released from prison. Bar Jonah was even more dogmatic now than he had been before the judge sent him away. Before Bar Jonah was released from Bridgewater, Tyra was full of hope that he had changed. Ober and Sweitzer had assured her that he had matured. He had learned from his mistakes. The spirit of the Lord was alive inside him. He would be able to get out of prison, get married, get a job, and raise a family. But after the Oxford incident, Tyra was devastated. She didn't know what to do. Montana was in the middle of nowhere. Bob said there weren't many people out there. It might be a place where Bar Jonah wouldn't be able to get into too much trouble. Tyra thought she could keep a better eye on him. She'd also have Bob close by to help.

Sandy suggested they turn in early saying it had been a long day. She sent her boys to stay with one of her friends, thinking it was best, she said. Tyra slept on the couch. Bar Jonah was smoking back in the boys' room. Sandy couldn't get down to sleep.

The prison letters she received from Bar Jonah were lying open on the bed beside her. She read the letters over and over. She didn't recognize the man in the letters as the man smoking in her son's room. His letters were professions of love and desire. He had never had any kids of his own and he loved kids; it was time to settle down.

When he was younger Bar Jonah said he had tried to choke a couple of teenagers, who jumped him one night in a parking lot. The court saw it different because they were teenagers and he was a man. Like a lot of guys in prison he got convicted for something he didn't do. He was the victim, but he had come to forgive the boys who lied. It wasn't until two Christian doctors came along that he had a hope of ever getting out of prison. But the Lord had sustained him throughout the time he was locked up. Bar Jonah hung his head in shame when he told Sandy about being horribly raped by a bunch of kids when he was a kid. That had changed his life, he said. It was even worse when he was raped in prison by a bunch of sadistic black guards. When he told the story at dinner, Sandy watched Tyra's eyes get big as she looked at him in disbelief. Sandy was uncomfortable with Bar Jonah wanting to sleep in the boys' room. But figured that maybe he had got used to bunk beds in prison and was just more comfortable there. But when he said he wanted to share the bed with one of her sons, and not her, Sandy had become scared. She finally fell asleep, imagining what it would be like to actually meet the kind of man Bar Jonah had portrayed himself to be.

The next morning, Sandy was up early. When Tyra walked into the kitchen, Sandy fixed her a cup of coffee and said she seemed like a real nice lady. She was sorry she wasn't going to have a chance to get to know her. Sandy was going to tell Bar Jonah to leave.

Sandy fixed a breakfast of biscuits and gravy with a side of grits and told Bar Jonah that he had to go. It was clear it was not going to work out between them. He didn't say anything. After he finished eating, he got up, told Tyra they had to get going, and walked out the door. Tyra apologized to Sandy and thanked her for her kindness. As Sandy watched Tyra and Bar Jonah drive under the yellow and pink fluorescent Happy Meadows sign, she silently said to herself, Lord, if I can be forgiven, forgive me for what I almost did ...

Tyra said she tried to talk to Bar Jonah about treating people better, but he would have no part of it. Sandy was the problem. She said she wanted to get married. She wanted help raising her boys. Then he offered to help her out and marry her, be a father to her kids, and she backed out. Why couldn't Tyra see how he tried to help people? He always gave people the benefit of the doubt. People not returning the courtesy was just one of the crosses the Lord had given him to bear.

Long haul

The trip to Montana was arduous. Tyra said she drove ninety percent of the way. Bar Jonah was only willing to drive for a few hours the entire trip. He liked driving in South Dakota because it was flat, with no traffic to speak of. Just outside of Rapid City, Bar Jonah insisted on stopping at Mount Rushmore. He said he had never seen this fabulous, sculpted mountain and wanted to take in the sights.

* * *

It's pretty desolate once you leave South Dakota and cross over into Wyoming. A few towns are scattered here and there,

Gillette and Sheridan being the largest. It was now getting well into September and as they continued to drive northwest the elevation was increasing. The weather could change on the passes at a moment's notice. Tyra didn't want to take a chance and have to drive in a sudden snowstorm.

She decided to stay overnight in Gillette. Only two more days of driving and they would be in Great Falls. That night after dinner Bar Jonah went out for a walk. He was gone for several hours. Tyra guessed he got back about two in the morning. He was just getting a feel for the town, he told her. He slept in the next day, an hour past checkout.

Bar Jonah was grumpy when Tyra was finally able to rouse him out of bed. It had been a late night and he needed his sleep. It was chilly that morning, somewhere in the mid-forties. On their way out of Gillette, they stopped at a local breakfast spot. Bar Jonah had the Paul Bunyan breakfast, three eye-up eggs, three pieces of sausage, three pieces of bacon, hash browns with a side of gravy, four pieces of toast, orange juice, and four cups of coffee.

* * *

As you begin to drive farther west on I-90 towards Montana, the landscape begins to change. The rolling hills and mesas of northeastern Wyoming begin to be gradually replaced with the splendor of the Northern Rockies. A little ways after you cross the crest of the Wyoming-Montana border, the Beartooth Mountain Range comes into view. There, jagged peaks are often obscured by a light fog. As dusk was approaching, Tyra said she had expected to see Butch Cassidy come riding out of one of the canyons.

Montana is the fourth largest state in the US, but it has less than a million people. For many, driving across the state is almost like a vacation in itself. The splendor of the mountains, the endless sky, and antelope, deer, bighorn sheep, bald eagles, beaver, otters, black bear, brown bear, and grizzly bear dot the seemingly forever landscape. At night you can reach up and scoop up a spoonful of the Milky Way.

The major cities in Montana all take several hours to drive in between. "Close by" means an hour and a half or so. It is not uncommon to be one of only a few cars on the road. The emergency gates at the exits off I-90 give visitors a hint of what winter weather can be like. Bar Jonah was taken with the vastness of the state. Tyra said he wanted to stop at every rest area. But he was different on these stops. He wasn't approaching kids or their families. He just walked around, taking in the surrounding landscape. Every now and then he would ask a trucker where a fold in the countryside ended up. How far back off the road did it go? Most of the time they said they didn't know; they were just driving through. He wondered to himself at what point would you be invisible to someone driving by.

* * *

Bozeman is just under 5000 feet in elevation. At night in September it can get down into the twenties. Snow is not uncommon either, especially in the mountains. Tyra thought about driving straight through to Great Falls but instead decided to stay in Bozeman that night.

The next morning they got an early start. Bar Jonah was up at dawn and wanted to get going. There was a new life waiting for him in Great Falls. He was looking forward to starting his antique business. This was an opportunity to make new friends. On the drive he had been writing all the way. When Tyra would look over, most of what he was writing didn't make any sense to her. He was drawing a lot of lines, up and down the page, like he was making some kind of grid. Then writing down what looked like random letters of the alphabet and words that didn't mean anything.

The city of Butte sits right at the I-90—I-15 interchange. Butte is an old copper mining town with a tarnished history. It is the home of the Berkeley Pit, an open abyss copper mine.

The pit is a mile long by a half-mile wide and about 1780 feet deep. There is about 900 feet of water that is heavily acidic. The pit is laden with arsenic, cadmium, zinc, and sulfuric acid. It was opened in 1955 and closed in 1982. Since it closed the water level has risen to within 150 feet of the groundwater. The Berkeley Pit has become one of the largest superfund sites in the US. In 1995, a large flock of Canadian snow geese landed in the Pit. The next morning there were 342 carcasses scattered about the water.

From the highway you can see some of the old drilling rigs rising up from the landscape. Bar Jonah and Tyra took a quick detour and drove up the steep hills to uptown Butte. Tyra commented to Bar Jonah the city looked like a place that time forgot. There were just a few more hours to Great Falls.

The Missouri river is a tributary of the Mississippi river and is the longest river in the United States. It likely originates at Brower's Spring at the upper reaches of the Jefferson before joining the confluence of the Madison, Jefferson, and Gallatin rivers in southwest Montana. It is 2,540 miles long and drains about one-sixth of the North American continent. Joliet called it the Pekistanoui River, making reference to an Indian tribe who lived upstream. They were known as the Oumessourita, which was pronounced the OO-Missouri, meaning those who have dugout canoes. The Missouri flows through deeply carved mountain canyons emerging from the mountains just south of Great Falls.

Bar Jonah wanted Tyra to stop at every scenic turnout she could, so he could stand and gaze at the mighty Missouri. He would stand off the road staring, not speaking, looking far away. Holter dam is about forty miles south of Great Falls. Bar Jonah insisted on stopping. They pulled off of the road. But the signs said it was more of an arduous drive than Tyra wanted to make. Bar Jonah said that was okay, he'd come back another time.

CHAPTER SEVEN

Great Falls

It was mid-September. Bar Jonah and Tyra were finally pulling off of I-15 onto 10th Avenue South and driving into Great Falls. The trip had taken more than three weeks. Tyra pointed out the old fighter jet mounted on a pedestal on the north side of the highway, announcing that Great Falls was the home of Malmstrom Air Force Base. Malmstrom is the largest missile command center in the US. It monitors the missile silos that dot the landscape around north central Montana. Bar Jonah could not have cared less. When they pulled up to Bob's white duplex on 1st Avenue, Tyra said she felt like she was ready to collapse. The drive had been extremely hard on her. She wanted to sleep for days. Bar Jonah told her he would need the car the next day; he had things to do.

The next morning it didn't take long to unpack; Bob helped. Tyra did not have to move everything by herself. The trailer was loaded with mostly broken toys and Bar Jonah's papers and letters from Bridgewater. He had thousands of pages of his writings. He said he was going to be a journalist. The toys were mainly trucks, toy guns, some robots, a big stuffed gorilla, and his specialty, police badges. This was his inventory. Just about anyone else would have tossed the stuff in the trash. Bar Jonah said he had to find a place to start his antique toy business.

Bar Jonah wanted to take Tyra's car immediately after they unhitched the trailer. Bob insisted he help unload. He didn't care if Bar Jonah's back hurt, he had to help. He was a thirty-four-year-old man. "Take some responsibility," Bob would say.

Setting-up business

Great Falls is an easy place to get around. Bar Jonah liked the grid type layout of the city. As long as it wasn't rush hour, you could get from one end of the city to the other in no time flat. After talking with a few people, Bar Jonah quickly found the old creamery, which had been converted into the American Antique Mall. Dealers rented space and set up tables. Just like Bev's back home. But this was inside. He wouldn't have to work out in the wind and rain. On his drive he also mapped out all of the elementary schools: Whittier, Lincoln, Longfellow, Riverview, Meadow Lark, McKinley, and Valley View. They were all pretty close to each other, convenient, easy to get to, one right after the other. Not like back east where everything took so much time. This way he could visit more than one school a day. He wouldn't be so worn out by the time he got back home.

About a week after Bar Jonah got to Montana, he received a certified letter from his attorney at Day, Berry and Howard. Inside was a check for 6000 dollars. The state of Massachusetts had agreed to pay him for the time they had kidnapped him. Three days after Bar Jonah received the check he went to Bob, saying that he needed fifty bucks right away; he had bills that were due. Bob was incredulous. You just got 6000 dollars, Bob said. Bar Jonah told Bob the money was gone, he had bought some guy's entire stock of toys. He now had plenty of inventory to start his antique business. When Bob saw the boxes and boxes of beat-up and broken toys, he said "You paid 6000 dollars for this bunch of crap?" Bob said it was in worse shape than the stuff Bar Jonah hauled from Massachusetts. It was all garbage.

Late September mornings in north central Montana are downright cold. This was good for Bar Jonah. He could wear his blue police jacket and stay warm as he patrolled the schools. Some of the teachers became so familiar with him hanging around the schools that they smiled and waved as he walked by. He was always so friendly to the kids. Even as the snows began to come, he would take his walks. On the mornings when it was too cold, Bar Jonah would take Tyra's car.

* * *

The antique mall needed painting badly, not to mention that the driveway could use a good mowing, where clumps of grass were growing through the cracked blacktop. Inside, tables were set up, piled high with junk, being passed off to unsuspecting buyers as undiscovered treasures. Within a week after he arrived in Great Falls, Bar Jonah rented space and started his toys and collectables business. The set-up was a white fold-up table with two six-foot pine planks sitting atop a couple of cinder blocks. The shelves were covered with cars, trucks, guns, and police badges. Just like his set-up in Massachusetts. Except now his inventory was bigger and more varied, thanks to the money he had gotten from Massachusetts. He was now an independent business owner.

You've got to be kidding

Michael Redpath, a probation and parole officer for Cascade County, was surprised when the heavily bearded, unkempt obese man walked into his office. He said his name was Nathaneal Benjamin Levi Bar Jonah from Massachusetts. He was told by the Massachusetts authorities to report to Probation when he arrived in Great Falls.

Bar Jonah sat down and told Redpath about his history. Redpath said he was astounded. He looked at Bar Jonah and said, "How in the hell did you get here?" Bar Jonah told him an agreement had been made with the prosecuting attorney in Massachusetts that allowed him to come to Montana with his mother. He was living with her in Great Falls and had just started up his own business. Redpath immediately called the probation department in Dudley. They said they had never heard of Nathaneal Benjamin Levi Bar Jonah.

Redpath contacted the interstate compact office in Helena, Montana. It would be their job to track down documentation and figure out what was going on. If Bar Jonah was reporting his history correctly, he was clearly a threat. Montana sure as hell didn't want him.

A few weeks later, in early October, Redpath received a file from the compact. From what Bar Jonah had told him, he was expecting a substantial amount of information. But the information Redpath received reflected nothing about Bar Jonah's background. The file only outlined the assault in Oxford.

Constance Perrin, supervisor of Montana's interstate compact, wrote to Dudley, Massachusetts demanding more information. She added in her letter, "We are also requesting the most recent psychiatric report that is available on this subject. Please advise us if Bar Jonah was required to register as a sex offender in Massachusetts." As soon as she received the additional information, Montana would determine if they would agree to monitor Bar Jonah's probation. She added at the end of the letter, "Your cooperation is greatly needed and appreciated."

The Dudley court forwarded a copy of Perrin's letter on October 15, 1991, to Richard Boulanger, Bar Jonah's counsel of record in Massachusetts. He also represented Bar Jonah in his successful appeal for release from Bridgewater. A letter from Paul Simone, a Dudley District Court probation officer, accompanied Perrin's letter. In his letter, Simone stated, "I cannot find anywhere in the court records if a psychiatric evaluation has ever been done". Simone went on to say, "I brought this problem before Judge Teshoian and he urges your office to make Mr. Bar Jonah aware that if supervision is rejected in Montana, he will have to be available for further court proceedings in this Commonwealth." Further, Simone wrote in his letter to Boulanger, "Perhaps some communication from your office to Mr. Bar Jonah would be helpful." The court records do not reflect if Boulanger ever responded to Simone's request or if he ever followed up with Bar Jonah. However, it is known that Boulanger rightfully assumed his work with Bar Jonah was finished after his representation ended, having not been further retained.

When the second file on Bar Jonah arrived in Perrin's office, she commented to a co-worker that she didn't think Massachusetts understood what the words "additional" and "cooperation" meant. There was little more in the file than before, plus nothing about his years in Bridgewater.

After Redpath and Perrin discussed the situation, and against their better judgment, they made the decision to accept supervision of Bar Jonah. The decision was based on the belief that Massachusetts simply would not take steps to extradite Bar Jonah if supervision in Montana was rejected. There was no reason to believe that Massachusetts would be any more responsive after the fact than they had been before. Redpath and Perrin thought at least probation was a way of keeping an eye on him.

During the two years Redpath supervised Bar Jonah, there was no mandate from Massachusetts for Bar Jonah to register as a sexual offender, for psychological treatment, or for a sexual offender evaluation to be conducted. Ordering psychological testing and a psychiatric evaluation is the minimum of what you do in a case like this, Redpath said. Yet, Bar Jonah's probation was ordered by Massachusetts to be "standard rules," which meant basic monitoring, monthly reporting for a few minutes, and periodic home visits.

Bar Jonah spent most of his time developing his antique business. Visiting yard sales and flea markets were part of his weekly routine. This was an opportunity to get to know families in his neighborhood. Bar Jonah liked to show up unexpectedly at his neighbors' houses. This way he could surprise the kids. He loved it when they ran up to him, jumping up, bouncing off his belly, so excited to discover what kind of surprise he had brought for them. Bar Jonah was in a real neighborhood community. Bunches and bunches of welcoming families. Great Falls was a great place.

The men of the families Bar Jonah befriended were mostly long gone, leaving too many kids and overworked, lonely moms. Sometimes an uncle might be somewhere in the distant picture. Bar Jonah preferred mothers whose recollection of the children's fathers was fleeting or better yet, unknown. They appreciated the attention he paid to their kids. He was particularly good with little boys who didn't have a dad. Bar Jonah understood, saying his dad was not there for him when he was growing up either, plus his father used to beat him with a thick black leather belt. Bar Jonah said he never understood someone who hurt children. He wanted to get married and have kids of his own. He just hadn't found the right woman yet. Sometimes, the kids' mothers jokingly told him he'd better hurry. You aren't gettin' any younger, they would say.

Bar Jonah told Redpath that the time on probation gave him time to clear his mind. How could he keep up with the demands of his business if he didn't have the opportunity to have time by himself? A businessman has to think things through, to plan for the future. There were no demands from Massachusetts for Redpath to keep much of an eye on Bar Jonah. He had other probationers who were far more of a pain in the ass and demanding of his time.

* * *

There are vast vacant wildernesses that are easily accessible by highway or country roads within a fifty-mile radius of

Great Falls. Bar Jonah particularly liked the Holter reservoir that is fed by the old Holter dam. It's about forty miles south of Great Falls, off of I-15, easy to get to and in those days, not many people around. Bar Jonah made several overnight drives to eastern Idaho and Washington, northern Wyoming, and North Dakota. Business trips he would say, when Tyra questioned where he had been. Alberta was a couple of hours north of Great Falls, just up I-15. A couple of questions and a friendly smile were all it took to cross the border over into Canada.

During a meeting with Redpath right before Christmas, Bar Jonah said it was Jesus Christ, his Lord and Savior, who shepherded his release from Bridgewater. Otherwise he would have been there for life. If it wasn't for Jesus, Bar Jonah would not have an opportunity to make amends for his past mistakes. He had tracked down all his past victims in Massachusetts and sent them a letter, apologizing. They were all doing real good now, Bar Jonah said. Redpath found Bar Jonah not only unlikable, but he also didn't trust him. He put the word out to the GFPD to keep an eye on Bar Jonah. Redpath knew, regardless of Bar Jonah's bullshit that he was going to reoffend. It was only a matter of time and opportunity.

The day after the meeting with Redpath, out of the blue, Bar Jonah wrote a letter to the *Great Fall Tribune* testifying to the miracles of Jesus Christ:

> *I've seen God take a hopeless situation like when all avenues were closed it seemed like I'd never be released. Yet God told me I would and I believed Him even though the evidence of my release was not there. Then totally out of left field I got 2—Yes 2—Christian psychiatrists who believed in me. That was a miracle in itself to find 2 Christians in that profession in Massachusetts. The state had a lot of evidence on their side, yet the judge sided with me.* (Great Falls Tribune, 1991)

The following Sunday, Bar Jonah joined the Central Assembly of God church in Great Falls.

* * *

The Royal Rangers is the Assembly of God's youth group. They do activities with the kids, like overnight camping trips and Sunday afternoon cookouts. They are also an evangelical Boy Scouts. A few months after Bar Jonah joined the Great Falls congregation, he became a youth leader for the Royal Rangers. The work of the Royal Rangers was well known to him, he assured church leaders. He had been a Commander in the Royal Rangers back east and had his certificate to prove it. His life was dedicated to guiding the little lambs to God. It was while he was a youth leader in the Royal Rangers that Bar Jonah first met Zach.

* * *

In January 1992, Tyra began pushing Bar Jonah to do more with his time, telling him he needed to get a job. Bar Jonah countered that he already had a job as an independent business owner. Tyra then suggested to Bar Jonah that he start babysitting. He was always so good with kids, she would say. Tyra had recently met Jenny Brydon at church. Jenny was the manager of the Bitterroot Apartments at 400 5th Street N. At one point, Jenny said the apartment complex was looking for someone to shovel the sidewalks after an evening snow. Tyra thought Bar Jonah would be perfect for the job. He told Tyra he would think about it. Bar Jonah walked the neighborhood and saw that the Bitterroot Apartments are just around the corner from Whittier Elementary School. He went back home and told Tyra he would take the job, but she would have to drive him to work in her 1987 white Toyota Corolla on the mornings it snowed. Tyra was now seventy-six.

CHAPTER EIGHT

Shawn

In late August 1992, Julie Watkins met Bar Jonah through the American Antique Mall. He had become somewhat of a character at the mall. Everyone knew him. His straggly beard, dirty hair, and rumpled clothes drew their attention. But, there was always real concern in his voice when he asked his customers how their families were. He seemed so sincere when he said he was always there to help with their kids if they needed it. Bar Jonah was always handing out his business cards, *"BJ's Collectables, Specializes in Collectables and Teddies"*. He was a hard worker, always at the mall on the weekends trying to sell his toys to the kids. Picking up some extra cash here and there, he would say.

Julie Watkins liked antiques too. She was one of the antique mall's best customers. Always looking for a good buy. Her son, Shawn, who was always in tow, had just had his eighth birthday. His dad had been out of the picture for a while. An organization that would provide an adult mentor for Shawn had been a consideration but Julie never seemed to have time to contact them. Every time she went to the mall, Bar Jonah seemed to have some new toy he wanted to show Shawn.

Most of his stuff looked pretty broken up, but she was still appreciative when he called Shawn over to his table. She later told detectives that Bar Jonah was always so attentive to Shawn. Taking a lot of time to talk to him like he was a real person, not just a kid. Shawn really liked the attention too, especially when Bar Jonah would get down on the floor and play cars with him. He didn't seem to care that other people looked at him funny. Bar Jonah would just look up and loudly go "Vroooooom," pushing a toy car towards Shawn. Shawn laughed, pushing the car right back. On one visit to the mall, Julie noticed the sign Bar Jonah had tacked up advertising his new babysitting service.

Julie continued to befriend Bar Jonah, thinking he was lonely and needed a friend. But the most important thing was that Bar Jonah was so good with Shawn. Julie began inviting Bar Jonah over for dinner. He seemed pleasant enough in a social setting, even if he was opinionated and always seemed to need a bath. She was also impressed with his devout religious beliefs and his special relationship with God. She commented on the letter he wrote to the *Tribune*, saying how impressive his openness was. His attitude was kids shouldn't have to suffer just because they are kids. He dropped his head in obvious pain, when he confided to Julie, that a gang of local hoods raped him when he was a kid. Bar Jonah said he made the decision right then to dedicate himself to the protection of children, so they wouldn't have to go through what he did. His selfless commitment to kids was also evident in his work with the Royal Rangers. Julie knew that because she had heard about Bar Jonah from other parishioners at the Central Assembly of God church, which she and Shawn attended.

In early October, Patrolman Dan Nelson of the GFPD contacted Pastor Dahl at the Assembly of God. Nelson knew something of Bar Jonah's background after hearing his name from Redpath. Nelson told Pastor Dahl that Bar Jonah should not be allowed around young boys. He also told the pastor that his son would not be involved with the Royal Rangers as long as Bar Jonah was one of its leaders. The church decided to keep an eye on Bar Jonah but not to remove him from his Ranger duties, because he was so good at bringing children over to God. However, Pastor Dahl knew that Julie Watkins and Bar Jonah had developed a friendship, having seen them around church together. Dahl called Julie when he learned of Bar Jonah's past from Nelson. Pastor Dahl warned Julie it was not a good idea to allow Shawn to be around Bar Jonah or at least to make sure that she was supervising them when they were. Dahl told Julie he just wanted to prevent something from happening to Shawn. Julie told Dahl that Bar Jonah was her friend. As a matter of fact, he was one of her best friends. He would never harm Shawn. She trusted him so much that she was going to ask him to babysit Shawn. Even though Dahl knew something about Bar Jonah's background, and took it on himself to call Julie, he still refused to remove Bar Jonah from his duties with the Rangers. A few days after Dahl's call to Julie she stopped over at the antique mall and asked Bar Jonah to begin babysitting Shawn after school. Bar Jonah was touched by her confidence in him.

Bar Jonah babysat Shawn from early November 1992 through June of 1993 when Julie decided to move to Havre, Montana to be closer to her new boyfriend Steve. Steve was financially secure and could provide a better life for Julie and Shawn. Later on one of the detectives who knew Julie said she was always looking for a date and only wanted to date men with money. But Julie insisted on continuing her friendship with Bar Jonah. He frequently made trips up to Havre, about an hour north of Great Falls, to have dinner with Julie, Steve, and Shawn. Steve didn't like Bar Jonah and told Julie he didn't want him around Shawn.

Julie told Steve he was being foolish. Bar Jonah was a good man who had had a rough life. She would not abandon her friend. Plus he was so good with Shawn.

On December 18, 1993 Julie and Steve planned to go to a Christmas party down in Great Falls. Julie asked Bar Jonah, if it was not too much trouble, could Shawn stay overnight. She would pick him up in the late afternoon the next day. Bar Jonah agreed, telling Julie that he would love to have Shawn spend the night. The wind was blowing in a storm on the afternoon that Julie dropped Shawn off at Bar Jonah's. It was going to be a big one, Steve said to Julie as she got out of the car to walk Shawn up to Bar Jonah's apartment. Bar Jonah opened the door, at the sound of the knock. Julie hugged Bar Jonah and told him Shawn was excited about spending the night. Bar Jonah leaned down and told Shawn they were going to have a lot of fun. As Julie turned to walk out the door, Shawn jumped into her arms yelling that he wanted one more kiss. Julie and Steve picked Shawn up the next afternoon about 3:00.

Shawn had always loved going to Bar Jonah's. He really enjoyed how Bar Jonah played with him. Running through Bar Jonah's cluttered apartment, ducking and hiding behind the torn recliner and jumping up and down on Bar Jonah's brown and black, threadbare sofa. Bar Jonah didn't care, he never yelled or anything, Shawn would tell Julie. Shawn was uncomfortable, though, when Bar Jonah insisted on going into the bathroom with him.

Over the weekend the week right before Christmas, Shawn kept pulling at his penis. When Julie had some friends over, one of them commented that she saw Shawn sitting on the couch openly playing with himself. Yes, kids play with themselves, but this was so sudden. Plus, Julie told her friend that Shawn had really changed in the past few weeks; she didn't know what was wrong with him. He had gone from being an easy kid to one who wouldn't mind.

Julie took Shawn into his bedroom and began telling him that it was okay to touch his penis, but he should do it in private. Not in front of other people. Julie was surprised when

Shawn kept pulling at himself while they talked, saying his penis hurt, it wouldn't stop itching. Even though he protested, Julie had Shawn pull down his underwear. She was surprised when she saw his penis. The head was red and swollen. How long had his penis been itching, she asked? He wouldn't say. Julie was reassuring, saying she'd take him to the doctor, they'd get the itching stopped. She felt guilty not realizing that he had been so uncomfortable. Shawn suddenly became hysterical, screaming he didn't want *anyone else* touching him. Julie was confused, *anyone else*, she didn't understand. She asked Shawn what he meant by anyone else, who had been touching him? He said Bar Jonah.

The first thing Julie did was to call her pastor, Steven Dahl, and ask him for his advice about what to do. Julie said she immediately felt like physically hurting Bar Jonah. Dahl told Julie he didn't know that Bar Jonah's past problems had been sexual. He had heard Bar Jonah had just held somebody for ransom back east. Dahl suggested to Julie that she keep Shawn away from Bar Jonah. Julie told Dahl that Bar Jonah had told Shawn that if he said anything that he would go back to prison forever. Shawn felt horribly guilty about telling Julie. Shawn didn't want to get Bar Jonah in trouble. Dahl asked Julie's permission to let him call Bob. Dahl knew Bob from church. Bob would be able to find help for Bar Jonah.

As soon as Dahl hung up the phone with Julie he called Bob Brown. Bob was taken aback and "hurt" by Julie's accusation. He couldn't imagine Bar Jonah doing such a thing. Bob told Dahl that he was "going to have to do something about this" and have a talk with Bar Jonah. Dahl asked if he could go with Bob to talk with Bar Jonah. Bob agreed. Bob tried to call Bar Jonah but couldn't get him on the phone. Dahl and Bob drove over to Bar Jonah's apartment and knocked on the door, but there was no answer. The next morning Bob and Tyra went to Bar Jonah's place without Dahl. Bar Jonah told them he didn't remember anything happening, but if it did he must have blacked out again. But Bar Jonah was enraged that Pastor Dahl had called Bob. Dahl should have stayed out of it; this was none of his business.

That afternoon Bar Jonah showed up at Dahl's office. He stood in front of Dahl's desk and screamed that if he could he would press charges against Dahl and file a lawsuit against him. Dahl told Bar Jonah he would no longer be able to work with the Royal Rangers directly. The church would no longer take the chance. But, Dahl said, Bar Jonah could continue to help the church by doing fundraisers, through toy sales, in the church basement. Bar Jonah slammed the door when he left Dahl's office.

Dahl called Julie and told her about his encounter with Bar Jonah. She said she wanted to call Officer Nelson and report it to the police, but that her phone bill was too high, she couldn't afford to call. Dahl offered to call Nelson and ask his advice. Nelson told Dahl that he didn't think Bar Jonah would get sent back to prison for life. Since Bar Jonah was still on parole, Redpath would probably be able to handle the situation. Nelson called the GFPD and reported what Shawn said Bar Jonah had done to him. While Dahl was talking on the phone with Nelson, Julie Watkins was talking with Bob. Julie had called Bob, saying she was concerned about Bar Jonah. Bob encouraged her not to pursue a complaint against Bar Jonah. Bob said he would see to it that Bar Jonah got counseling from one of the church psychologists.

* * *

Detective William Bellusci was assigned the case. Bellusci was a long time veteran of the Great Falls PD, having come up through the ranks from patrolman to gold shield detective. Bellusci handled mostly sex cases for the department. He was forty-four, but looked older in his grey polyester suits. His thumbs were usually tucked into the waistband of his trousers, as he talked over the cigarette hanging off his lip.

Bellusci took Julie's and Shawn's statements. Shawn said he had been afraid to tell his mother because he didn't want Bar Jonah to go to jail. Bar Jonah had told Shawn that a long time ago he lived in another state. One day it was raining real hard, Bar Jonah had told Shawn. He had to get out of the rain, so he jumped into a car that wasn't his. Inside the car were two boys. One of the boys started acting up and crying. Bar Jonah didn't like it when kids didn't behave and he especially didn't like it when kids cry. So he picked the brat up and put him in the trunk. Bar Jonah stole the car and drove it away. The other little boy started crying too. So, Bar Jonah told Shawn, he choked the kid a little bit, stopped the car and put him in the trunk with the other kid. Then he drove away again. The kids were making a lot of noise in the trunk and distracted him. Then he ran into a tree. The police came and found the boys in the trunk and made Bar Jonah go to prison for a long time. Bar Jonah told Shawn that he didn't want to be responsible for getting him in trouble again, did he? Shawn said Bar Jonah told him he shouldn't tell anyone about their special time together. It wasn't for anyone else to know. During Bellusci's interview of Shawn, he also described in detail the big scar on Bar Jonah's right leg.

* * *

On January 19, 1994 Bellusci drove to Bar Jonah's apartment. When Bar Jonah answered the door, Bellusci identified himself as a police officer and read him his rights. Bar Jonah denied fondling Shawn's penis when Bellusci confronted him with the accusation. But, Bar Jonah did say, that if he did it, he must have blacked out. That had happened to him before. Bar Jonah also said, "But if I had done it, I just would have gone ahead and killed the kid." There was a possibility, though, he had had an erotic dream and touched Shawn while they were sleeping. Bar Jonah said he wasn't sure. During the interview with Bellusci, Bar Jonah admitted to previously kidnapping and trying to kill a couple of kids in Massachusetts. Bellusci peered at Bar Jonah over his glasses and said to himself, "Who the fuck is this guy?"

On January 20, 1994 Dean Chisholm, Cascade County Attorney asked District Judge Joel A. Roth to issue an arrest warrant for Bar Jonah, setting his bail at $25,000. Bellusci received the warrant and arrested Bar Jonah at the antique mall that afternoon. Bellusci had put Bar Jonah on Montana's radar.

* * *

Bar Jonah was taken to the Cascade County jail where he was fingerprinted and mug shot. He was appointed a public defender, H. William Coder. The judge decided Bar Jonah was a risk to the community and should remain in jail until his trial. He also ordered him to undergo a psychological and sexual offender evaluation.

Coder entered a motion on March 1 to have Bar Jonah's bail reduced to $10,000, stating the $25,000 posed an undue hardship on the defendant and his family. Plus Bar Jonah would agree to have no associations with any minor child, would live with his mother, be in every night by 9 p.m., and obey all of the laws of the state of Montana. District Judge John McCarvel agreed the bail was unreasonable and reduced it to $10,000. During the hearing, Bar Jonah also entered a plea of not guilty.

Bob and Tyra were displeased with the way Coder was handling Bar Jonah's case. He wasn't doing enough to get Bar Jonah out of jail. In early May, Bar Jonah notified the court that he was firing Coder and had retained attorney Patrick Flaherty as his legal counsel. Flaherty was a high dollar Great Falls attorney with criminal defense experience. He was a member of the Assembly of God church, a devout Christian who routinely said "Praise God" when he was talking with clients about the worst of their circumstances. Flaherty was the attorney for the Montana Chapter of Operation Rescue and volunteered countless hours to pro-life causes.

Shortly after Flaherty got out of law school, he ran for county attorney up near the Montana Highline. It wasn't long after Flaherty won the election that the county and Flaherty didn't see things eye-to-eye. The county filed a motion and successfully recalled Flaherty from office. When the sheriff delivered the order to Flaherty to vacate his county office, Flaherty steadfastly refused. The sheriff's deputies picked-up Flaherty in his office chair, carried him out into the middle of Main Street, sat him down, and ordered him not to re-enter the county attorney's office.

Flaherty worked with private investigator Mark Metzger. Metzger was a former Los Angeles police officer who came to Great Falls to get away from the big city and decided to set up his own shop. Metzger contacted Julie Watkins on May 10, 1994 as part of Flaherty's investigation of the charges against Bar Jonah. During Metzger's interview with Watkins, he discovered that Julie was sympathetic to Bar Jonah and the difficulties he had been through in his life. Especially the rape Bar Jonah had suffered when he was ten and the horrible assault by the black prison guards. Julie understood. Metzger asked Julie if she would be willing to write a letter of support for Bar Jonah. She said she would. When Flaherty received the letter he gave a copy to the Cascade County Attorney, at the time, Dean Chisholm.

Julie Watkins's handwritten letter read:

> My name is Julie Watkins and I want to say that my wish has always been for Bar Jonah to get probation and to receive counseling. I feel very strongly that Shawn testifying would have an adverse effect on him emotionally. He does not want for Bar Jonah to be in jail and never did. He would still like to be Bar Jonah's friend under a supervised situation such as my being present for the most part. Shawn harbors no ill will toward Bar Jonah. I feel Bar Jonah has been through a lot in his life and jail would only increase the problems he has and counseling would

help with all of the adversity he has had to face. I still feel Bar
Jonah is a good person for the most part but needs to have con-
trol in his life that would make him get the help he needs. These
are my own words and beliefs and I have not been influenced
in any way.

Julie Watkins, May 1994

Flaherty appeared with Bar Jonah on June 2, petitioning the
court to further reduce Bar Jonah's bail. Judge McCarvel
denied Flaherty's motion saying the $10,000 bail was far
from unreasonable. Judge McCarvel again ordered a sexual
offender evaluation plus set the trial date for August 15, 1994.
Since Bar Jonah couldn't come up with the bail he would
remain in custody until trial. As Flaherty began to prepare his
defense of Bar Jonah, he began to look at how to handle Julie
and Shawn. In his work product notes, Flaherty said that his
impression was that Shawn was an angry kid who resented
Julie sleeping around. He hoped he didn't have to bring that
into the case.

Interconnections Counseling Group, which was affiliated
with the Mt. Olive Assembly of God church in Great Falls,
agreed to conduct the sexual offender evaluation. In their conclusions, the counselors said Bar Jonah suffered from Post-
traumatic stress disorder as a result of the assault he suffered
when he was ten and the gang rape by the prison guards. Plus,
he also experienced dissociative episodes, where he would disappear inside himself and lose track of time. They questioned
if he suffered from multiple personality disorder.

The sexual offender portion of the evaluation looked to see
if Bar Jonah became sexually stimulated by sexually explicit
stimuli involving children or depictions of violence associated with sexual activity. Bar Jonah's score was off the chart.
A polygraph was also conducted as part of the evaluation. The
polygrapher asked Bar Jonah, "Did you touch Shawn Watkins
in a sexual way?" Bar Jonah responded, "No." The polygrapher

wrote in response to Bar Jonah's answer that, "It is the opinion of the examiner that the subject responded with deception."

Interconnections recommended that Bar Jonah be mandated to undergo treatment for being a sexual offender. A few days later, Bar Jonah began seeing a therapist at Interconnections to work on the leftover psychological residue from the sexual assaults he had suffered from the neighborhood bullies and the brutal prison guards.

* * *

Under the Montana constitution, an accused has the right to a speedy trial. The unwritten understanding is that the trial must take place within eighteen months of an accused being charged with a crime. The eighteen months is not a hard and fast rule but is based upon how the pleas and motions filed by both parties have proceeded before the court. Bar Jonah had been in jail now for six months. Flaherty was beginning to plan his strategy for trial. Bob, in the meantime, was calling Flaherty and wanting him to attack Julie Watkins's character, saying she was a slut because she slept around. This made her an irresponsible mother and not a good Christian woman. Flaherty told Bob that under no circumstances would he proceed that way. Bob also was calling Mark Metzger demanding to be present for any subsequent interviews Metzger had with Julie Watkins. Metzger said Bob demanded to interrogate Julie himself. He would get the truth out of her, he said. Bob called Metzger so many times that Metzger finally told Bob that if he called again he would report him to the county attorney for witness tampering. Bob finally backed off. Tyra had friends who knew both Bar Jonah and Julie Watkins from church. Tyra's friends knew Julie didn't hold herself up to the Christian standards the church expected of an unmarried woman. They agreed to testify on Bar Jonah's behalf, saying that they believed Shawn was a liar. Bar Jonah would never harm a child. Lois, Bar Jonah's sister, also wrote a letter in support of Bar Jonah saying that for a short while, after Bar Jonah was released from Bridgewater, he lived with their family. They never had any concerns Bar Jonah would harm any of their children.

There were multiple delays with judicial wrangling back and forth between the prosecutor's office and Flaherty. The August 15 trial date was eventually postponed with no new date being set.

While he waited for Flaherty to take care of things, Bar Jonah sat in jail with his three cellmates, Boone Yeager, Reno McLaughlin, and Keith Corwin Bauman who was known as "Doc". Yeager was a big, hairy, burly guy who another inmate said, "smelled like he never quite wiped his ass right."

In 1993, Detective Tim Theisen had just graduated from polygraph school. Yeager was the first suspect Theisen hooked up to what polygraphers call the box. Yeager was charged with sodomizing his one-yearoold daughter. Theisen took the approach of not trying to coerce a confession by browbeating a suspect, which he believed could potentially invalidate the results of the polygraph, but by establishing an empathic rapport with the accused. When Theisen was polygraphing Yeager, Yeager couldn't get it to come out of his mouth that he had raped his infant daughter. Theisen said he looked at Yeager and said "Yeah, I understand, here you've got this girl who's naked and you're a man. You just lost control of yourself." Yeager was nodding his head up and down but not saying that he had savagely sodomized his daughter. The polygraph needle was indicating Yeager was being truthful but there was no relevant question to associate his truthfulness to. Theisen looked at Yeager and said, "Look, I know you can't talk about it, here is a pen and piece of paper, just go ahead and write it down, sign it and get it off of your chest." Yeager took the pen and paper and wrote out a full confession. Theisen said he felt like he was going to vomit after he walked out of the room with Yeager's confession in hand. "You just have to get beyond your own sensibilities, no matter how personally disgusting it is with some of these guys if you are going to get them off of the streets," Theisen said.

Reno McLaughlin was in his early thirties when he put a shotgun in his five-year-old-daughter's mouth, telling her if she didn't suck his penis he'd blow her head off. Bauman was charged with luring young boys into his home for what he called "playtime." He liked to joke that he had kneaded more boys than a baker making hot cross buns.

The jailers regularly wrote up Bar Jonah, Bauman, Yeager, and McLaughlin for circle jerking each other and sucking each other off. Yeager, McLaughlin, and Bar Jonah wrote letters back and forth for many years after Bar Jonah got out of jail. Yeager and McLaughlin were eventually sentenced to twenty years in Montana State Prison. Apple-cheeked Doc Bauman, who comported himself like a fretful misunderstood *gentilhomme*, was released on probation.

* * *

After a series of exchanges between Flaherty and Assistant District Attorney Julie Macek, a deferred prosecution agreement was reached. A deferred prosecution simply states that if a defendant adheres to a prescribed set of conditions and doesn't get into any more trouble during the time the deferment is in force, then the charges will be dismissed. All the parties signed the deferred prosecution agreement on April 24, 1996. However, there was never any action taken on the agreement. Flaherty, seeing an opportunity to best serve his client, filed a motion to dismiss all charges because of a lack of a speedy trial. On May 29, 1996 the Cascade County Attorney's office agreed and all charges against Bar Jonah were dismissed.

Macek wrote in her statement to the court:

> Now comes Julie A. Macek, Chief Deputy Cascade County Attorney, and moves this court for its order dismissing the charge of sexual assault, a felony, included in the

105

information previously filed in this matter. The defendant has filed a motion to dismiss for speedy trial. The state believes that it would prevail on the issue of speedy trial due to the number of delays requested by the defendant, and the waivers of speedy trial, which were filed by the defendant. Nevertheless, the state believes that although there was probable cause to file these charges, upon review of the entire factual situation, the state does not believe that sufficient evidence currently exists upon which to obtain a conviction, as the mother of the child victim does not want him to testify, therefore, a dismissal of this matter would be in the interests of justice.

In November 1994, Brandt Light was elected as County Attorney. During his campaign, Light charged that the previous administration was weak on crime. They were not protecting the best interest of the people. Too many criminals were getting by with too much, he would say in his campaign speeches. The prosecutor's office in Cascade County had been known for its inefficiency. Light ran on a platform of doing things differently. He promised that the interest of the people and the safety of the community would always be his first priority. After Light won the election that November, he hired Julie Macek as his assistant district attorney. By all accounts the prosecutor's office was in a state of disarray carried over from the previous administration. Macek was not made aware of the Watkins case until late in 1996. By this time it was far too late to mount an effective prosecution before the time on the case ran out. Mark Metzger made the statement that the prosecutor's office had actually lost the Watkins file but there was never any proof this occurred. When Bellusci was asked about the Watkins case he refused to comment, only saying, "I want to keep my pension."

A memo drafted by Julie Macek explaining the timeline and outcome of the case was found in Bar Jonah's private files.

The same letter was placed outside of the public record in the Cascade County Attorney's office. The memo read:

> This case was dismissed—I inherited this case from Dean Chisholm in the prior administration. The file indicates that at the time the parties began negotiating for a deferred prosecution agreement, the defendant was required to obtain a sexual offender evaluation. There are a multitude of documents regarding plea negotiations in the file. When I got the file there was no pending trial date and it had sat since November [1995]. I attempted to negotiate an acceptable deferred prosecution agreement and we were not ever able to come up with one that everyone could agree upon. I did not reset it for trial, as we had no way of trying this case due to the facts set forth below:
>
> The defendant did as part of this case spend six months in jail. He obtained a sexual offender evaluation and has been in counseling since the time of the evaluation. This appears to be the best we can do.
>
> This case involves an allegation by an eight-year-old victim of sexual assault, fondling of his penis. There are no other witnesses of the actual event. There is no medical evidence. There is an expected delay in reporting. Although the defendant has an extremely bad criminal history, he repeatedly denied the allegations. This would be a case in which the entire case depended upon the child's testimony.
>
> The mother of the child had sent a letter to Chisholm, which is in the file indicating all she wants is for the defendant to be on probation and get counseling. She further states that she feels very strongly that having her son testify would have an adverse effect on her son. I also spoke with her on the phone and she confirmed the

fact that she does not want her son to testify and that she
believes that all the defendant needs is counseling.

Based upon the fact that the mother does not want her
son to testify we do not have a case to present to the jury.
Unfortunately, I have no other way to go with this case
other than to dismiss at this time.

When Julie Watkins found out, she was stunned. She said she
had no intention of not allowing Shawn to testify. She had
reconsidered the comments in her letter and had informed
Metzger that she was in fact going to allow Shawn to testify.
Bar Jonah had molested her son. He had to pay for what he
did. When Julie Watkins learned that part of the official version
of the dismissal was blamed on her, she was outraged. Julie
packed everything up and moved her and Shawn to Southern
California shortly after the charges were dropped, fearing that
Bar Jonah might seek revenge.

CHAPTER NINE

No bars

The morning after the dismissal, Bar Jonah woke up pleased. Zigzagging his way through the cluttered apartment, he pushed toys and boxes of Christmas ornaments out of the way with his short fat feet, cussing when he caught a long jagged toenail on the straw hair of a doll lying in his way as he walked to the bathroom. Bar Jonah lit a cigarette while he used the toilet, dropping it into the toilet bowl when he was done. Then he shaved and slicked back his hair. After he finished in the bathroom, he went to the kitchen and poured himself a cup of coffee. He toasted three bagels, and as always heaped them with garlic cream cheese, sat down and read the school lunch menus in the *Great Falls Tribune*. Getting up from the table, he brushed the crumbs off his podgy belly onto the floor as he walked back into the bathroom. He smiled into the mirror and said to himself, "Montana isn't any smarter than Massachusetts." The small apartment echoed the resounding belch from Bar Jonah's full stomach. "Compliments to the chef," he said.

Bar Jonah went back into the living room and sat down for a few minutes in his recliner. He squared back his shoulders, took out a cigarette, lit it, took two puffs and then tossed it into an opaque glass ashtray with gold leaf trim. The wispy ashes made the picture of the Statue of Liberty stenciled onto the bottom of the ashtray look like the Mother of Exiles was covered in blowing snow. Bar Jonah remembered yelling at Tyra over dinner the night before. He had said he tried to tell her all along that he was innocent but she didn't believe him. It wasn't enough that she and Bob got family friends to agree to testify as to Bar Jonah's good character. He knew Bob was trying to turn Tyra against him with his lies, making her doubt him.

Bar Jonah had one last piece of business to take care of before he left to do his rounds. He was furious at Flaherty for the way he let him "rot in jail" for so long, wasting his time by going back and forth with Julie Macek. Flaherty also failed to show up for an appointment with Tyra and Bob the day after Bar Jonah was released from jail without even so much as a phone call. He had some kind of an excuse about being called unexpectedly to meet with a judge. Bar Jonah knew Flaherty was lying. He was incompetent and Bar Jonah was going to tell him so. On his personalized stationary, with his picture sketched in the upper left hand corner, Bar Jonah wrote Flaherty a letter telling him that canceling the appointment with him and his family was a great inconvenience. Bar Jonah had been locked up for months and had a lot of things to catch up on. His business had suffered, not to mention his good name. Flaherty did a poor job and had used poor judgment, not to mention the fact that his Christian ethics were not up to par. He had not earned the $3000 that Bar Jonah's family had paid him. Bar Jonah thought that Flaherty should give some of the money back. If he was any kind of Christian he would. Bar Jonah addressed the envelope, slipped the folded letter inside, hocked thick spit on the flap to moisten the glue, and used his thumb to seal it closed.

The springs groaned, as Bar Jonah pushed himself up and out of his chair. A few quick steps and he was out the door.

He stopped and slid the letter to Flaherty under the rounded bump of the wooden clothes pin that he kept clipped to his mailbox. When Bar Jonah flipped open the lid to his mailbox, he pulled out a letter that had Montana State Prison as the return address. It was from Boone Yeager. Boone was asking how Bar Jonah's court case had turned out. He had not yet heard through the prison grapevine. Boone also wanted Bar Jonah to know that he had been thrown in max for a while because of an altercation with his cellmate. But things were better now. Once Boone had done his time in max he was moved to the lesser-restricted "G" block with a new cellmate, his old friend, Reno McLaughlin. Bar Jonah sent him a short note back to say everything had turned out just fine. He was now, for the first time in seventeen years, a *completely* free man. And, it felt good. Not to be in jail, no probation, and most importantly, no one looking over his shoulder.

Smorgasbord

The loaded school buses got in about 7:30 a.m. Bar Jonah liked to get there just a little before. He joked with his now best friend, Doc Bauman that he liked to get the best seat in the house. It was important to hit a different school each morning, if he had time. This way the kids could count on him being there. But, they could be demanding too, wanting more of his time than he had to give. Sometimes it just depended on the weather. Sometimes he would give some of the boys treats or matchbox cars. But he would never give them anything with sugar, saying, no, it wasn't good for them. In the afternoons, the empty buses started lining up about 2:45 p.m. Bar Jonah sometimes walked up and down the sidewalk waiting for school to end, sticking his head in the door of the buses, saying hello to the drivers. Sometimes he brought doughnuts. They were adults; they could have sugar. He even brought toys and trinkets for their kids too. There was no point in leaving them out.

Whittier Elementary was Bar Jonah's favorite school. Whittier sits on a comfortable tree-lined side street where an alley, right next to a yellow two-story house, comes right out to the front of the school. When the buses pulled up in front of the school, bunches of swarming, rapturous, squealing boys would pile off, running, swinging their backpacks, chasing each other, yelling with excitement. They were all so polished and fresh, done up like precious little lambs first thing in the morning. If it was warm out, Bar Jonah made his patrols by walking, but if the weather was bad he drove. Either way, he liked to walk among the kids as they ran toward the school. Dozens and dozens of kids ran past him, brushing against him, hearing his voice telling them to slow down and be careful. Especially on icy days, they could slip and fall, he would caution.

Sometimes Bar Jonah said he patrolled the hallways dressed in his blue police jacket. A few of the parents talked among themselves about the fat, sloppy man walking around the school talking with the kids. They felt easier though when they saw him talking with the teachers. There were no complaints filed or concerns expressed to the school. None of the teachers expressed any concerns either. In fact, Bar Jonah's presence at the schools became so common that several teachers thought he was a volunteer or actually an undercover police officer who was there to help make sure the kids were safe.

BJ's Collectibles

Westgate Mall (Vendor's Market)
1807 3 NW
Great Falls, MT 59404

Specializes in Collectible Toys & Teddies
Home Phone (406) 771-0317 evenings

Ten-year-old Bar Jonah with his father on vacation.

Bar Jonah aged ten.

Bar Jonah aged ten.

Bar Jonah aged eighteen.

Bar Jonah's high school graduation picture.

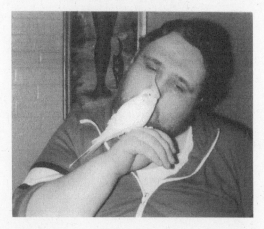

Bar Jonah aged seventeen with a bird.

Tyra holding Bar Jonah's high school diploma.

Bar Jonah being booked into Bridgewater State Hospital.

Judge Walter Steele.

Doc Bauman with his pet cat Puddin.

Zach Ramsay at the time of his disappearance and an aged progressed picture.

Signed photo of Montel Williams, which Montel gave to Rachel.

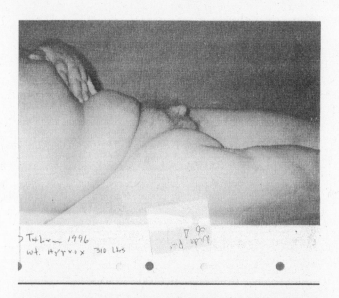

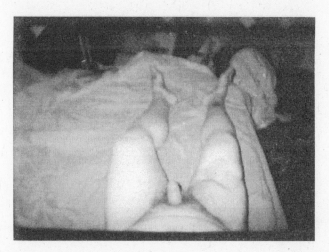

The only known photos of Bar Jonah naked. There is speculation that Zach may have taken this photo. There was also speculation by Det. Cameron that this photo was taken in a "hidden room" in the basement of Bob's basement.

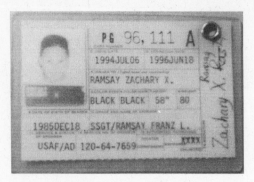

Zach Ramsay's military ID.

Zach in front of Whittier elementary school.

TEDDY BEAR, CAST METAL
AND
COLLECTABLE TOY SHOW

CENTRAL ASSEMBLY OF GOD

2001 Central Avenue
Great Falls, Montana 59401

Friday / Saturday, Nov. 19 & 20th, 1993

Farm   Construction   Trucks   Cars   Banks

TEDDY BEARS   Collectible Toys & Dolls

Admission - $1.00
Kids Under 12-FREE
Doors Open 9:30 a.m. - 4 p.m.
Set Up - 7:30 a.m
Exhibitors - $25.00 per Space
Admission fee Benefits Royal Rangers

MAIL RESERVATIONS TO:

Nathanael Bar-Jonah
1000 4th Avenue North #6
Great Falls, MT 59401

1-406-771-0317

Reserve Your Spaces Early

CHIT CHAT   CHIT CHAT

SHARE THE
GOOD NEWS

BEAR MOBILE

GOD ALWAYS
LISTENS

121

CHAPTER TEN

Doc

When Doc was released from jail, a few weeks before Bar Jonah, he went back to his place at 1615 7th Avenue. Doc liked to call his house a loving sanctuary for lost boys. He was their golden glowing nimbus guiding them out of the turbulent waters of life on the streets. "Come home with me and let me offer you my love, hot meals and a warm bed; I only want to be loved in return," Doc would exclaim, sounding desperate and pitiful. He said his passion to emancipate vanquished lads from their life of toil and tears was the bane of his existence. No matter how he tried to camouflage his disability of caring too much for the disenfranchised and downtrodden, it always seemed to come out when his heart was snared by a fetching, curly headed, dark-complected boy. Doc liked to think of them as winsome rascals. Over the years, so many susceptible boys would find Doc's certitude, in his declaration of devotion to their wellbeing, alluring and reassuring.

When Bar Jonah and Doc shared a cell they discovered how, by a bizarre twist of fate, their lives had unknowingly crossed paths many years earlier. While in jail, Doc and Bar Jonah became the best of friends. Sitting on a bunk in their cell, Doc whispered to Bar Jonah that they were of one mind when it came to loving boys. Before Doc left their cell for the last time, he told Bar Jonah he would reserve a permanent seat for him at a local neighborhood bar, called the HiHo Tavern.

Like most seedy bars, it had a dark and dank feel. An odor of old, sweet hop-filled piss permeated the aged barn-sided walls. Stools that had dropped many drunks were lined up like wooden soldiers standing at attention along the front of the bar. A mirror caked with years of smoke reflected life in the tavern as a sepia-tinted silent movie, playing itself out over and over again, night after night. There, Doc and Bar Jonah would meet, drink, and talk about what fuckers the Great Falls cops were. From the very first late night discussions in their cell, Doc saw Bar Jonah's great potential; he wanted to mentor him, to bring him further along.

Doc was a well-known character around Great Falls. He would tell people he was a medical doctor who also had his PhD in child psychology. This allowed him to deeply understand children and their special needs, Doc would say. His bright red velour suits, usually adorned with a red fuzzy felt hat, and sometimes a feather, always seemed too big for his rail-thin stature. Even though Doc was born in 1929, he didn't really need his ever-present cane, which he kept covered in red felt to match his hat. Doc also wore amber aviator sunglasses. Not to keep out the sun, but to prevent others from seeing his eyes constantly scanning for young boys. Doc was a pedophile, with a fifty-year history of molesting young boys.

He would find boys with no place to go and lure them into moving in with him. Making promises that they could do as they pleased, plus he'd give them plenty to eat and a roof over their head. It was better than living on the street. Doc was born to a hardscrabble life in the Texas Hill Country and spent most of his early years there. By the time he enlisted in the Army about 1946 they were just beginning to talk seriously about bringing electricity to the Hill Country. Doc used to joke with his army buddies that he had never even seen a bar of store-bought soap until he joined the service. He said that his mother had scrubbed the color right out of his skin during his once-a-week baths, leaving him with magnolia white skin. Doc was proud of his service to his country. He never let anyone forget that he had saved a lot of boys' lives on the battlefield. "Sergeant!" the wounded would scream in terror and pain, after being hit by a Gook bullet. Doc would hear the boys' cries, throw his hand up, grip the top of his red-crossed helmet, shove it down tight on his head, and dodging bullets, go running toward the wounded. Sometimes it was too late, Doc would quietly say, recalling his anguish at the catastrophic wounds some of the boys died from. Others that Doc was able to bring back from the brink of death still sent him Christmas cards of thanks every year.

Doc eventually ended up going to Massachusetts in the 1970s. In the early '80s, Doc migrated to El Paso County, Colorado and finally settled in Great Falls sometime in the mid-1980s. He thought of himself as a philosopher of sorts and a champion of the men who loved boys.

* * *

NAMBLA, as the North American Man Boy Love Association is known, is an organization of pedophiles. The goal of NAMBLA is to end what they refer to as the oppression of men and boys who have mutually loving relationships. NAMBLA was organized in February 1979 at the end of what was called the Man-Boy Lovers Appreciation conference, which was held in Boston. The MBLA conference was the first thinly-veiled formal gathering that brought together pedophiles from as far away as Bangkok and as remote as Alaska. In 1979, the internet was not available for social networking, so all communication between members was done by mail, telephone, or word of mouth. The keynote speaker at the conference was the still-frocked Father Paul J. Shanley. Because NAMBLA is a secret criminal society, information is sketchy and often contradictory. However, it is rumored that at the end of the MBLA meeting, thirty-two of the participants formed NAMBLA. Doc Bauman liked to sit in the HiHo and brag that he was one of the thirty-two. No one would ever say for sure, but Doc always held fast that he was one of the "gifted minds" that came up with the original idea for men who love boys to organize en masse. "We deserve love too," Doc would expound, while waving his hand like a sentry at the castle of Elsinore announcing the arrival of Horatio.

In the early 1980s, members of the newly formed NAMBLA were fed up with the way men who dedicated their lives to loving boys were being treated, especially in Massachusetts. The members of NAMBLA made Bridgewater State Hospital a particular place of interest. Twenty members of NAMBLA protested in front of Bridgewater in the spring of 1983, with signs denouncing the unwarranted treatment of men being held prisoner by the state of Massachusetts. Bar Jonah said he watched the protest from the dayroom at Bridgewater. Doc told Bar Jonah that not only was he carrying one of the signs, but he was one of the organizers of the protest. Bar Jonah and Doc reached out simultaneously and locked their curled hands together in solidarity.

* * *

In his twenties, Doc had supposedly worked on the railroad as a conductor. He told a few of the older boys he was knocked off the back of a passenger car one day, when the train lurched suddenly. Doc bragged that he had received a settlement and permanent pension from the railroad. It wasn't hard to make things look a lot worse than they were. The settlement is what Doc said allowed him to go to medical school and get his doctorate in child psychology. Sometimes there are advantages to being injured on the job, Doc liked to boast. The time that Doc said he was in medical school were the years that he was having trouble with the authorities in El Paso County. The cops picked him up for soliciting a child for prostitution and conspiracy to commit a sex act on a child. Both charges were, what Doc would say in his chronically hoarse voice, "brummagem." The boys he had befriended were castaways. Doc liked to say that the curse he had been charged with, of being a coxswain for the wayward, was going to be the death of him. But, it was his lot in life. What could he do?

* * *

When visitors walked through the gate of Doc's jagged, planked Hansel and Gretel fence that wrapped around his yard at 1615 7th Avenue N, they began to catch the faint hint of an odor. It was subtle, but familiar enough to cause them to stop and ask, "What's that smell?" But, when Doc opened the door to his house on the north side of Great Falls, one was immediately besieged with the unmistakable smell of cat shit. The odor didn't come from dirty litter boxes. In fact, there weren't any in the entire house. Rather the profound overwhelming stench came from hundreds of mounds of cat shit, piled three feet high, spread throughout the house. Doc told his friends he knew his house stank, but he didn't care. He loved the sixty cats that lived with him. Doc would always caution visitors to be careful not to let any of his cats outside when they opened his front door.

When Bellusci and his partner went to Doc's house to arrest him on the 1994 sexual assault charges, Bellusci tried to push open the kitchen door. But the door would only open about a foot because of the piles of cat shit blocking the door. Bellusci was able to push the door open enough to squeeze through. His partner tried to squeeze through the opening right after Bellusci. But his gut protruded out too far. Bellusci had to walk through the house, donned in high rubber boots and a respirator, cussing with every step, and let his partner in through the front door.

Bar Jonah never seemed to mind the retching odor at Doc's place either. When he walked into Doc's house, Bar Jonah would roll his head back, close his eyes, and fill his lungs with the pervasive stench of cat shit and piss.

The other mounds in Doc's house were toys. Thousands of toys, perfectly preserved in their boxes, dolls, trucks, guns, cars, racetracks, and airplanes, were stacked floor to ceiling. Anything that would appeal to a boy, Doc had. Doc's living room was adorned in a Christmas and Halloween motif while one of his bedrooms was permanently decorated with big stuffed Easter bunnies. Doc kept dozens of Easter baskets, filled with dried out candy and years old colored eggs sitting atop pale green plastic grass, for his boy visitors to choose a treat from. Doc didn't permit anyone to sleep in the Easter bedroom, it was only for show.

A small bedroom off the kitchen was where Doc slept with whomever the boy was he was sharing his house with at the time. In that bedroom was a small twin bed covered with an army man quilt and a dozen overstuffed drab green pillows. Doc also kept an old ivory-handled Harrington and Richardson, .22 single-action revolver in a drawer beside his bed. These were street urchins, after all; you had to be careful, he would say. You could give them your love and care for them, but because of the way they were raised, sometimes they'd turn on you like a snake. Doc would sit at the HiHo with Bar Jonah and joke that he was a devotee of recycling long before it became a cultural fad. He liked to take in a boy who was newly discarded by his family, and turn back out the boy he had lost interest in.

Doc said he used the Socratic method to bring men of like minds further along the path of enlightenment. He wanted to help them to identify and eliminate any contradictions they may have had about loving boys. Doc always said he had nothing more loving to offer a boy than the time they spent in bed together. And, like Bar Jonah, he called boys lost little lambs wanting to be found. Doc desired to leave a permanent mark on the boys he cared for, the boys that he groomed. It was Doc's way of leaving as many of his "successors" behind, as he possibly could, to carry on his legacy.

Bar Jonah and Doc used to get together for sex too. They gave each other hand jobs and blowjobs and would lay in bed for hours, talking about the boys they had known. Often the bed was littered with pictures of boys that they had collected over the years. Bar Jonah would say it was sex of convenience, that he wasn't gay; he just hadn't met the right woman to settle down with. When they first met, Bar Jonah was in his early thirties. Doc was in his late sixties. Patrons of the HiHo use to hear Doc loudly complain that Bar Jonah's sex drive wasn't what Doc had experienced with other men Bar Jonah's age. Bar Jonah snuffed it off, saying he was just more patient than Doc.

Ropes and choking always seemed to become part of the conversation when Bar Jonah talked about sex, Doc said. It so happened that one day Doc got an article in the mail on autoerotic asphyxiation, from one of his long-time friends in Colorado. Doc didn't have any interest in almost dying during sex, so he passed the piece along to Bar Jonah. Bar Jonah told Doc he knew all about it, but he'd take it anyway. After he read it, maybe he would write the author and give him some pointers. Doc also handed Bar Jonah a copy of an article he had copied from a law journal called "Child Witnesses: Translating Research into Policy" (Stephen Ceci & Maggie Bruck, 1993). Doc said the article talked about the way lawyers can make kids out to look like liars on the witness stand, without pissing off the jury. Doc told Bar Jonah that what the authors talk about in the article had saved his butt several times.

Even though they were the best of friends, Doc was also afraid of Bar Jonah. Doc said he was an old man now and could not defend himself anymore. He was afraid of being hurt, that was one of the reasons why he preferred weak and brittle boys. Bar Jonah only slept over at Doc's house a few times. The last time Bar Jonah stayed, Doc woke up in the middle of the night to Bar Jonah grabbing him by the hair and shoving his dick into Doc's mouth. Doc in the twilight of sleep initially thought the moment was erotic. Then Bar Jonah forced his dick all the way down Doc's throat. Even though Bar Jonah's dick was small, Bar Jonah held Doc's head so tight against his pubic bone that Doc could barely breathe. Doc began to panic and tried to pull his head away. Bar Jonah held his head tight against him. Doc managed to turn his head sideways enough to catch a breath. In that moment Doc felt Bar Jonah come in his mouth. Anytime they had sex after that night, Doc told Bar Jonah he couldn't stay, he had to go home.

In early 1993, Rachel Howard moved from Fairfield, Montana to 1617 7th Avenue, in Great Falls. Rachel told one of her friends from church how much she liked the cute little wooden storybook fence that the strange little old man, in pink fuzzy suits, had built around his house. Her son, Zach, thought it was pretty neat too.

Hardee's

In the summer of 1995 Bar Jonah decided that in addition to his antique and snow-shoveling business it would be a good idea to have a job he could build a future on. He told them at the 10th Avenue Hardee's he had been a chef back east and was looking eventually to get into management and build a career. A few days later they hired him for the midnight shift. Bar Jonah's job was to work in the back and chop up chickens for the next day's crew. A few months later he was promoted to manning the deep fryer. His name badge read, "Nathan, Biscuit/Chicken Man". He eventually became a shift supervisor, being responsible for making sure that all the equipment was spot cleaned and sanitized. In 1997, Sgt. John Cameron was assigned to the graveyard patrol, "midnights to 7 A." Cameron said when he rolled into the 10th Avenue Hardee's for his 2 a.m. lunch break that Bar Jonah always seemed to wait on him.

CHAPTER ELEVEN

Zachary Ramsay

Maple trees dapple the sunlight that falls across the front of the wood frame and brick houses that line the neighborhood streets where Zach Ramsay used to play. Before the weather turns foul, kids ride their tricycles up and down the sidewalks going a million miles an hour. Brake lights are always coming on, alert to dashing little feet pursuing a ball thrown by a future major leaguer. An alley that runs behind 4th and 7th Avenue is always neat and well tended. No boxes of trash or old cars on blocks taint the view or make the alley seem unsafe.

In 1996, Zach was 4' 6" and weighed 85 lb. He had a dark complexion, black hair, and dark brown eyes. His mother, Rachel Howard, is white and his father, Franz Ramsay, is black. They were divorced. Rachel and Zach lived in Great Falls. Franz was in the Air Force and stationed in Colorado. In a photograph taken in 1988, when Zach is about two, he is sitting on a tan plush rug, cradled in his father's arms, dressed in a red, white, and blue shirt. His tongue is pressing against his two new front teeth like they are a novelty. His full cheeks are puffed out by his broad smile.

Zach was a handsome boy, who, by all accounts, was known for his kind and gentle nature. He was also an artist. Zach kept track of his life in black spiral-bound notebooks, where he drew pictures of football jerseys with numbers of his favorite players and headless men. Heavy lines in some of his drawings outlined the crotch of his characters illustrated by what appeared to be blood. The genitals in several of the drawings were cut out with a knife. A knife was drawn off to the right on the same page, elliptical hash lines encircling the tip indicated the sharpness of the point. Droplets of blood were dripping from the blade. There were also what appeared to be drawings made by someone else in his notebooks. Also in Zach's journals are what looks like coded writing and twisted words that seem to wrap around each other. No one thought anything about it at the time. It was just something a kid would do. Some of Zach's drawings of robots have long claw-like fingernails holding onto a rope and many more pictures of knives. More than thirteen years later his drawings would become one of the important links between him and Bar Jonah.

On Tuesday, February 6, 1996, Zach got up as usual. That morning he was particularly looking forward to going to school. It was the Good Guy breakfast, where kids brought their dads to have all the pancakes they could eat in the school cafeteria. After Zach pulled on his favorite football jersey, he stood in front of the mirror, turned his head around and saw "RAMSAY" reflected in big gold letters across his back. He sat down on the floor, and rocking back on his butt, tugged on his blue jeans. Finally, he snugged up the laces and double-knotted his black sneakers. He was all ready now, wrapped up warmly in his blue denim coat with green plaid sleeves and his ever-present backpack.

Rachel had moved from 7th Avenue to 4th Street, so Zach could be closer to school. This way he could walk right down the alley and in a few short blocks come right out at Whittier. Right before Zach walked out the door Rachel looked at the clock, 7:34 a.m. As Zach was closing the front door behind him, he looked up at the top of the stairs and yelled goodbye to Rachel. Rachel said it never dawned on her that she would never see him again.

Marvin, Melissa, and Helen Henry, who lived behind the alley off of 5th Street, saw Zach walking down the alley to school, crossing 5th St. at 5th Ave. Carol Henry said she also saw Zach in the alley. As he was crossing 5th Avenue, Carol said she yelled at Zach when a late 1980s four-door, off-white car almost ran him over. Zach jumped out of the way and kept walking into the alley heading toward 6th Avenue.

Mrs. Margaretta Richardson lived in the Bitterroot Apartments, a block over from Rachel. In a thick German accent, Mrs. Richardson said when she first spoke to Zach, he asked her where she was from. Zach said she sure didn't sound like she was from Great Falls. Mrs. Richardson laughed out loud. She got to know Zach because he would frequently be walking down the alley coming home from school right when she arrived home from work. She was always impressed with how polite and courteous he was. Whenever they saw each other, Zach would run up and open the door. He always offered to help Mrs. Richardson carry her packages to the elevator. "I asked him his name one afternoon and he told me it was Zachary. I told him I was Mrs. Richardson. I also told him he had the prettiest smile I ever saw. I will never forget him." The morning Zachary disappeared, Mrs. Richardson happened to pull back the curtain on her kitchen window and see Zachary standing in between the two garages that sat at the edge of the alley. "He was just standing there looking around, like he was waiting for someone, turning his head from side to side," she said. Over the years, Mrs. Richardson felt guilty she didn't hold the curtain back just a little while longer.

Patrick Hall, who lived close to where the alley cuts into 6th Avenue, saw a boy matching Zach's description crossing 6th Street, with a fat adult male following a few feet behind.

Michael McIntire was getting ready to go to the Good Guy breakfast with his daughter. While she was getting ready, he took the trash out about 7:15. The alley ran behind Mr. McIntire's home on 5th Avenue. He lifted the top of an aluminum trash can and tossed in a white plastic bag. When he looked to his left, he saw Bar Jonah leaning against a large green dumpster smoking a cigarette. McIntire said "Hello," as Bar Jonah flipped his cigarette across the narrow alley. Then Bar Jonah looked at McIntire and nodded. McIntire was not surprised to see Bar Jonah. He had been hanging around the alley for about a month, talking and playing with some of the kids. McIntire said on some days Bar Jonah showed up about 2:30, just before the kids got out of school and stayed until 3:30. When Mr. McIntire and his daughter went out to leave for the Good Guy breakfast, he looked to the right and saw Zach just walking into the alley. Bar Jonah was still standing beside the dumpster. Somewhere between where the alley cuts into 6th Avenue and comes out on 7th, ten-year-old Zachary Ramsay vanished.

* * *

The Good Guy breakfast was a success. Teachers walked around greeting their students and shaking hands with their dads. Fathers stood in line, with their arms around their kids' shoulders, gently nudging them along, plates at the ready for pancakes and maple syrup. The boys and girls were laughing, looking up proudly at their dads feeling competitive about whose dad was the best.

Zach's teacher, Mrs. Davis, knew he was looking forward to the Good Guy breakfast. A few days before, Zach couldn't stop talking about how excited he was. He was going to get up especially early, he said, just to make extra sure *they* got there on time.

Mrs. Davis also knew Zach's mother had broken up with her boyfriend a week before and Zach's dad was in Colorado, so

134

she didn't know who Zach was going to bring to the breakfast. That morning, all of Zach's classmates were there, sitting at the same table. As the hands of the clock inched closer to the end of the celebration, it was obvious Zach was not coming. When he didn't show up for class right after breakfast, Mrs. Davis called the principal, Diane Long.

The secretary from the Great Falls Vocational College office came into Rachel's class about 9:00 and handed her a note. It simply said, "Zach is not at school, call Whittier right away." Rachel called the school. Mrs. Long asked Rachel to come to the school. She was concerned that Zach had not shown up for the Good Guy breakfast. Rachel decided to go home instead. When she arrived at home, Rachel unlocked the door and went through the house yelling for Zach. Had Zach gone back home, was Rachel's first thought. Then Rachel walked the alley, calling Zach's name. She went back home and finally drove to Whittier about 10:00 a.m. The police were already at the school. Rachel gave the officer a play-by-play account of that morning and then drove back home. She said she wanted to be there in case Zach came back.

Detective Bellusci was in his car when the call about Zach came over the radio. He did a U-turn and immediately headed over to Rachel's. As soon as Bellusci heard the call he said he had a bad feeling. "I couldn't explain it but I thought this is a kid we're never going to find." When he arrived, Rachel met him at the door wearing sunglasses. She didn't take them off. Bellusci said it made him uncomfortable not being able to see someone's eyes when they were talking. He asked Rachel to take her sunglasses off. She reached up and pulled them off with one hand. Her right eye was purple and the white of her eye was blood red. Bellusci asked her if she had been in a fight or if her boyfriend had beaten her up. Rachel just said no.

Two nights before Zach disappeared, Rachel and her boyfriend Carl Dekooning were having sex. Rachel said that when Carl was on top of her, he reached around, grabbed her by the hair, put his mouth over her right eye and began sucking. She tried to push him off, but he kept sucking on her eye. Rachel said she felt like her eye was going to pop out of its socket. She screamed and shoved Carl off of her and onto the floor. Rachel ran to the bathroom and looked in the mirror. The mirror told Rachel that she looked like she had been punched. She had blood pooling in the corner of her eye near her nose. Carl heard her screaming and ran into the bathroom. Rachel was crying hysterically and started chasing Carl through the apartment saying they were through; this was the final straw. Bellusci stared at Rachel in disbelief trying to focus on the fact her son was missing.

* * *

Bellusci tried to reassure Rachel that Zach probably became distracted by something and would turn up at a friend's house. Kids do this kind of thing all the time. However, Bellusci didn't believe what he was saying. Rachel told Bellusci Zach had been pushing her to get him an older friend; he had really wanted an adult male friend in his life. Zach's father was a master sergeant in the Air Force and stationed at Peterson Air Force Base in Colorado Springs. Zach and his dad didn't have much of a relationship, Rachel told Bellusci. There had been a lot of blood shed between Rachel and Franz over the years about custody and child support. In fact Rachel was about to take Franz back to court again.

Carl had moved out of Rachel's just two days before and never really seemed to hit it off with Zach. Carl was a whiney, difficult man, Rachel said. But he was easy to control, mostly with sex. He also walked with a decisive limp, from when he tried to kill himself years earlier, by crashing his motorcycle into a concrete bridge stanchion. Carl told Rachel he was so fucking inadequate that he couldn't even succeed at killing himself. Rachel constantly reassured Carl that he was adequate enough to kill himself, if he really wanted too.

A few days after Carl and Rachel became involved, Rachel thought it would be a good idea if they moved in together. But Carl was being his usual wishy-washy self. So Rachel took matters into her own hands. She went over to Carl's place, and while his pasty, built like a toothpick, waifish wife and kids were at home, Rachel packed Carl up and moved him out of his place and into hers. He didn't have much, some heavy canvas work clothes, hunting gear, not much else. Rachel told Bellusci that a few nights before Zach disappeared Carl took Zach to the park. Carl also had Zach show him the path he took down the alley to school. Rachel didn't understand, because Carl had not taken any interest in Zach before.

Rachel's boyfriend prior to Carl was Jeff Partain, who had killed himself a few months before Zach disappeared. He rolled his car, while in a drunken stupor, into the Missouri river and drowned. Rachel didn't seem to mind much. Like all the men in her life, he had been a pain in the ass too.

* * *

Detective Bellusci, knowing about Bar Jonah's background, suspected he might be involved with Zach's disappearance. About 11 a.m., Bellusci had patrol officers Rodriguez and Schalin go to Bar Jonah's apartment. The blinds were drawn. There was no answer when they knocked. Rodriguez put one of his business cards in the door jamb asking Bar Jonah to call him.

Franz Ramsay and his wife Cynthia arrived on the 1:40 p.m. flight into Great Falls coming out of Peterson Air Force Base in Colorado. Rachel was waiting for them at the Great Falls airport. The plan was for Rachel to drive them to the Great Falls police station where they would all be routinely polygraphed.

Rachel said that on the drive to the GFPD Franz didn't say anything about Zach, except to complain that Rachel had not bought Zach name-brand shoes. Rachel sarcastically defended herself, saying that if Franz paid his child support on time she wouldn't have to scrimp on what she bought Zach. Franz called Rachel a liar and demanded to know how she was spending the child support he was sending. Rachel was relentless in her accusations and demands.

Franz had had enough of Rachel and asked Bellusci if he would take him and Cynthia to a local hotel. They didn't want to get back into the car with Rachel. Franz told Bellusci that Rachel was crazy. He didn't know how but he believed Rachel was somehow responsible for Zach's disappearance. At 2:30 p.m. Bellusci, still suspicious, went to Bar Jonah's door himself, but again there was no answer. He didn't know that he had missed Bar Jonah by ten minutes. At 2:20 p.m. Bar Jonah had gone to the Doctors Convenience Care Center across the street from his apartment at 1216 1st Avenue. Bar Jonah was complaining that he had hurt his left index finger and had a sore right leg. Before Bellusci left, he slipped his business card in the door jamb too. "I am trying to contact you," he wrote on the back.

At the time Zach disappeared, Bob was still married to his wife Jill. When they heard the news reports that an eight-year-old boy was missing, Jill said they became concerned that Bar Jonah was involved. They were especially suspicious because Tyra's sister, Rosanna, had recently died. Tyra had left for her sister's funeral in Massachusetts on January 26; she would not return until February 16. Bar Jonah would have had complete access to Tyra's white Toyota Corolla, even though she had told him he that he was not to use her car while she was gone. He didn't listen. He never did.

About 4 p.m. on the day Zach disappeared, Bob went over to Bar Jonah's apartment. He said that the apartment was a complete mess. The bathtub was particularly dirty he said, covered with mud and small broken twigs. There were muddy footprints from the main door leading into the bathroom. Bob spent the next hour cleaning up the bathtub and scrubbing the mud off of the carpet. He had just replaced all of the flooring in the apartment. Bob was pissed Bar Jonah was not keeping the place clean. He tossed the debris and the rags he used for cleaning the place into the dumpster. The trash men hauled the dumpster away the next morning. Bob also checked the garage where Tyra kept her car but he said he couldn't tell if Bar Jonah had used the car. The garage had an electric door opener and the remote was kept above the sun visor in the Toyota. Bob said he had no way of knowing if the door opener had been used or not.

Bellusci organized neighborhood searches and acquaintances of Rachel were questioned. The neighborhood was searched and researched. Every dumpster was checked. Rachel said it was as though Zach had simply vanished off the face of the earth. The local television stations broadcast alerts that Zach was missing, flashing his picture on the screen several times during the day. The police were asking people to check the trunks of their cars and any abandoned refrigerators. What lukewarm leads they had were quickly turning cold. There was no trace of Zachary Ramsay to be found. He *had* vanished off the face of the earth.

Late in the afternoon on the day Zach disappeared, Bellusci wanted Rachel to go on local television and make a plea for Zach's safe return. Bellusci said it might do some good. The television crews came and set up outside of Rachel's apartment. They were ready to go. But Rachel was not there. Bellusci went looking for Rachel and found her in her bedroom, carefully putting on her make-up. She told Bellusci she would not go on television unless she looked her best. Rachel's comment pissed Bellusci off. When Bellusci talked with Rachel, she did not appear distraught. She wasn't crying, her eyes weren't red. Rachel later said, "I'm a strong bitch and my boy needed to see me strong. There was no way I was going to look upset on television." Rachel did not sleep for two days after Zach disappeared. Right before noon on the 7th, Rachel said she received a phone call. The caller did not identify himself. He told Rachel to come to Paris Gibson Park, near downtown Great Falls, at 10:00 p.m. The caller said he had information about who took Zach. Exhaustion began to overtake Rachel as the day wore on. As 8 o'clock approached Rachel lay down on the couch and fell asleep. She woke up at 2 a.m. realizing she had missed the meeting. She didn't think it was important to tell Bellusci about the phone call.

Rachel received a call from Bellusci a few days after Zach disappeared. Bellusci had a picture of Bar Jonah he wanted Rachel to see. The question of whether or not Rachel knew Bar Jonah kept running through Bellusci's mind. Rachel and her kids had been members of the same church as Bar Jonah. Moreover when Zach was younger he was a Royal Ranger. How could they not know each other? Bellusci asked Rachel if she would come down to the station to take a look at the photo. Rachel refused saying she had too many things to do, but Bellusci could bring the photo to her and she would take a look at it. Bellusci arrived at Rachel's about an hour later. Rachel said she had never seen Bar Jonah.

* * *

On February 8, Bellusci finally spoke briefly to Bar Jonah by phone. Bar Jonah agreed to come in for an interview eighteen days later, on February 26. He was to be at the police station at 1:30 p.m. He never showed up. February 8 was the last day the police made any attempt to contact Bar Jonah. Four years later, when Detective Cameron took over the investigation he found an entry in Bar Jonah's 1996 calendar for 1:30 p.m. on February 26 that read, "1:30 GFPD." The entry was scratched through in pencil and Patrick Flaherty's name was written in instead. Until then, no one knew why Bar Jonah didn't show up for the meeting.

Instead of meeting with Bellusci, Bar Jonah had decided to meet with Patrick Flaherty. When Flaherty arrived at his office, on the morning of February 26, he found a handwritten note rolled up and stuck in his door. It was from Bob. The note said the police had contacted Bar Jonah and he had agreed to meet with them. Bob didn't think it was a good idea for Bar Jonah to meet with the cops alone. Flaherty didn't either. Flaherty's working notes show that he called and left a message for Bellusci on the afternoon of the 26th, telling Bellusci that he and Bar Jonah would meet with him. Flaherty said he never received a return phone call from Bellusci. The meeting between Bar Jonah and Bellusci never took place.

At 12:30 that day, Julie Doney called the police and said she wanted to report some suspicious activity around Whittier School. Doney stated that approximately two and a half weeks before her eleven-year-old son, Dustin, was walking home from school on 3rd Ave. A big fat man pulled up to the curb and told Dustin his mother was in trouble and needed him right away. The fat man was a policeman, he would take him to her, he said. Dustin yelled that the man was too fat to be a policeman and took off running. When he looked back he saw the man driving away.

* * *

In a public statement, a week after Zach disappeared, Great Falls Police Chief Robert G. Jones said, "It's going to take a long time for our community to return to normal". Normal in Great Falls meant a sharply defined sense of right and wrong and a mistrust of authority. It also meant that no one had any problem with the Ten Commandments being chiseled into a granite slab in front of the courthouse. But most of all it meant kids didn't disappear without a trace. Not a single member of the Great Falls police department had ever dealt with a case of child abduction where it was not resolved with the child being found alive, the same day. In Montana there is also a sense of vigilante justice at the business end of a Winchester. When the

Great Falls Tribune interviewed a local dentist, Dr. David Comer, he said if he found out who took Zach, "I'd shoot him myself and never give it a second thought" (Belkin, 2000).

Prime suspect

On Wednesday morning, February 7, the day after Zach disappeared, Bellusci and FBI Special Agent James Wilson drove to Rachel's apartment. As they were driving up they saw Rachel's two other children, four-year-old daughter Simone and two-year-old Isaac, playing unattended a block away from home. Bellusci and Wilson looked at each other and felt unsettled. As of yet, they did not know who had taken Zach or if he was alive or dead. When Wilson expressed his concerns about Rachel's other two children playing out of her sight, Rachel said, "Oh the kids will be fine, I'm checking on them." Wilson said that Rachel clearly had no idea where her other two children were. Her nonchalant attitude raised Bellusci's and Wilson's suspicions of Rachel. How could she let her other kids be out of her sight, even for a moment, with Zach missing? They thought she was either involved in Zach's disappearance or just plain stupid. Bellusci decided to walk the neighborhood while Wilson stayed and talked with Rachel. Wilson said he began to ask Rachel about the kind of men she dated. Rachel looked at Wilson and said, "Let me tell you one thing, I would never even consider dating a man unless he let me give him a blow-job first." Wilson looked dumbfounded at Rachel.

The special agent in charge of the Great Falls FBI office was Scott Cruz. He was pushing Wilson to aggressively pursue Rachel as a suspect. When Wilson and Bellusci began questioning Rachel, they discovered that she was attending Great Falls Vocational College, majoring in interior design. She had an 8 a.m. math class on the morning Zach disappeared. Rachel dropped Simone and Isaac off at their babysitter's about half an hour after Zach left for school. She got to her class at 8:15. The professor didn't think anything about her tardiness because Rachel was always late. About 9 a.m., the secretary in the college office called Rachel out of her math class and handed her a note. Rachel's friend Jamie Schmidt was in the hallway when Rachel read the message that Zach had not shown up for school. The principal at Whittier wanted her to come to the school right away. Rachel told Bellusci she went back home before she went to the school. She wanted to check her apartment just in case Zach had come back home for some reason. It didn't make sense for her to go to school if Zach wasn't there.

Mrs. Long had met Rachel at Whittier once she arrived. The school's police resource officer was there also. Rachel told Mrs. Long and the police officer that nothing was out of the ordinary before Zach left for school that morning. In fact, Zach was excited about going to the Good Guy breakfast. Rachel said she thought his teacher was going to sit with him at breakfast since his father wouldn't have anything to do with him. Zach emphatically told Rachel to be sure *not* to forget to pick him up a little early, because he was going to get a special artist award at the Paris Gibson Center that afternoon. Rachel left school about 9:45, picked Simone and Isaac up at the babysitters and went straight back home. Rachel had an airtight alibi. She was sitting in class at the time Zach went missing.

As Bellusci and Wilson continued questioning Rachel, they discovered she could not firmly account for four hours of her time on the night Zach disappeared. Between 9 p.m. and 1 a.m. Rachel could only say she had been out looking for Zach. Her mother, father, and brother had been at Rachel's apartment until about 9:00. Rachel said she'd had enough of them and wanted them all to leave. A few minutes after her family left, Rachel called Cathy, her babysitter, who lived right down the alley behind the Bitterroot Apartments. Rachel wanted Cathy to come over and stay with Simone and Isaac for a while. Rachel said she had to go out and look for Zach; she had to do something. In fact, Rachel went scouring the alleys around the area where Zach had walked to school. Rachel said she looked in every trashcan and dumpster in a ten block radius. When Rachel got back home about 2 a.m., she didn't go to bed. She stood by the window staring into the darkness. At one point in the early morning she looked out the window and said out loud, "Okay, the joke is over, it's fucking time to bring my kid back." Then she went up to Zach's room, crawled under his desk, pulled his clothes around her, rolled up into a fetal position, and began sobbing. Rachel said no one was going to see her cry because she had to be strong for her boy. Rachel didn't think she would need any witnesses that could verify she had been digging through trashcans and dumpsters at two o'clock in the morning. The fact that she didn't have any made Bellusci and Wilson more suspicious.

Bellusci told Rachel they needed to eliminate suspects, would she take a polygraph. Rachel readily agreed. Bellusci took Rachel to the Great Falls police station about 4 p.m. The police polygrapher was already set up and waiting for Rachel. The polygraph took about an hour. When Rachel came out of the room she looked at Bellusci and said, "Well I guess I didn't do too well." Bellusci said, "No, you did just fine, you passed with no problem." Later that day Bellusci had arranged for Rachel to go on television and make an appeal for Zach's return. Rachel was late for the press conference because she told Bellusci it took her longer than she expected to get her make-up on. She wanted to look her best for the cameras.

It was pushing into the afternoon of the 7th and nothing was happening. The cops needed to quickly turn up some leads. Bellusci decided to bring in search dogs. Really they were cadaver dogs that were trained to "alert" by rolling around or barking when they scented any kind of biological material. Bellusci contacted dog trainer Denny Adams. Adams was well known in the Great Falls Detective Division having worked with the department for many years. Adams had also been Bellusci's superior officer when they were both with the Air Force Office of Special Investigations. The blood between Bellusci and Adams wasn't the best. Adams thought Bellusci was difficult to deal with and would sometimes take investigations in the wrong direction. "There was a lot of politics in the PD," Adams said. The old detectives were always at odds with the new upstarts. But it wasn't just Bellusci, according to Adams, who was hard to deal with; it was all the detectives. Adams also said that Bellusci had had enough of the politics in the early '80s, and quit the PD for a short time to sell real estate. However Bellusci remained a reserve officer. He also kept his badge number, 100, which Adams said pissed off the other detectives.

Adams brought in his dogs about 10:30 p.m. on February 7. Rachel and her parents, who had come over earlier in the evening, sat in the living room while Adams took the bloodhounds throughout the house. Bellusci complained to Adams during the search that the dogs were not certified cadaver dogs. Adams countered that there was no certification for cadaver dogs. The search was nerve-racking, not only because they were looking for evidence that Zach had possibly been killed in the house, but also because of the tension between Bellusci and Adams.

Adams first took the dogs upstairs and got Zach's toothbrush to get an uncontaminated scent. Adams started taking the dogs through the house. He also pulled lint out of the dryer and looked in the refrigerator to check for any traces of blood. When they went back to the first floor, the dog alerted in the area under the stairs that was littered with clothes. Bellusci said out loud that he had never seen anything like it. The dog just started rolling around in a pile of dirty clothes, yelping. Bellusci bagged the clothes to have them checked for blood, urine, or fecal matter. The police and Adams also noticed that a section of carpet had been cut out of the stairs leading out the back door of Rachel's apartment. A couple of officers found the carpet in the dumpster behind Rachel's. They took it as possible evidence. On February 8 Adams took his dogs down the alley. Where the alley comes out onto 7th, the dogs alerted again. But there was nothing to be found. Adams worked the area for the next three weeks. The dogs never alerted again.

Adams also took his dogs to Carl DeKooning's place in Belt, Montana. Carl had moved back in with his wife, after Rachel threw him out of her place. Adams checked the inside of the house and walked his dogs all over the property. When Adams took his bloodhounds to check Carl's old pick-up truck, he saw that Zach had spray painted "ZACH RULES" across the inside of the tailgate. The bloodhounds didn't show any signs of alerting. About a year after Zach disappeared, Carl put a 12-gauge shotgun to his chest and pulled the trigger. It blew out one of his lungs and imbedded a handful of double-aught buckshot in his pericardium. But somehow he lived. Another year later, Carl got drunk and drove his pick-up at 80 mph down an old back dog-legged road. Not quite making one of the knee bend turns, Carl flipped his truck several times, landing upside down in Belt creek. When the cops got there, they found Carl's head bobbing up and down against the creek bank. A few weeks later, Rachel saw a small article about Carl's death in a local paper. She guessed he'd finally figured out how to kill himself right.

Getting stranger

A few days after the final search down the alley, Rachel showed up at Denny Adams's ranch, saying she wanted to talk to him about who took Zach. Rachel immediately brought up Franz's name but also added that she thought an alien abduction was possible too. Adams thought she was strange and he didn't trust her. He also thought Rachel was taping their conversation. Rachel had on a bulky knit sweater and sweat pants. She kept excusing herself and going to the bathroom. Adams said he was always careful about what he said to Rachel. He didn't know how Rachel might twist things around.

Later in the year, Adams took his dogs to work another case in Minnesota. During the course of the investigation one of his dogs was poisoned and died. Adams was devastated. Not only was one of Adams's prized bloodhounds killed but his marriage was also on the rocks and headed for divorce. Adams decided to start afresh and move to South Dakota. When the word got out that Adams was leaving the area, Rachel called him. He told her his dog had been killed during the course of an investigation and that he was getting a divorce. Rachel thought Adams was secretly telling her that he was afraid for his life because he had worked on Zach's case. She started telling people that Adams was leaving Great Falls because *two* of his dogs had been poisoned. *They* were sending a message to Adams that he should stop looking for Zach, or *else*. Adams had to leave Great Falls or he would be killed. For many years after Adams moved to South Dakota, he continued to keep a three-foot poster of Zach's picture in the back window of his pick-up truck.

The Ladies

The morning after Zach disappeared Rachel received an anonymous telephone call. Someone on the other end of the phone told Rachel she should contact Darlene and Delores Gustovich. The Gustovichs' green business card read "Psychics International". "The Ladies" as they were known around Great Falls, had consulted in several high profile murder cases, including the Bundy case and most recently the "Lil' Miss" murder case out of Billings, Montana.

* * *

Rachel called The Ladies and was able to schedule a reading for later in the afternoon. Rachel asked that a sheriff deputy accompany her and listen to the reading in case some clues were revealed. Bellusci responded to the whole thing by saying he had no idea that Rachel was involved in the occult.

The reading took about an hour. Darlene and Delores sat down at their kitchen table with Rachel and asked her to hold their rosary for a few moments. Rachel took the clear-beaded rosary and pressed it between the palms of her hands. The silver crucifix was draped over the back of Rachel's right hand. Rachel sat with her eyes closed, silently praying, lifting the rosary close to her heart. She handed the rosary back to Darlene who raised it to her lips, gently kissing Jesus. Delores, as she received the rosary from Darlene, did the same. The Ladies closed their eyes. It didn't take but a few seconds until Darlene began to see Zach, in a car near Judith Gap, Montana, which is about an hour southeast of Great Falls. The session was recorded on a cassette and given to the sheriff deputy. Darlene also saw Zach near an area called the Dearborn. Most important, like Rachel, Darlene and Delores sensed that Zach was alive. The police and the FBI went to Judith Gap and combed the area. Nothing was found. They also took Denny Adams and his dogs to the Dearborn area, which they searched extensively. There was no response from his dogs. Darlene said that a few days later, when the sheriff gave them the tape back, there were sections that had suspiciously been erased. The Ladies were frustrated. They wished they had made notes because they felt there were important clues on the tape about Zach's whereabouts that were lost forever. They also couldn't understand why the cops had erased part of the tape.

* * *

About fifty miles south of Great Falls, near Holter Lake, runs the Dearborn River. The Dearborn flows into the Missouri just north of the small fishing village of Craig. The Dearborn Inn, a local hangout, known for its steaks and beer, is a way station for tourists. The Dearborn area is made up of about 600 heavily wooded, difficult to traverse acres. The area used to be known as the Seven-Bar-None Ranch owned by the Cooper family. As an adolescent, actor Gary Cooper learned to chop wood at five in the morning and ride horses in the rugged mountains up that way. It was a skill that served him well in "High Noon."

* * *

Over the next two weeks The Ladies continued to do daily psychic readings with Rachel. Darlene and Delores began to develop a powerful sense that Zach was somewhere in the Dearborn area. Darlene said she could *see* him there. She said Zach wanted to come home, but he was being brainwashed and being held against his will. Rachel said she felt she had to go to the Dearborn. She needed to search the area herself. Shortly into the third week of Zach's disappearance, Rachel drove out to the Dearborn.

* * *

Once you go past the Dearborn Inn, you get into some very rough country, usually requiring a four-wheel-drive vehicle to traverse the old, narrow, logging roads. The area is also known for harboring a lot of folks who want to be left alone or forgotten about. Survivalist types live next to skinheads, nudists, and drug dealers in small cabins, many of which don't have running water. Signs posted that trespassers will be shot let you know that uninvited visitors are not welcome.

Rachel was driving her red Oldsmobile Delta '88. When she passed the Dearborn Inn, she gunned the Olds. The ground had thawed in the late morning sun and turned the cold road into a thick muddy soup. Rachel started climbing the incline, initially without too much of a problem. At a junction in the road, Rachel turned right. The road quickly became almost impassable. She continued gunning the car, driving as hard as she could, when her tires began spinning and steam began rolling from under the hood. Rachel finally found a place where there was enough clearance that she could maneuver the car to turn it around. With the plume of steam making it difficult to see, Rachel made her way back down the mountain. A jeep, bouncing left then right on its stiff springs, was making its way up the road. Rachel pulled off to the right and stopped. As Rachel sat along the side of the road, waiting for the jeep to pass, the misty fog spewing from the Olds, was almost totally obscuring her car. The two men who were in the jeep stopped and offered to stay with her until her car cooled down. One of the men told Rachel she shouldn't be up in that area, saying she could find herself dead real fast. The men also wondered how in the hell Rachel had made it up as far as she did in an Oldsmobile. Rachel thought the two men were nice enough, but was sure they were cops who had been sent to follow her. In fact, one of the men was a cop, Dan Nelson. But he wasn't following her. He had a hunting cabin up in the mountains and was by chance going up to check on it. But he did recognize Rachel, as her picture had been all over the *Great Falls Tribune* in recent weeks. Rachel stood by her car smoking a cigarette and making small talk with the men. When her car cooled down she said her polite goodbyes and tore the rest of the way down the mountain road.

* * *

By the time Rachel got back to the Dearborn Inn, her Olds was caked in mud. She went inside the inn and yelled over the top of a blaring Patsy Cline if anyone could take her back up into the mountains. She said she was looking for her son. Rachel was sure he had been kidnapped and was being held in one of the cabins; she just didn't know which one. But, Rachel said, she would be able to identify the cabin by the energy it was emitting. A burly-bearded man, in well-worn overhauls, said he'd be glad to run her up the mountain. The man said he'd help her look around for her kid too. She didn't "wanna to be up there alone; it wudn't a good idea," he said. They went out, climbed into his banged-up, primer-spotted pick-up truck and made their way back up the road. When they came to the fork in the road, he suggested they go left instead of right. The man drove past his own cabin, waving to his wife who was out front getting some firewood. She threw up a hand when she saw her husband and Rachel drive on past. The man looked at Rachel and said it was a good thing it was cold out because he and his wife were nudists. If Rachel had come up a bit later in the year, she would have found them naked. Rachel laughed and said she didn't care if they had clothes on or not. As they got to the crest of the road, near the top of the mountain, Rachel had a feeling that the dry cabin up ahead was where Zach had been. There was a force outside of herself that Rachel felt was directing her.

* * *

They are called dry cabins because they have no running water. They are just small huts that hunters use as way stations to get dry and take a quick rest, after a long day out scouring the mountains for big game. When they pulled up to the cabin, Rachel and the man got out of the car and walked up to the door. Rachel tried to open the door and found it was locked. That's odd, she thought. No one ever locked their houses in this part of the country, much less locking up a cabin in the middle of nowhere. Rachel picked up a rock, broke one of the small windows in the door, reached in and lifted the door latch. Once she and the man were inside they found remnants of leftover food and half-frozen glasses of water. Someone had recently been staying at the cabin. Against the back wall, lying on a scarred-up wooden table, Rachel saw the pack of magic markers she had bought Zach a week before he disappeared. She grabbed the man by the arm and rushed out of the cabin. They jumped back into the pick-up and drove back down the

151

mountain. However, Rachel in her frenzy forgot to take the markers. The man said he didn't want to give her his name.

* * *

Shortly before Rachel went to the Dearborn, her father had driven over to get a drink at a local bar in Great Falls. As he was parking his truck, he glanced into the back window of a red pick-up truck that was parked in the space in front of him. In the back of the truck sat Zach. He was sure of it. Rachel's father panicked, asking himself what he should do. He went to a pay phone to call Rachel. She'd know for sure, but there was no answer. By the time Rachel's father got back to the bar, the red pick-up truck was gone. Rachel's father was desperate with grief. His chance to rescue his grandson had slipped through his fingers. He had to tell Rachel right away that Zach was alive. Knowing that Rachel had gone to the Dearborn, Rachel's father sped down 10th Avenue making his way for the highway.

When he arrived at the Dearborn Inn, Rachel's father, for whatever reason, decided to park behind a clump of trees. He didn't know why but thought it seemed like a good idea. As he looked out the front window of his rig, he saw the same red pick-up truck from the bar now parked in front of the Dearborn Inn. Zach was still sitting in the back seat. A few parking spaces down sat Rachel's red Oldsmobile. Rachel's father was beside himself. He was ready to get out of his truck when he saw *Bellusci and Wilson* walking out of the Inn. Rachel's father decided to drive a little further up the dirt road away from the Inn. When he did he ran into Rachel and the burley bearded man coming back down the mountain. He waved his hand out of the window, flagging them to stop and told Rachel what had just happened. Rachel jumped out of the man's truck and into her father's rig. They speeded back to the Dearborn Inn. But again it was too late. The red truck and Zach had disappeared again. So had Bellusci and Wilson. It was then that Rachel knew that somehow Franz was behind this cat and mouse game. Because he was in the Air Force, he was able to get the cops and FBI involved too. This had to be bigger than Zach, Rachel thought.

* * *

The Ladies thought so too. They were now being followed everywhere they went by black Suburbans with tinted windows and government plates. Rachel was also being followed. Darlene and Delores had talked and decided between them that, regardless of risk, they would dedicate their time and money to helping Rachel find Zach. Zach was most certainly alive; they could feel it. A few days after the Dearborn incident, The Ladies had another sense that Zach had been secreted away in some caves several miles out on old Highland Road.

* * *

The Deaconess Hospital complex sits directly off to the left, as soon as you turn off onto 26th Street. Cars routinely stop for patients crossing the street, anxiously making their way to the same day surgery center. The traffic on the road near the hospital quickly goes from bustling to none as the pavement, about a mile down the road, turns from blacktop to gravel. About 4 p.m., Rachel and The Ladies decided to drive out to the caves. This was the day they were going to find Zach. Shortly after the road turned to gravel, Darlene looked in her rearview mirror and saw a black Suburban with tinted windows and government plates closing in on them. The rocky road bed that day was intermixed with ice and Darlene was driving fast to get away from the rapidly approaching Suburban. When she looked out the rear window, Rachel said, the Suburban was just ready to slam into the back of The Ladies' car. Then, Rachel and The Ladies began calling out for their angels to protect them.

* * *

For a moment Darlene thought she was losing control of the car. It seemed to be sliding all over the road. Then, Darlene said, the car began to levitate. It hovered for a few minutes about fifteen feet in the air and then rotated 180°. "I couldn't believe it …," said Darlene. The Suburban had stopped. Whoever was in the Suburban had to be amazed by what was happening, Rachel said. The Ladies' car softly descended back to the road, but now pointing in the opposite direction. Darlene pressed hard on the gas pedal. Rachel and The Ladies heartedly laughed and waved, as they sped past the Suburban. If there was ever *any* question in Rachel's mind about Zach's disappearance being a conspiracy, it had now been put to rest. The question remained though, in all of the women's minds, about who was the mastermind behind the plot and *where* was Zach? Fortunately, Rachel said, on that day the angels had heard their call and kept them out of harm's way.

Over the next two years, The Ladies and Rachel, almost daily, went looking for Zach. In that two-year period, The Ladies put over 100,000 miles on their car and never charged Rachel anything. They also slipped Rachel a little money here and there to help out with her mounting debt.

* * *

Bellusci was skeptical of anyone who said that had actually seen Zach in the alley. The witness reports seemed sketchy to him. Even though many of the people who reported seeing Zach said they knew him, Bellusci and Wilson knew eyewitnesses are notoriously unreliable. The day after Zach disappeared, Bellusci and Wilson casually talked with four-year-old Simone, Zach's sister. Simone told Bellusci and Wilson that she remembered waking up and eating oatmeal for breakfast. Zach was excitedly running around the apartment yelling to Rachel not to forget that he was getting a special artist award at the Paris Gibson Center after school. She had to pick him up early he said. Simone said she was finishing her breakfast when Zach came into the kitchen to say goodbye. Zach always told her goodbye. Rachel was standing at the top of the stairs, which came down right to the front door, getting ready to go to school. She was going to be late as usual. Right after Zach walked out the door, Rachel yelled down and told Simone to look out the window and see if Zach had his coat on. Simone told Bellusci and Wilson she went to the long rectangular window, to the left of the front door, pulled the curtain back and looked out the slightly frosted glass. She saw Zach across the street, just stepping up onto the curb. Simone yelled back to her mom that Zach had remembered to wear his jean jacket with the green plaid corduroy sleeves. Simone said this was the last time that she ever saw her brother.

* * *

When Simone would recall that morning much later in her life, she would slip her hand under her blouse and rub the tattoo on her left shoulder that says "ZAC". Simone would tenderly smile when she remembered Zach drawing robots in his notebook, then point to them and say, "Simone, this is you as a robot." Tearfully, Simone said, "If only I had watched Zach a little while longer the morning he disappeared, I may have been able to stop him from going away."

CHAPTER TWELVE

The investigation continues

Bellusci and Wilson took the names of everyone in Rachel's life. Hundreds of hours were spent investigating and ruling out every name Rachel had given to them, including Zach's father, who was stationed in Colorado at the time Zach disappeared. But for Rachel, there was still only one suspect, Franz. Bellusci and Wilson understood from Rachel that Zach had asked her to terminate Franz's visitations. Rachel said Zach never wanted to see his father again. However, Bellusci had talked with Zach's teacher who contradicted Rachel, telling Bellusci that Zach had told her he wanted to go live with Franz. Rachel also told Bellusci that a few years back Franz had taken Zach to Germany without her permission. According to Rachel the base commander in Germany had to intervene in order to get Zach back. Rachel also accused Franz of abducting Zach "ten times over the past eight years." Supposedly, when Zach was three years old, Franz kidnapped him and took him to Alabama. Rachel told Bellusci and Wilson that the FBI in Alabama had to get him back. There were never any kidnapping charges filed against Franz because, Rachel said, he was able to manipulate the legal system through the military. The day Zach disappeared, Rachel's mother was in the hospital, not expected to live. The decision whether or not to terminate life support fell to Rachel. Surprisingly, Rachel's mother made an unexpected recovery shortly after Zach vanished. But Rachel didn't tell her mother about Zach disappearing for three weeks for fear of causing a major setback.

* * *

Rachel and her mother had had a contentious relationship for many years. Her mother had regularly accused Rachel of having too many men always hanging around. She was also critical of how Rachel was raising Zach. Zach was a difficult boy to parent because he was always distracted by something. Zach's grandmother wanted him on medication. Rachel refused, saying he wasn't that bad and she could manage him naturally with diet and supplements. Rachel's mother constantly chided her, saying that if she wouldn't set limits with the boy then he should go live with Franz. Franz was a military man who could provide the discipline Zach needed. Rachel's mother accused Rachel of being undisciplined and chaotic: that wasn't what Zach needed. Rachel would throw it back in her mother's face and accuse her of being crazy. The arguing was endless.

* * *

For a long time Rachel couldn't understand how Franz got so much information about her. He always seemed to know who the new man was in her life. Or worse yet, the kind of problems they were having. Rachel figured Franz had hired a private detective and was having her followed or digging through her trash. Detailed, personal information would appear in the legal documents Franz filed against Rachel when he would take her back to court and try to get custody of Zach. Rachel was at a loss about out how Franz was getting the information to use against her. The latest salvo of legal papers between Rachel and Franz was an attempt by Rachel to terminate Franz's visitation rights in January 1996. Rachel said Zach had come to her saying he didn't want to see his father again. Franz's retort contained verbatim information that Rachel had only told one person, her mother. When Rachel confronted her mother, she confessed Franz had agreed to pay her in exchange for information he could use against Rachel in order to get custody of his son. Rachel said she didn't know if any money had actually changed hands, but she did know her mother had agreed to sell information to Franz.

* * *

In April, a man and his daughter were walking down the alley at 9th Street and 3rd Avenue. The man glanced over at a dumpster and saw a blue denim coat with green plaid sleeves, laying spread out on top of the trash. The coat was in perfect condition, looking like it had just been cleaned. The man called the GFPD and told them he thought it was suspicious, because the coat looked like the one that had been described in the papers as belonging to Zach Ramsay. Bellusci went to the scene and found the coat exactly as the man had described it. It looked to Bellusci like it had been placed on top of the trash, not to be thrown out, but to be noticed. Bellusci bagged the coat and went back to the police department. He called Rachel and told her they may have found Zach's coat. Rachel called her mother and told her about the call from Bellusci. In a few minutes Rachel and her mother arrived at the GFPD. Bellusci watched them come up the sidewalk and escorted them to an interview room. The coat, now in a clear plastic evidence bag, was laid out on a table. Bellusci cautioned Rachel and her mother not to touch the coat. Rachel started screaming that it was Zach's coat. She was sure. Her mother yelled that it wasn't, accusing Rachel of not being able to recognize her own son's coat. Rachel retorted that she was *sure* it was Zach's. Her mother didn't know what she was talking about. Zach was her son, *not* her mother's. Finally Bellusci had enough of Rachel and

159

her mother's bullshit. He said he had everything he needed and told them to leave. Bellusci was pissed. He didn't believe Rachel when she said it was Zach's coat. He grabbed a cup of stale coffee and went back to his desk, sat down, and smoked what he considered to be a well-deserved cigarette. The report came back from the lab that the coat was clean, no fibers, no nothing. Later on Rachel said she couldn't remember ever being called to ID a coat, especially with her mother. Rachel said she couldn't stand her mother at the time.

Short-lived leads

Over-the-road truck driver, Clint Michael Kayes presented himself to the Canadian border patrol in April 1996. It was three months after Zach vanished. Kayes told the border patrol agent he was obsessed with Zachary Ramsay. Zach was constantly on his mind and invading his dreams. He had even almost run off of the road several times because the image of Zach would appear to him when he was driving.

Bellusci left Great Falls for the border within the hour after the Canadian authorities contacted him. When Bellusci interviewed Kayes, he told Bellusci that he had been masturbating in his truck while fantasizing about Zach. He was tired and consumed with guilt. Bellusci initially thought he might have the first solid lead in the case. But when he searched Kayes's truck he found a credit card receipt that put Kayes, broken down, in Spokane, Washington the day Zach disappeared. Since Kayes worked out of Great Falls, Bellusci decided it would be prudent to have Kayes's home and cars checked for any evidence that might link Kayes to Zach. Nothing was found.

* * *

Several months after investigating Kayes, Bellusci received a call from Shawn High Pine, who was well known to the Great Falls Police as a sexual predator. High Pine told Bellusci someone had told him where Zach was buried. "I'll take you there and you can dig him up," High Pine told Bellusci. When Bellusci questioned High Pine about who told him where Zach was buried, he only would say he couldn't remember. It was late November 1996, ten months after Zach had disappeared. Again, Bellusci thought this might be it. High Pine was specific: he said Zach was buried under a bridge on Highway 2, along the bank of the Missouri, out near Chinook, Montana. "He's buried in the mud," High Pine kept telling Bellusci. Bellusci and Wilson went to the area with High Pine. The bank was sodden with thick mud. Bellusci called the volunteer fire department for the area, to come out and peel back layer after layer of mud and thick leaves with their fire hoses. But there was no evidence that Zach had ever been there.

* * *

Six months after Zachary Ramsay disappeared, the case was completely cold. Aside from the calls from the crazies, there was nothing that pointed to anyone as a suspect. There was no body and no physical evidence of any type to indicate a crime had even been committed. The only thing Bellusci and Wilson did know for certain was that a ten-year-old boy had vanished. At the end of the sixth month, Scott Cruz, special agent in charge of the Great Falls FBI office, told Special Agent James Wilson to bring Rachel Howard in for formal questioning. Cruz had been involved in the investigation from the beginning, but primarily was directing things behind the scenes. From all accounts, Cruz was a difficult man to deal with. Politically savvy, with a manipulative soft-spoken voice, Cruz was also rumored to be one who would stretch the boundaries of interrogative ethics.

Rachel arrived at the FBI office in downtown Great Falls about 8 a.m. She was expecting the meeting to be an update on the investigation. When she entered the office she was greeted by Cruz, who told her that before they started talking he thought she should take a polygraph to clear up any questions they had. Rachel readily agreed, not requesting the benefit of counsel or being suspicious of the request. She was taken into a small side office where Rachel said a FBI polygrapher was waiting. The polygrapher had Rachel sit down in a wooden straight-back chair and then proceeded to put the leads to the polygraph around her chest and on her fingertips. Cruz, Wilson, and Bellusci, who had got there late, came into the room. For the next six hours Rachel Howard was grilled. Rachel would later call the polygrapher a buck-toothed ferret-face little prick.

The polygrapher began asking Rachel control questions like, what is your name, what is your birth date, and how many children do you have. These were used to establish how she would look on the polygraph if she lied. If she were telling the truth the tracing on the polygraph would be a consistent vibrating line with no peaks or valleys. But if she were lying there would be up and down spikes that would stand out. Sometimes there could possibly be slight variations that could raise some question whether she was being deceptive. If this happened during the interrogation, the polygrapher would try to adjust his questions to a more accusatory tone to clarify if she were telling the truth or lying.

Cruz started out the interrogation by lying to Rachel. The FBI had satellite footage showing that Zach never left the apartment on the morning he disappeared, Cruz said. Rachel became hysterical when she learned about the satellite images. She started screaming for Cruz to run the tape fifteen minutes ahead, then they could see who took Zach. It would help them figure out how to get him back. Then Cruz told Rachel that he was lying. There were no satellite photos. He just wanted to see how she would react because he knew she had killed Zach and gotten rid of his body. Cruz said that's what she was doing when she told Bellusci and Wilson she was out looking for Zach on the night he disappeared. It would be better for her if she came clean and told them what had happened. Wilson added in his deep Texas drawl that Rachel would feel less guilty if she just went ahead and confessed. Bellusci said he knew she was a good person. Kids can be tough and things probably just got out of hand. Especially kids who have mental problems. Then the polygrapher asked her, "Did you kill your son?" Rachel responded with "No." During the six hours that Rachel was questioned, she said more than 100 times that she did not kill Zach. But the polygraph said she was being deceptive. Ferret face became increasingly frustrated as the day wore on. He paced back and forth in the small office, screaming accusations in the form of questions at Rachel. She would scream back her denial. Sometimes she would cry, other times she would become enraged. When Rachel asked if she could go to the bathroom she was told, no. They thought she would break down as her bladder filled. She wouldn't be able to take it anymore and she would confess. Rachel said she would have rather pissed her pants. As 4 p.m. approached, Cruz looked over at the polygrapher. The polygrapher looked back shaking his head left to right. Cruz glared at Rachel and told her she failed the polygraph. Now there was no uncertainty, they were absolutely sure she had killed Zach. Rachel became enraged. She stood up and tore off the leads to the polygraph, screaming, "You mother fuckers, then charge me with murder or I'm walking the fuck out of here." As Rachel was storming out of the office she yelled that if the FBI weren't interested in finding Zach then she would find him, alive, herself. Cruz, pointing his finger at Rachel, screamed back and said, "If *you* find him, I'll sit at my desk and eat a piece of bark."

Rachel took the elevator down to the lobby. When she tried to open the front door it was locked; she couldn't get out. Rachel looked up and saw a camera protruding from the ceiling. She raised her middle finger toward the camera. Rachel stormed back up to the FBI office and began pounding on the glass window screaming she wanted out of the fucking building. Cruz came out into the hallway and told Rachel he would unlock the door. Rachel made her way down the stairs. Cruz followed close behind, continuing to tell Rachel she would feel better if she confessed.

Beside the fact that Rachel had to pee, she also had not had a cigarette for more than six hours. She was an obsessive two pack a day smoker. When they got to the lobby Cruz unlocked the door and Rachel ran to her car. She jerked open the passenger side door and began fumbling in between the seats looking for her cigarettes. Cruz could not see what she was doing, only that he could not see her hands. In one movement, she raised her trembling hand and put a cigarette between her lips as she backed out of the car, stood up, and turned around. Her hands cupped the flame of her lighter, protecting it from a Great Falls wind cornering the building. Rachel inhaled the calming nicotine, infusing the smoke swirling deep into her lungs. When she raised her head she saw that Cruz was standing about ten feet back with his hand resting on the butt of his gun. Rachel began to laugh hysterically through her tears and screamed, "You thought I was going for a fucking gun. You thought I was going to shoot you, you stupid fuck." Cruz responded, "Well, maybe." After a few deep drags, Rachel flipped her cigarette butt into the street, got into her car and drove straight to The Ladies.

The police and the FBI had no other suspects. Rachel had not confessed during the six-hour interrogation. Even though there was nothing more than Rachel's odd behavior and a failed polygraph, administered under duress, Cruz, Wilson, and Bellusci were convinced that Rachel Howard had killed Zach.

* * *

Shortly before Christmas, 1996 the Great Falls Police Department began tapping Rachel's phones. They also began "bird dogging" Rachel by secretly placing a small homing device under the front fender of her car during the Christmas holiday, on the anniversary date of Zach's disappearance and on his birthday. The cops were convinced she would lead them to where she had stashed the body.

Rachel's troubles

Rachel Howard is 5' 10" and about 175 lbs. She is a smart, beautiful, voluptuous woman with high cheekbones, auburn hair, and smooth skin. However, Rachel's façade looks better on the outside than she is stitched together on the inside. If you could unzip Rachel and peer inward she would look like a major metropolitan freeway at rush hour. She burns with an unrelenting, frenetic energy.

At seventeen or eighteen, Rachel couldn't remember exactly, she took her first overdose. She didn't come close to dying, she said, but it messed her up pretty bad. Rachel got married when she was nineteen, mainly to get away from her mother. The marriage was incredibly volatile. One night her husband came home late and Rachel accused him of fucking another woman. He denied it. Rachel had been drinking and had a beer bottle in her hand. She slammed the neck of the bottle on the kitchen counter and with the skill of a fine swordsman slit her own throat. Rachel said a plastic surgeon happened to be on duty in the ER that night, so the scar on the left side of her neck is barely visible and doesn't look like a welding bead.

In the late '80s, when Rachel's second husband was stationed in Okinawa, Rachel took a massive overdose. She barely survived that one. Rachel doesn't remember much about why she actually took the OD, other than to say that she was depressed. It's probably best that she also doesn't remember having the charcoal line shoved down her throat, when the ER doctors pumped the remnants of the drugs out of her stomach. Rachel was committed to an Air Force psychiatric hospital on base for two weeks. A couple of years later, she slit both of her wrists.

Those scars stand out more than the scar on her neck, when she pulls her hands back and tauts her wrists.

* * *

For eighteen years, Rachel worked as a process server for the Great Falls Police Department. Rachel had a deserved reputation of being wild. The cops who remembered her during that time said she was known as an easy lay. Not someone you would want to get involved with, but a tigress in bed. One of the cops told a story about Rachel getting pissed off at one of her boyfriends and throwing a Molotov cocktail at his car. Yet for all her wildness, she was also extremely fragile.

Rachel tried her best over the years to have stable relationships not only for herself but also for her kids. They just never seemed to work out. The sex was good, but the men that happened to be attached to their penises were for the most part losers. Franz was the most successful of the men Rachel had been with. He was a naturalized American citizen born in Guyana, and he was on a career path in the Air Force. But it was only a few months after Rachel and Franz married that their relationship went to hell. Rachel's second husband, Vincent, is also black and was also in the military. He is the father of Rachel's other two children, Simone and Isaac. Rachel said Vincent drank too much and had a problem with anger when he was drunk. Their relationship ended badly too.

During the time Rachel was being investigated for Zach's disappearance, she went back to the police station to see if any of her old contacts might be able to help. But the cops knew about Bellusci focusing in on Rachel as his only suspect. When she asked several of the officers she used to know for help, Rachel said one responded by saying, "What missing kid, there's no missing kid, you know where he is, you nigger-loving slut." Rachel walked out of the GFPD in tears, feeling empty and deflated.

* * *

Franz had been completely ruled out as a suspect in Zach's disappearance. In fact he had never been considered a suspect in any viable way. But because his son had disappeared the FBI had to rule him out as having any culpability. Franz, along with his wife, Cynthia, promptly agreed to take a polygraph, which they each passed with no ambiguities. The FBI in Colorado had gone to Franz's apartment shortly after Zach disappeared as part of their investigation. Rachel said that the FBI told her there was a baby at the Franz's apartment when they arrived. Franz and his wife didn't have any children at that time. The FBI left Franz's apartment, thinking nothing of a baby being there. The Colorado agents went back a few days later to do a follow-up interview with Franz and his wife. When they arrived a ten-year-old girl answered the door. When Rachel was told about a girl, she knew then that Franz had Zach. He had dressed him up in a disguise. Three months after Zach vanished, Rachel called Franz. Unbeknown to Franz, Rachel taped the conversation. The conversation wsas pleasant enough, but at one point during the call Rachel said she heard a boy's voice in the background say, "Is that mom." Rachel knew it was Zach's voice. Rachel took the tape to Cruz whom she said never did anything with it. Instead he accused her of trying to create a smokescreen and divert the focus of the investigation off of her and onto Franz. Rachel, however, continued to be convinced that Franz was behind Zach's disappearance.

* * *

A week before the anniversary of Zach's disappearance, Bellusci called Rachel and asked her if she had arranged a vigil for Zach. Rachel said she had not. In fact she had not made any plans. Bellusci, the GFPD, and Officer Nelson quickly arranged to have a candlelight vigil for Zach on February 6, 1997 at St. Ann's Cathedral in Great Falls. Rachel was quoted in the *Great Falls Tribune* saying the ceremony was important to her because it represented a connection with God and "To me that's the only thing that will bring him home." However, Rachel almost missed Zach's vigil, arriving only a few minutes before the first candle was lighted.

* * *

Rachel was scheduled to appear on the Montel Williams show in New York, on February 5, 1997, one day before the first anniversary of Zach's disappearance. Rachel thought she was going on the show to make an appeal for her Zach's return and maybe to bring some new life to the case. During the show, Montel grilled Rachel, all but accusing her of killing Zach. Rachel was raw and frayed by the time Montel's grandstanding performance was over. Before Rachel left the studio, Montel came up to her and handed her a black and white, autographed picture of himself. In the photograph Montel's chin is leaning on his clinched fist, a Cheshire cat smile is framed under a well-groomed Oil Can Harry mustache. The photograph is signed "Thanks for Coming, Montel."

By now, Rachel was certain Zach's disappearance was part of a massive conspiracy that didn't just involve Franz. She was convinced the FBI and the Great Falls Police Department were part of a child kidnapping ring that stole children to appear in pornographic movies. Everything was muddled. She didn't know how things fit together. But she knew she was on the right track.

The night after the Montel show, Rachel went to the Bear Bar on Second Avenue in New York City. An hour after she arrived, the bartender pulled her aside and said the cops were in the bar looking for her. The bartender told Rachel she had seen the Montel show that afternoon. She understood and told Rachel she would protect her. She took Rachel by the arm and led her into the ladies' room. "Don't come out until I tell you it's safe," the bartender said to Rachel, as she closed the bathroom door behind her. Rachel knew the cops had been sent by the FBI to hassle her, because they were all part of the conspiracy. Tucking herself into a stall, Rachel slid the well-used chrome latch to the left, locking the door. She sat on the toilet and pulled her legs up to her chest, so no one could see her feet, sitting still, silently breathing. This had to be huge, Rachel was imagining, trying to put the pieces together in her head. *Everyone* seemed to be part of what was now clearly a cover-up. Rachel didn't know how long she hid in the bathroom at the Bear. Finally, the bartender came back and told her the cops had left, it was now safe to come out. In her hands, the bartender was holding a white sweatshirt. Three bears, adorned in top hats and canes, danced underneath *The Bear Bar*, embroidered in an arc, stenciled across the top of the shirt. Rachel wore her Bear Bar sweatshirt the next day to the airport, where she passed out at the gate while sitting in the terminal, waiting for her plane. Rachel said she woke up an hour after her plane had taken off, sprawled out in the seat, with her feet propped up on her suitcase. She panicked. Rachel had to be back in Great Falls for Zach's vigil later that day plus she had no money left. She had spent what she had brought with her at the Bear. No matter how much she tried to explain to the ticket agent, the airline refused to put her on another flight that day. If she wanted to get back, Rachel would have to buy another ticket.

Montel Williams's producer received the frantic call from Rachel demanding another ticket. She was screaming into the phone, that the only reason she had missed the plane was because the police harassed her the night before. *That* was why she drank too much. After much haggling the producer finally acquiesced and agreed to buy Rachel another ticket. When Rachel arrived back in Great Falls, she went directly from the airport to Zach's vigil. The service closed with the choir of St. Ann's Cathedral singing *Amazing Grace*. A photograph of Rachel, in a prayerful pose, holding a candle, appeared on the front page of the *Great Falls Tribune*. Rachel said her hair and make-up looked a mess in the photograph.

"You've got to be fucking kidding me"

Bellusci, Wilson, and Cruz decided to watch who attended the service. They were hoping that Zach's assailant would not be able to resist the temptation of attending. Bellusci and Cruz parked down the block where they could see who entered the church through their binoculars. Wilson was about a half-an-hour late getting to the stake-out. He parked in a spot down by the river and walked back to the car that Bellusci and Cruz were in. Bellusci, Cruz, and Wilson made sure they observed each person going into the vigil. Ten minutes before the vigil was scheduled to begin, Bellusci saw a small compact car pull into the spot right besides Wilson's car. He called Cruz and Wilson's attention to the car, since there were parking places closer to the church. A young sandy-haired man in his early 20s sat in his car for a few minutes and looked around in all directions. Bellusci, Cruz, and Wilson had their binoculars trained on the man, deciding his behavior was suspicious. The vigil had started and the young man made no attempt to go into the service. Several more minutes passed when the young man opened his door, got out of his car, unbuckled his pants and began masturbating, quickly ejaculating onto the side of Special Agent Wilson's car—his personal car. Wilson started yelling, "Fucking gross, oh man, how fucking gross." Since it was not a federal crime to masturbate in public, Bellusci had to respond. Bellusci got out of Cruz's car, walked down to the parking lot and approached the masturbator. The young man was just pulling his pants up, when Bellusci identified himself as a police officer. Bellusci said he asked the man what the fuck he thought he was doing. The young man responded that he was there to feed the ducks *and* that he liked to jerk off in public areas. It got him off, he said. Bellusci held the man until a patrol unit rolled up to the scene and took him into custody. When Bellusci went to the young man's home, he found that he had a wife, a kid, and an underground tunnel that went from the enclosed back porch of his house out to his garage. The man later told Bellusci the tunnel was there just in case the cops ever came looking for him so he could make a fast getaway. The young man turned out to be the stepson of the over the road truck driver, Clint Michael Kayes.

CHAPTER THIRTEEN

The plot thickens—Zack

In early 1997, the Great Falls Police Department received a phone call from Italy. A neighbor of Douglas and Kathleen Ditch, who were stationed at Aviano Air Force Base, in Italy, saw a story about Zach Ramsay on Italian television. The neighbors of the Ditches were shocked. Zach Ramsay, they said, was not missing; he was living next door to them. The GFPD checked with the Air Force Office of Special Investigations and discovered that in fact the boy living with the Ditches was named Zack. Zack spelled with a "*k*". But eerily, Zack shared the same birthday as Zach Ramsay, December 18, 1985. Plus, Zack was born in Butte, Montana, about three hours south of Great Falls.

The FBI asked the Office of Special Investigations to videotape Zack in his classroom. Zack was a spitting image of Zach. The FBI had a forensic odontologist compare the dental records of Zach against Zack. The dentist determined there was no possibility they were the same child. However, Rachel was not convinced. She contacted the neighbor of the Ditches in Italy, and had them make her a separate videotape of Zack. When Rachel watched the tape she was convinced the boy in Italy *was* her son. Zack was later fingerprinted and his DNA was checked by the FBI against Zach's, and as with the dental comparison, Zack *was not* Zach. But now, in her mind, Rachel had positive proof that Zach was still alive and he was being kept from her. This had become an increasingly complex shell game. It was an Air Force family that Zach was living with. Franz was in the Air Force. Again there was no one else who could be behind this except for Franz. Even if he didn't take Zach himself, Rachel was sure he had paid someone to set it up. When Rachel took the tape to The Ladies they too were convinced, saying they could feel Zach's presence in the videotape. Rachel began connecting the dots. Anyone who had ever been associated with Zack's family in Italy now became part of the intricacy of the conspiracy. However, the trail always led back to one person, Great Falls attorney, Joan Cook.

* * *

Cook had represented Franz for many years when Rachel took Franz back to court about custody issues or child support. Cook was a highly successful attorney with political and financial means. Rachel was convinced that Cook was the mastermind behind what Rachel was now calling a kidnapping. Franz wasn't smart enough to figure all of this out on his own. It had to be Cook who had made all of the arrangements. Rachel also believed that Cook had a private pilot who worked for her, based out of Seattle. She tracked down where the pilot lived and went to his house. Rachel discovered he had five locks on his door. Why would anyone need five locks on their door unless they were hiding something? As Rachel continued to ponder the questions she was asking herself, more of the answers to the puzzle began to come together. Rachel concluded the only thing that made sense was that her former boyfriend, Carl Dekooning, was the one who had snatched Zach in the alley. Zach had taken Carl on his route to school just a few days before Zach disappeared. Carl would know that Zach would go with him without protest, even if Zach didn't like him. It would have been easy to get him into a car. Carl then probably drugged Zach and passed him off to Cook.

* * *

Rachel never believed that Carl was really dead. She had thought all along that the story had been made up. At that time, she just didn't know why. While she was still reading the article in the paper about Carl Dekooning being killed, Rachel was picking up the phone to call Darlene. When Darlene answered the phone, Rachel told her that she was reading that Carl had died in a car wreck. Darlene said she didn't understand how that could be, because she just saw Carl the day before walking into Joan Cook's office. Rachel had shown Darlene several pictures of Carl. There was no mistaking, Darlene was sure it was Carl. Now Rachel knew that the story about Carl's death had been made up to get him out of the picture. Franz had probably arranged to have Carl held in one of the abandoned missile silos up near the Canadian border.

* * *

Once Cook got hold of Zach, she took him to the cabin where Rachel found his markers, up in the Dearborn. That would have been where Franz met Zach to let him know what was going on. It was also at the cabin where Franz would begin to brainwash Zach against Rachel. After Franz met with Zach, Cook would have to get him out of the country. But Cook had underestimated that taking some kid no one ever heard of would draw such national attention. Clearly, the other kids that Rachel was convinced that Cook had kidnapped had not been a problem.

Franz's father had been the procurement officer for the country of Ghana, before coming to the United States. The old man still had relatives living in Ontario. Cook's private pilot must have flown Zach directly to Toronto. Probably to a private airstrip that Cook had used before to avoid immigration. Rachel figured that Franz must have known the Ditches from the Air Force and had it prearranged for them to pick up Zach in Canada and take him directly to Italy. Everything was orchestrated by Joan Cook and bankrolled by Franz. As Rachel continued to search for connections she discovered that a Joan Cook, from California, had connections to a business called Enterprise Entertainment. This, Rachel thought, was connected to the production of child pornography. The California Joan Cook also ran a low-income counseling business. Rachel knew the counseling business was a charade. Most likely it was an easy feeder for Cook's child porn operation. Desperate people probably sold their kids to Cook. Rachel even knew someone in Great Falls who told her that Cook also was the head of an underground railroad for children. If a non-custodial parent wanted their kid they only had to pay Cook's fee and the job would be done.

* * *

Rachel knew this was huge. Her original suspicions that the police and the FBI were involved were confirmed. There could be no way that Cook could run this kind of operation without the authorities being mixed up in it. Cook was probably slipping money to Bellusci and Wilson and then they passed it around. It wasn't long after Rachel had finally figured out the scheme, that the black Suburbans now began driving past Rachel's house. The vehicles had all different stickers in their back windows that were coded to indicate whether they were dropping off or picking up a kid. The black helicopters also began circling overhead, shining bright spotlights directly onto Rachel's house. Rachel's beliefs were like those of a sailor who can see in her compass that her ship is swiftly moving in the wrong direction. A direction that will dramatically set the ship adrift, only to be blown about by the prevailing wind of the moment. Unfortunately, Rachel was powerless to stop the momentum and correct her course. To admit she was disoriented in her belief was to admit Zach was dead. To admit Zach was dead was to admit there was no God. To admit there was no God, was to admit all was lost.

CHAPTER FOURTEEN

Pam Clark

In April 1995, Pam Clark got a job at Hardee's. She had come from North Dakota with little money and no friends. Pam was black, overweight, and had a tongue that seemed to get constantly confused, jumping around in her mouth from one subject to another. Every few minutes, Pam bounced around a dozen different subjects, none of them connected and almost always coated with a bizarre flavor. Bar Jonah had just been promoted from the biscuit/chicken man to chief fry cook. He was demanding an assistant. The workload was too great, he would say. Not only did he have to chop up the chickens, but he also had to dip them in breading and drop them in the deep fryer. Pam came across as friendly and outgoing. To Bar Jonah, Pam seemed like the perfect assistant.

The first thing Pam noticed when Bar Jonah talked was that he hardly had any teeth. The few teeth he did have were a displeasing shade of brownish-green. She thought he probably had a hard time eating meat or salt water taffy. For a fleeting moment, it ran through Pam's mind how repulsive it would be to kiss him. Even with the smell of deep-fried chicken skin permeating the air, Pam could still smell stale cigarettes and tooth decay on Bar Jonah's breath.

Right away, Pam felt compelled to tell Bar Jonah a secret about herself. It was what she was most proud of. Pam noticed how his right eyebrow twitched when she told him she was a *Lyalorishas*, Mother of Orisha, a Santeria High Priestess. Pam was pleased she didn't have to tell him what kind of religion she practiced. Bar Jonah already knew Santeria was Spanish for the "Way of the Saints", or as it was more commonly known, voodoo. As Pam was dumping a basket of breaded chicken breasts into the deep fryer, Bar Jonah began telling her the history of the Santeria. He seemed to know history even she didn't know. Pam had learned the way of the Santeria from her Momma and her Momma had learned it from her Momma before her.

Bar Jonah leaned over and told Pam that the Yoruba people believed that all humans have *Ayanmo*, or manifest destiny, to become one in spirit with the *Olodumare* or the divine creator. But those who fail are destined for the spiritual realm of the *Orun-Apadi*, the forever forsaken. Pam tried to avoid the odor coming from Bar Jonah's mouth when he leaned into her and said to eat a piece of chicken, while he continued to talk. Santeria was born when Nigerian slaves were kidnapped and brought to the Caribbean to work on the sugar plantations. They tried to combine their Yoruba beliefs with the Roman Catholic beliefs in which they were being indoctrinated. Part of the Yoruba beliefs, he said, also involved the tradition of entering a trance-like state to communicate with those who had passed on. However, Bar Jonah talked mostly about the tradition of sacrifice.

* * *

Bar Jonah had recently become a member of the Mount Olive Assembly of God church. Within a few hours of their meeting, Bar Jonah insisted that Pam join too. The church was devout in their belief that the Bible was the living Word of God. Bar Jonah said they would welcome Pam like they had welcomed him.

The pastor respected different beliefs; all that mattered was that the path led to Jesus. Rachel Howard and Zach Ramsay were also members of the Mount Olive church. Pam started attending regularly. Soon she met a man from the church who had posted an ad on the bulletin board saying that he had a small apartment for rent. It happened to be just up the street from Bar Jonah's place.

* * *

Pam's new apartment was small, with a kitchenette, a tiny bedroom, bath, and an L-shaped living room. At the end of the "L", Pam set up her altar of many sacrifices. It stood about four feet tall, three feet long and two feet deep. The altar was completely covered in years of dense candle wax. Under the wax, veins of dried blood were visible from the many animals that had surrendered possession of their souls under Pam's knife. Over time, the walls and the ceiling surrounding the altar became completely covered in black soot from the hundreds of candles constantly burning in the apartment.

Bar Jonah constantly asked Pam how she sacrificed the animals. How did she go about killing them? She always gave him the same answer. Tie their back feet together and hang them upside down with a rope. Then pull their heads back and cut their throats; otherwise, they'd suffer too much. They weren't supposed to suffer when they offered up their life.

* * *

Within a few weeks after meeting, Pam and Bar Jonah became inseparable. It didn't take long for her to fall in love with Bar Jonah. Tyra was overjoyed. Her son was *finally* dating a woman. Pam and Bar Jonah regularly began going to Bob and his wife Jill's for dinner; Tyra was always included too. Pam and Tyra liked to sit next to each other and bump each other's shoulders when they got to laughing. Pam would get amazed at how much and how fast Bar Jonah ate. She yelled at him constantly,

181

telling him to slow his eating down, as he shoved huge bites of food into his mouth. Tyra would speak up and tell Pam to leave him alone, he'd always ate that way, ever since he was a baby.

* * *

Pam took an immediate dislike to Bob. She thought he was an odd duck and had complete control over Jill. Pam also thought he was a queer, but didn't want anyone to know. At one of the dinners Pam said that Jill got pissed at Bob, threw her chair back against the wall, and stormed out of the house, saying she was never coming back. Pam didn't remember what the argument was about but said they argued every time she was there. She also said Bar Jonah didn't like Bob either. Bob always tried to control Bar Jonah's life. But he was good for a few bucks, so Bar Jonah said he played up to Bob's self-importance.

Bar Jonah and Pam liked to take drives on the weekends, particularly up to Holter Lake. It is a breathtaking glacial lake that sits atop the northwest foothills of the Big Belt Mountains. Surrounding the lake are narrow white sandy beaches. In the wintertime, the few cabins scattered around the lake are mostly abandoned. The great lake spills over Holter dam into the reservoir below, which flows back down into the Missouri river.

Often they would drive for hours and never say a word. It was as though Pam wasn't even alive. Bar Jonah would sometimes mumble to himself, making up words that didn't make any sense. He *never* touched her, he never kissed her, he never reached out to hold her hand, and certainly there was never any kind of sexual contact. Sometimes Pam stayed overnight at his apartment. On rare occasions, they would even sleep in the same bed. But he insisted that she stay on her side of the bed. At one point, Bar Jonah told Pam he wanted children. Especially a boy, one of his own. Pam chided him saying,

"You're almost forty years old, what's you goin' do with a kid"?

* * *

It bothered Pam that Bar Jonah would spend hours watching cartoons. He didn't just watch the cartoons though. He also talked to the cartoon characters. Sometimes he yelled and screamed at them It was not unusual for Bar Jonah to go to the video store and bring back a dozen superhero cartoons, watching all of them, one right after the other. Pam also discovered that Bar Jonah liked cake, whole chocolate cakes. He always tried to have a chocolate cake in the refrigerator. There was cake when there was nothing else in the house to eat. No matter what the weather, if he woke up in the middle of the night and there was no cake in the house, he would drive to an all-night market, buy a chocolate cake, come home, fix a pot of coffee and eat the whole thing.

* * *

In early December 1995, while on a drive to Holter Lake, Bar Jonah leaned over and asked Pam to marry him. Bar Jonah had decided that he wanted to give Pam the honorable shelter of his name. She was overjoyed and tearfully said yes. Pam had been with a lot of men. Most abused her in one way or another and told her she was insane. Even though Bar Jonah was odd, he wasn't physically abusive and he mostly let her alone. She'd have a warm place to stay and plenty to eat. It was better than she'd ever had before. When Tyra found out Bar Jonah and Pam were engaged, she called Pam and offered to pay for her wedding gown. Pam was elated at Tyra's generosity and gesture, welcoming her into the family. When Pam told Bar Jonah about Tyra's offer he said, "No." It was the bride's responsibility to pay for the wedding gown. If she wanted one, she'd buy it herself. Pam had to learn to pay her own way. A couple of weeks before Christmas, Pam and Bar Jonah went to look at wedding gowns in the mall. In the formal shop, Pam came out of the dressing room adorned in a lacy white wedding dress. She'd just had her face done up and her eyes were sparkling, looking momentarily triumphant. Pam turned towards Bar Jonah, who was sitting cross-legged, in a molded plastic chair with thin chrome legs and waited for him to tell her how beautiful she looked. But he sat motionless, with his head down. He didn't look up at her or speak. She tried on two more dresses and then decided it was time to leave. Pam took long heavy strides as she walked angrily ahead of Bar Jonah, her long shirt flying out over her broad high-tipped hips, as she and Bar Jonah made their way back to Tyra's car, which Bar Jonah had borrowed so he wouldn't have to spend money for gas.

Bar Jonah was now introducing Pam as his fiancée when they went to church or anywhere for that matter. All the people from Hardee's knew Bar Jonah and Pam were engaged. Bar Jonah bragged they were going to have a big wedding. All his relatives from Massachusetts were going to come for the celebration, he said. He was the most popular member of his family. They all wanted to help him celebrate the joyous occasion.

During the Christmas Eve dinner, Bar Jonah got furious with Tyra because she refused to give him the money she had offered to spend on Pam's wedding dress. He said Pam could buy her own dress and Tyra should give him the money because he needed to buy more toys for his business. It would help him out.

* * *

Between January 26 and February 16, Bar Jonah kept completely to himself. When Pam went over to his apartment and pounded on his door, he refused to answer. On the rare occasion when he did answer, he was enraged and ordered Pam to leave immediately. Pam said there was no point in bothering him. She didn't see her fiancée again until he showed up at her door on February 17, the day after Tyra had returned from Massachusetts. That evening at dinner, Bar Jonah brought up Zach Ramsay out of the blue, saying someone probably chopped him up and threw him all over the forest. No one would ever find him, Bar Jonah said. Pam, happy to be back with Bar Jonah, sat untroubled, imagining the day they were going to be married.

* * *

As the spring of 1996 approached, Pam became increasingly concerned about how Bar Jonah was behaving around kids. Bar Jonah wouldn't touch Pam in any way, yet whenever they were around a small boy, he would be all over the kid. He seemed to be getting bolder and more brazen in his desire to be with children since the Ramsay kid had disappeared. When Pam saw him at the antique mall and church, he couldn't keep his hands off of the little boys. Even at Hardee's, Bar Jonah would come out from behind the counter and sit down with mothers, who brought their boys into the restaurant. He would talk with them and slip them a couple of extra toys that the restaurant might be handing out. One night Pam said Bar Jonah came home and told her that one of the shift bosses told him he had to stay away from the kids. There had been some parents who had complained. Bar Jonah said he pushed the boss into a freezer and told him they could go out back and settle it right now. The boss man backed off. He never told the big boss about Bar Jonah shoving him. At the antique mall Bar Jonah refused to leave the kids alone too. He constantly lured them over to his table, hugging them as they eyed the toys on the shelves. Pam thought Bar Jonah was acting like no one could tell him what to do. He didn't have to answer to anyone.

Pam didn't like to be bothered with anything that disturbed her view of reality.

It was harder and harder for Pam *not* to see what drove Bar Jonah's world. Pam started demanding to know why Bar

Jonah was always sitting around putting pictures of kids in binders. She would say there was something wrong with that. Not to mention that it took a lot of time. They could have been doing something together, Pam would complain. He used the pictures for advertising in his toy business, he would say. Pam couldn't understand how, especially so many of them. He also never advertised. One afternoon when Pam got the mail, she saw that the July edition of *Boy's Life* had come, along with a large heavy cardboard packet, sent from the Great Falls Board of Education. When Pam opened the package, she found three yearbooks, from three different elementary schools in Great Falls. Pam set the opened package on the kitchen table, wondering why Bar Jonah needed more pictures of kids he didn't even know. As soon as Bar Jonah stepped foot into the apartment, he recognized the yearbooks and became enraged. Pam had no right to open his mail, berating Pam for her disrespect. She had no fucking right, he screamed. Pam said she didn't understand why he wanted the yearbooks: he didn't know none of the kids anyhow, she whimpered back. It was none of her business, he told her.

Pam was having more crying jags now and Bar Jonah knew this was going to be one of them. He grabbed the yearbooks off of the table and told Pam to shut the fuck up and stay out of his business as he walked past her, disappearing down the hallway, into his bedroom. About a half-an-hour later Bar Jonah caught the sound of the teakettle whistle. For a few minutes he didn't think anything about it. Then he realized that he had heard the whistle for longer than he should have. Bar Jonah jerked open his bedroom door, walked down the hallway, and saw Pam sitting on the brown and plaid couch, staring at the living room window. The venetian blinds were closed. The room was completely dark. Bar Jonah turned off the burner and sat the empty, burnt bottom teakettle aside. He walked over to Pam, pushed on her shoulder and yelled that she looked like she was nuts. "Snap the fuck out of it," he said. Bar Jonah tried several times to rouse Pam. But she didn't move or blink her eyes. Bar Jonah stepped back, glared at Pam's dark silhouette and imagined how she would look dead. Shaking his head, Bar Jonah walked to his bedroom and lamented how hard it was on him to be living with someone who was insane.

Not with my kid

Pushing into late September, Tyra heard from her pastor that a fellow parishioner's home had caught fire and burned to the ground. The family was desperate for anything anyone could spare. Tyra called Bar Jonah and Pam. "We should take some food to the family," Tyra said. Bar Jonah agreed. That was all part of being a Christian. That evening, Bar Jonah, Pam, and Tyra knocked on the door of the trailer that someone from the church was letting the family use as a goodwill gesture. Debbie Cotes opened the door to three people bearing a freshly baked apple pie. Cotes tearfully asked the pie bearers into her temporary but warm home. Cotes's son, Lucas, was an eleven-year-old, blond-headed boy, who sat on the couch while Tyra, Pam, and Debbie were talking in the kitchen. Bar Jonah right off went over and sat down beside Lucas. Debbie was stuck how Bar Jonah barely acknowledged her, as he made his way through the stacks of smoke infused clothes to get to her son. She could see how easily Bar Jonah engaged Lucas, who Debbie always saw as shy and somewhat withdrawn. Before Tyra, Pam, and Bar Jonah left, Bar Jonah approached Debbie and told her Lucas told him he wanted an action figure doll. Bar Jonah offered to find one for Lucas as he made his rounds at the toy fairs. Debbie thanked Bar Jonah. The next day Bar Jonah showed up at Debbie's door, saying he thought he would stop by and see if there was anything she needed. She said, no, everything was fine, given the circumstances; everyone had been very generous. Bar Jonah insisted on coming inside. Debbie finally agreed and let him in. As soon as he saw Lucas, he pushed passed Debbie and asked Lucas to show him his bedroom. Bar Jonah wanted to see his toys: he liked toys too. Debbie said she didn't think it was a good idea for Lucas and Bar Jonah to go back to the bedroom, using the excuse that the place was still a mess with boxes stacked everywhere, filled with the remnants of what she was able to salvage from the fire. Bar Jonah became increasingly insistent. Debbie adamantly said no. Bar Jonah left, telling Debbie he had a lead on the action figure doll. Debbie thanked him, growing increasingly leery of Bar Jonah.

A few days later, Bar Jonah again showed up at Debbie's door with the doll, holding it above Debbie's head for Lucas to see. Lucas was ecstatic. Debbie paid Bar Jonah for the doll, thanked him, and expected him to leave. Instead he pushed by her, went over, sat down on the couch and told Lucas how much he wanted to play with him. He helped Lucas cut the plastic packaging from the doll and began imitating a boxer's movements with the action figures arms. Lucas was laughing. "He's funny," Lucas said. Debbie allowed Bar Jonah to play with Lucas for a few minutes, never leaving them alone. She then said, "Ok, it's time to stop. Lucas has to do his homework." Lucas protested, so did Bar Jonah, they were just beginning to have fun. Debbie was insistent. Right before Bar Jonah walked out the door, he stopped, put his arm against the thin doorframe, looked into Debbie's eyes and said, "You know that kid, Zach Ramsay, they'll never find his body, it's gone."

* * *

Bar Jonah didn't show up again for a few weeks. Then he started dropping by. Always wanting to play with Lucas. Debbie always said no. It wasn't long before Bar Jonah began coming by with Tyra, carrying boxes of food from the church. Debbie had to constantly keep an eye on Bar Jonah. As soon as Tyra would engage Debbie, Bar Jonah would corral Lucas, always trying to sit close to him or get Lucas to take him into his bedroom. This continued throughout all of the next year. On Christmas Day,

1997, Tyra called Debbie and told her she, Bar Jonah, and Pam, had something for her. It was a huge pot of chili. They wanted to drop it off and have a bite to eat with her and Lucas. Initially Debbie said no. Tyra continued to insist, saying that Bar Jonah had made it *especially* for them. Debbie reluctantly agreed. Bar Jonah carried two big pots into the trailer. He went over to the stove, turned on the gas, and sat the pots on the burners. In a few minutes, the pots were boiling and the trailer was filled with an odd smell. Debbie said it smelled like shoe leather cooking. Bar Jonah scooped out several ladles of chili for everyone and sat the bowls on the table. Lucas tried his first. He dipped his spoon into the chili, blew one of the kidney beans back into the bowl and put the spoon into his mouth. Lucas immediately yelled, yuck, and spewed his mouthful chili back into the bowl. Debbie, took a bite, picked up a napkin and spit out the barely chewed meat. Debbie said the deer meat tasted rotten. Bar Jonah had killed the deer, butchered it, wrapped it, and cooked it himself, he said. He *knew* how to butcher meat; it was his specialty. Debbie told him to take it away. It wasn't something she and Lucas would be eating. Pam and Tyra ate theirs quickly, commenting how sweet they thought the chili tasted. Bar Jonah was incensed that Debbie and Lucas refused to eat the chili. He pouted and said they had hurt his feelings. He was just trying to do something nice for Debbie and Lucas. Look how he got repaid. It was the first time he had shared any of his special meat with anyone.

Mr. Popcorn Head

As the weather continued to warm up, Bar Jonah began spending more and more time in one of Bob's two garages that opened out onto the alley. Sometimes he would even sleep in the garage. Pam demanded to know what he was doing out there for so many hours. He told her it was none of her business. On a late Saturday afternoon in early June, Bar Jonah called Pam and told her to come over, he had something he wanted her to see. When Pam arrived and saw what he had done, she was aghast. Bar Jonah had transformed the garage into what she called his "paradise for children". It was packed full of toys of all kinds for both boys *and* girls. He had even built a crude hand puppet theater out of wooden crates. It was all for the kids in the neighborhood. "Now they will come to me", he said. Tyra was impressed with the effort Bar Jonah had put into making the garage look so nice. She was proud that Bar Jonah was showing more and more initiative.

The word among the local kids spread quickly. The back alley Saturday afternoon puppet shows with Mr. Popcorn Head was becoming the talk of the neighborhood. Before too long the puppets knew the names of all of the kids that showed up for the shows. Mr. Popcorn Head always welcomed each child when they came running up to the garage. Bar Jonah would especially greet the mothers when they drove up and dropped their kids off. He assured them their boys and girls would be safe. Parents had entrusted their children in his care for all of his life.

The boys and girls would start showing up about noon. The kids giggled and jumped up and down when they saw Bar Jonah lumbering down the back sidewalk toward the garage. As he began to lift the door, the kids could see a big furry gorilla, with long floppy arms, sitting on a Formica table. The eyes of the gorilla were positioned to be looking right at the kids. When the gorilla came into view, whoops and hollers could be heard up and down the alley. They would yell, "Oh wow, look at this ..." as they ran grabbing for the toys sitting on makeshift shelves of bricks and plywood nestled further back in the garage. There was a big fold-up table right in the center of the garage. The table sat directly over an area of fresh loose sand. On one of the walls Bar Jonah had painted a big eye with the words "The Land of Oz" printed above it. Bar Jonah took an interest in each child, putting his arm around their shoulders, letting them know he was their friend. Often he would lift some of the boys onto his lap, and hug them close to his chest letting them know they were loved.

A lot of the kids in the neighborhood didn't have dads. And if they did, they weren't involved too much in their children's lives. The kids mainly wanted someone to take an interest in them. But even more important, they wanted someone to listen to them. Bar Jonah always leaned down and put his ear close to the child's mouth; this way they didn't have to yell in order to be heard by an adult. He also whispered to them that he was their best friend, he would be their secret keeper.

* * *

Bar Jonah was a master puppeteer, manipulating the kids with the same ease he manipulated Mr. Popcorn Head's arms and legs. The puppet shows lasted for about an hour. They became so popular that some of the mothers who brought their kids stayed for the show and thanked Bar Jonah at the end, slipping him a few dollars for being such a good friend to their children. When some of the mothers watched Bar Jonah with their children, their own personal miseries kept them blind to the truth.

* * *

Dr. David Comer didn't think Bar Jonah was such an asset to the neighborhood. His dental office window looked right out onto the garage. Eventually the crowds in the alley got so big they spilled over into Comer's parking lot. Kids running around everywhere made it difficult for his patients to safely maneuver their cars into a parking space. Comer went to Bar Jonah and asked him to curtail the shows or have them when his office wasn't open. Bar Jonah shoved him and told him to fuck off. After that Comer started carrying a twisted stick of hard oak, known in Ireland as a shillelagh. "If he ever came near me again I was going to break his collarbone," Comer said.

Almost always, after the shows, Bar Jonah pulled the door shut and spent the night in the garage. Sometimes Pam would come over and beat on the door, pathetically saying she wanted to be with Bar Jonah. There were times when she would be crying. Rarely though, did she get what she wanted. Late in the afternoon on June 26, Pam took a letter out to the garage that Bar Jonah had just received from the False Memory Foundation. Pam yelled through the door that he had got a letter; she wanted to give it to him. There was no reply. Pam heard a scratching sound, looked down and saw three fingers wiggling through the gap at the bottom of the garage door. She leaned down and placed the envelope in between the squirming fingers. The envelope was quickly snatched through the gap under the door. Pam put her ear against the door and could hear the letter being torn open. She began yelling, telling Bar Jonah how much he meant to her, "Please let me in," she pleaded. Her pleas were ignored. Other than the cluster of fingers that had appeared under the paint-flaked white door, there was no other sign of life from the garage.

* * *

Bar Jonah was now also starting to take longer trips by himself to different antique shows. Packing up a small trailer with toys, he would head up I-15 towards Alberta. Crossing over into Canada was effortless. Early on, the border patrol would inspect his trailer, but once he became a familiar face, they smiled at each other as he was waved through the checkpoint. One time, when Bar Jonah was crossing the border he asked the lone border patrol officer about her kids. She said she had two young boys. When he returned from Canada, Bar Jonah brought the customs officer a couple of die-cast metal cars. Bar Jonah even took time to carefully lift the bright red hood on one of the cars and point out the shimmering chrome-plated engine.

CHAPTER FIFTEEN

The Lord is my shepherd

In July 1997, Bar Jonah moved out of 1216 1st Avenue S to a small, seedy two-bedroom basement apartment at 26th Street and 11th Avenue. He told Tyra he needed his own space and wanted to live on his own. Tyra said she felt apprehensive but thought he was ready. He had never lived by himself for more than a short while, and somehow he always managed to get into some kind of trouble. Tyra believed that the author of all sin worked awfully hard putting up roadblocks in Bar Jonah's life. Bar Jonah *must* be awfully special to the Deliverer for the Dark Angel to be so dedicated to continually be taunting him with sin. But Tyra had an unwavering faith that Bar Jonah would thumb his nose at the ways of the Devil. She knew that loving Jesus so much had given Bar Jonah the nerves of a steeplejack when he encountered the Son of Perdition. Bar Jonah trusted the Lord like a lamb in the meadow trusted the wise old shepherd to ward off the hungry wolves. Tyra thought he had been put through so much.

* * *

In August, Pam's landlord told her she had to move. The complaints from the neighbors were never ending. He said Pam was going to burn the place down with all the candles, and the sounds of screaming animals had gotten out of hand. Pam thought this was the perfect time for her and Bar Jonah to move in together. They wouldn't be doing anything wrong, she said, after all, they were engaged to be married. It wouldn't be no sin. Pam said she had respected Bar Jonah's wish not to have sex before they got married. But she thought God would understand if they lived together. Finally in early September, Bar Jonah abruptly agreed to let Pam move into his apartment. However, he told her to stay out of his bedroom, always locking the door before he left.

Sherri Dietrich

Sherri Dietrich was broken. The bad relationships had to end, Sherri said to herself. It seemed like her whole world was just going from one hell to another. She needed a new start. On August 15, 1997 Sherri pulled her fully-loaded, dull yellow rental truck with no radio and bad springs, into the American Antique Mall, after leaving Durango, Colorado on July 4. By the time Sherri arrived in Great Falls, she hadn't eaten in two days. She had planned on going to Walla Walla, Washington. She had a kid there. Sherri told herself she was going to enforce her parental rights and charge her ex with kidnapping. But on the drive she decided that she might spend some time in Great Falls, to get herself together before she headed over to Washington to take her kid back.

As Sherri walked around the mall, she saw a short, fat man with one shirt tail hanging out of his pants, leaning down and showing a young boy a box full of police badges. His arm was resting on the boy's shoulder. He could have one for free, Sherri heard him say to the boy, rubbing his back. After the fat man pinned the badge to the boy's flannel shirt, Sherri approached him about buying some of her belongings. Bar Jonah reached out and shook Sherri's hand, introducing himself. Bar Jonah and Sherri walked on out to the parking lot without speaking to each other. He wanted to see what kind of treasures she might have tucked away inside of the truck.

Sherri pushed back the metal bracket that held the C shaped hook, which slipped into the square hole that was cut into the frame of the truck, releasing the door latch. The ball bearing metal wheels clamored against the bent aluminum tracks, as Sherri threw the door upward with a woomph. The door bounced back down a bit as it slammed to a stop. The pocked-faced, has-been of a man working at the rental place, didn't tell her anything about how to tie the boxes together when she loaded up the truck. What the hell did she know. Now with all the tight curves and bumpy roads there had been lots of weight shifts; she had a topsy-turvy mess in the back to clean up. Bar Jonah looked at a few things that were strewn about and offered her a few dollars. They weren't toys but if nothing else, he thought he could unload them on a few of the other dealers. Sherri accepted Bar Jonah's offer by nodding her head up and down, in between rattling on with her endless tale of misery. Sherri talked so fast Bar Jonah had trouble keeping track of what she was saying. She had no money, no food, and no place to stay. Bar Jonah felt sorry for her; he too had known great suffering in his life. Bar Jonah looked at Sherri and said that a devout man should offer shelter to those without comfort. He said she should move in with him that day.

* * *

Pam had been out at the thrift stores all day. When she arrived home she noticed a yellow truck parked beside their apartment building. As Pam was fiddling to get her key in the door lock, a frumpy, middle-aged, peroxided blonde woman jerked opened the door, looked at her and said, "You must be Pam, hi, I'm Sherri." Pam stood at the door baffled. Who in the Lord's name was this? Sherri invited Pam into her own apartment. When Pam walked through the door, Sherri began spewing out the story about how she and Bar Jonah had met earlier that afternoon. Sherri tried to reach out and hug Pam, when she told her Bar Jonah had offered her a place to stay, at least until she got on her feet. Pam recoiled from Sherri's embrace. Bar Jonah had told Sherri she could sleep on his couch; it would be better than sleeping in the truck. Several hours later, after he got home from the antique mall, Pam confronted Bar Jonah, saying she didn't want Sherri there. Bar Jonah told Pam that if she didn't like Sherri being there, then Pam could leave. There would be no discussion. Many years later, Pam told the FBI that Sherri learned more about Bar Jonah that night than Pam had known about him in the two years they had been together.

* * *

After Pam confronted Bar Jonah, he stormed out of the apartment, slamming the door, screaming something about Pam always trying to tell him what to do. Pam was right on his heels, crying, begging him not to leave her. Pam walked up to Bar Jonah, wrapped her arms tightly around his neck and started retching. She reached out and took Bar Jonah's cheeks between her hands and told him that she was fine when they were together, but when they are apart it was like she didn't exist. Bar Jonah pulled Pam's arms from around his neck, got into his car, and drove out of the parking lot. Pam fell down to the pavement and began sobbing, holding her head in her hands, as the traffic streamed by, oblivious to her anguish. After a while, a brief rain shower made Pam pick herself up off of the blacktop. She walked across the street to the hospital and wandered aimlessly about the corridors. Pam ended up falling asleep, in a stiff, orange high back chair, in the corner of a hospital room of an unknown, unconscious old man. A nurse, who came into the room, thought Pam was a friend who had drifted off while visiting the old man, who was being held an inescapable captive by a deep sleep from which he would never awake. After several hours the nurse roused Pam and told her she had to leave, visiting hours were long over.

* * *

Sherri sat down on a chrome-legged, red vinyl kitchen chair with silver specks and lifted her feet up onto the table. She sighed and moved her head from side to side, looking around the apartment. On the kitchen wall there were yellow sticky notes with prices scribbled on them in pencil; $1.00 here, 50¢ there. She assumed Bar Jonah must have had an apartment sale, because each price tag corresponded with a picture or something on a table directly under it.

But, for a few minutes, Sherri sat transfixed, staring at the wall in the living room, thinking about the first time she'd sat on Santa's lap telling him about the Poor Pitiful Pearl doll she wanted, that walked and talked. Bar Jonah was someone who loved Christmas she thought. Clearly this was a good Christian man. Earlier that day, after Bar Jonah had offered her a place to stay, he trustingly gave her the key to his apartment and told her to go on over. When Sherri first arrived, she could hear "Jingle Bells" playing from inside the apartment. As Sherri pushed open the door, and light began to awaken the room, Sherri saw the decorations. Covering the wall were more than 20,000 angels, Christmas bulbs, and garlands. Nailed to the top of the wall near the ceiling was a strand of effervescent bubble lights, the kind she hadn't seen since she was a kid. Dozens of nativity scenes where a Mary and Joseph stood vigil over a baby Jesus adorned every table. Sherri said it was comforting, after coming from so much turmoil, to walk in and be overwhelmed by the spirit of Christmas in September. About an hour later, Bar Jonah came back home. He lit a cigarette and asked Sherri to sit down with him at the kitchen table. Bar Jonah wanted to tell Sherri about some ten-year-old kid, named Zach Ramsay, who had disappeared last year. Sherri said she'd never heard of him.

* * *

Zach was a little artist, Bar Jonah told Sherri. He and Zach would sit on the couch and draw in the black spiral-bound notebook Bar Jonah had bought for him. Zach had no one to talk to about his problems. Bar Jonah was always happy to lend Zach a sympathetic ear. Zach's mother, Rachel Howard, was having all kinds of problems with her boyfriend, Carl The Coon, as Zach called him. But this wasn't unusual, she always had problems with her boyfriends. Zach told Bar Jonah he didn't like Carl. Bar Jonah told Sherri that Carl couldn't take Rachel anymore and had moved back in with his wife and kids two days before Zach disappeared.

Bar Jonah said Zach always walked down a back alley to get to school, even when it snowed and the alley hadn't been cleared. Zach was startled on the first morning that he saw Bar Jonah leaning against the big green dumpster, with needles of hard frost clinging to his mustache, his black stocking cap pulled down almost over his eyes and smoking a cigarette. The boy acted like a whipped puppy; wanting to take the treats Bar Jonah offered, but was suspicious about getting too close. It helped when Zach saw Bar Jonah's badge. He was working as an undercover policeman, on duty by the dumpster to help kids. Sherri asked herself why Bar Jonah was telling her about this kid she didn't even know. But given what Bar Jonah had just done for her, she felt obliged to sit and listen.

Bar Jonah inhaled deeply as he lit another cigarette, smoke rolling out his nose. He motioned with his hand toward the other side of town, when he said there was an old man who lived down the alleyway. Zach used to visit the old man when he walked to school. The old man was a homosexual. Sometimes Zach would stop by after school and play games with the old man. After Zach started playing with the old man, he stopped playing as much with Bar Jonah. When Bar Jonah asked Zach to come over and play with him, he made up excuses and said he had to go home and do his homework. Bar Jonah knew he was lying. He cautioned Zach that lying was a sin that God would punish him for. It was beginning to piss Bar Jonah off, that Zach was spending so much time at the old man's house that he didn't want to play with him any-more. Zach confessed that the old man had a lot better toys to play with than Bar Jonah did. Sometimes the old man let Zach open up a new toy, still wrapped up tight in faded cellophane. Zach thought it was just like Christmas morning. Bar Jonah told Sherri he got more and more jealous when Zach would walk right past him and go into the old man's house, acting like he wasn't even there.

* * *

Sherri took a deep breath when Bar Jonah told her that he felt like a different man after he first met Zach, not like the man he had been before Zach smiled at him. Something inside him changed. Sherri thought Bar Jonah talked like Zach was a lover and not a little boy. Then Bar Jonah looked down; his eyes were empty. He didn't think he could ever heal from the rejection he felt when he saw the old man open his back door, gently dust the snow off Zach's shoulders, and greet him with a cup of hot cocoa. And Zach, not looking back, walked right on in.

Bar Jonah lit another cigarette and rolled the convex glowing tip against the head of a ceramic swan trying to take flight from the ashtray. He leaned back against the chair, looking almost contemplative, as he watched the blue cigarette smoke unfurl from his mouth against the uncovered flickering fluorescent light. Sherri felt relieved when Bar Jonah stopped talking, giv-ing her a moment to catch her wits. She had been around the tracks enough times to know when someone was leading up to something that didn't have a good ending. Then Bar Jonah started talking again. This time about "the policeman".

The policeman

The old man had a friend who was a policeman, Bar Jonah said. The two were very close but Zach was getting to be a real problem for the policeman. Bar Jonah said the policeman didn't like kids hanging around the old man's place when the policeman wasn't there, especially Zach. Sherri sat stock-still as she watched Bar Jonah's eyes become despondent and his face, without warning, turn red with rage when he described how the old man and the policeman would fight over the boy. Each one wanted Zach for themselves. The old man and the policeman finally agreed to always share Zach. Friends were not selfish with each other.

On the morning that the boy went missing, Bar Jonah told Sheri that the policeman nodded to Zach in the alley. That morning, Zach nodded back. Bar Jonah's voice softened, as he told her how Zach had made it right to the opening of the alley and then "poof," he just vanished, and was never seen again. The comfort Sherri had felt before, about Bar Jonah being a good Christian man, was now replaced by fear.

The person who took Zach dressed up like a policeman, Bar Jonah said. Zach wouldn't have gotten into a car with someone he didn't know. He knew the policeman. The policeman had to work especially hard to become friends with Zach; no one could ever know how close they were. Most kids trust policemen right off. That's what their mothers teach them. But Zach's mother taught him not to trust anyone, so he took longer. He turned down lot of rides before he'd get into the policeman's car. But once he did, Zach and the policeman would go places together and have fun. They could go on long drives together, because Zach's mother never knew where he was. Zach walked all over the city. Everyone in town knew him. Zach liked the policeman, because he really took an interest in him, giving him things, just like a real dad would. There were even sometimes when they would take naps together. The policeman got really jealous when Zach ignored him and went to play with the old man. Zach didn't like it when the policeman told him he *had* to stop playing with the old man. He even got smart-alecky with the policeman. Zach hadn't done that before the old man made him his friend too. The boy would have to be punished if he didn't stop being unfaithful.

* * *

That morning in the alley, Zach was crying and telling the policeman to leave him alone. The policeman was sympathetic. He understood; he always understood. They'd go to the Good Guy breakfast together. The old man won't go with you, like he said he would, so I'll take you, the policeman told Zach. Think about how jealous you'll make your friends, when you come with the policeman. The policeman smiled softly and put his thumb under the lapel of his blue police jacket. The Good Guy breakfast would be a celebration for him too. He had just got his "gold shield," as he pushed the shiny new detective's badge out for Zach to see. Everyone at school knew who the policeman was.

Zach was leery but the policeman's eyes were so pleading, that he got into his car anyway. Buckle up, the policeman said, he sure didn't want Zach to get hurt if they got into an accident. As Zach was latching the seat belt, the policeman turned into the alley at 6th Avenue. Before the policeman drove out of the alley on 7th, Zach was unconscious. Sherri had tears running down her face as she sat paralyzed. Bar Jonah went on talking. His face was blank. He was indifferent to her tears.

The policeman started driving toward Holter Lake, Bar Jonah told Sherri. He had a friend from church who had a small fishing cabin there. But the friend wasn't around in the winter and the policeman knew where he kept the key. Every now and then on the drive the boy started to wake up, but the policeman had slipped a noose around his neck before they left the alley. The way the policeman had fixed the seat belt held

201

the boy really tight when the policeman pulled hard on the noose. In a few seconds, the boy would pass out again. When they got to the cabin on the lake, the policeman picked the boy up and held him close to his chest so he wouldn't get cold as he carried him inside. Then he laid the boy onto the dusty floor of the cabin, leaned down, and rubbed his sandpapery cheek against the boy's face. The boy's eyes opened, surprising the policeman. He reached out and grabbed the outside waist zipper of the policeman's jacket, partly tearing it off of the policeman's coat. When the policeman tried to push the boy's hand back, the boy got the policeman's thumb and index finger and twisted it backwards, hurting the policeman. This made the policeman very mad. He jerked hard on the rope, strangling the boy as he pulled his head up off of the floor. The policeman was having to breathe hard, as he made the boy's head bounce with dull thuds against the oak planked floor when he punched him in the face, over and over again. This way the policeman made sure the boy would stay asleep and not make things harder than they need be. The boy had been so good up until now he didn't want him to spoil anything. Especially now, when it had all come together so perfectly, so right. The policeman had had problems with boys acting up before. But, he had more experience now.

When the policeman had taken the back seats out of his undercover police car, the plywood board had slid perfectly into the trunk and up into the passenger compartment. The boy was good and knocked out now, so the policeman could go and get the board out of the car without having to worry about the boy waking up again. He had so much to worry about, everything had to be done just right.

The door of the cabin was too narrow to get the board through without tipping it onto its side. The policeman had thought this might happen, so he brought extra rope, so the boy wouldn't slide off, as they were going back out of the door and down to the beach. Laying the plywood flat on the floor, the policeman rolled the boy onto the board. The boy rolled his head thickly from side to side, like it was encased in cold molasses. His nose was broken and bloody; his eyes swollen shut from the policeman's heavy blows to his face. After the policeman took the boy's clothes off, he picked up his underwear and stuffed them into the boy's mouth. He wrapped his hands and feet in heavy silver tape and tightly tied his body with a piece of oily rope to the plywood. The policeman tied the end of the noose to a longer piece of rope and wrapped it around the back of the board. He yanked the rope up from the bottom of the plywood and tied it to the boy's taped feet. This way if he woke up and wiggled around, he would choke himself. The policeman then took another piece of rope and wrapped it around the boy, from side to side, like a cocoon. He always said oily rope was best, because the knots won't slip. Once it's tied, it stays tied. The policeman had spent a lot of time studying knots.

After the policeman was done raping the boy a few times, he tipped the board up onto its side and pushed it through the door of the cabin. For a moment the policeman left the board resting on its side and stared at the image of the boy hanging bound and bloody to the board. The policeman thought of Jesus suffering on the Cross. The policeman leaned down and in a soft voice whispered into the boy's ear; he was taking him into the Land of the Skulls. And there, like a good soldier, the policeman would take away his misery and cleanse him of his sin.

The policeman finished sliding the board through the door, making a drag mark along the wooden floor on the small deck of the cabin. When the policeman dropped the board onto the two steps going down from the deck, it tipped up one end of the board. This made it easier for the policeman to get his fingers under the board to lift it. As he raised the board, the boy began to wake up again. He was a feisty rascal. That was one of the things the policeman would miss the most about the boy.

Suddenly, the boy seemed to be completely awake. Then he started hopelessly fighting against the ropes. He even tried to push the tape off of his mouth with his tongue. But the policeman had wrapped the tape tightly all the way around the boy's head.

The policeman looked at the boy as he was dragging him along and thought of how foolish moths were. Flocking to a bright light, only to be caught by something as simple as syrup smeared onto a long strip of paper. For a second, the policeman wondered what it was like to be the boy. Did he know that in a few minutes he would be gone? No more drawings, no more football, no more, no more, no more. The policeman kept saying it over and over again. But, he was sending him to a better place, a place without sin. Even though the boy had bewitched two good men, God would be merciful. The boy would not have to suffer very long in Hell, before God raised him up to be with Him.

* * *

When they got to the little beach, the policeman dropped the board onto the frosty mottled sand. The policeman watched the boy jerking around. He was foolishly going to fight until the very end. The policeman reached under his jacket, pulled out his stag horn handled hunting knife and started stabbing the boy. The first blows were just right, cutting the tendons in his arms and legs, this way he couldn't be such a wiggly boy. But when the policeman slammed the knife into a fleshy part of meat under the boy's armpit, it went all the way through the plywood. The policeman's thumb and forefinger twisted back against the hilt of the knife. It hurt the policeman. This made him mad all over again.

A rat-a-tat-tat echoed against the plywood as the policeman, in a flurry, began to stab the boy's chest with his knife. The boy's throat began to gurgle and the underwear still in his mouth poking out from behind the tape, started turning a wet red. When the policeman finally got bored, he grabbed the boy by the hair, pulled his head back and cut his throat. The policeman rocked to and fro chanting a short Hebrew prayer after he sacrificed the boy by the *shechita*. Then he grabbed handfuls of snow and packed it into the boy's gaping neck to slow down the bleeding.

Sherri said Bar Jonah talked like he was a zombie, sitting motionless, his eyes glazed over, his mouth moving, words coming out, but nothing was alive inside. This was not real, Sherri silently said to herself. Bar Jonah deeply breathed in the smoke from another cigarette as he continued.

* * *

As the policeman watched the white sand and spots of snow siphon up the boy's blood, he remembered Moses turning the waters of Egypt red, while Pharaoh stood feebly by. After the boy was finished bleeding, the policeman took time to fillet the meat from the flanks, shoulders, ribs, and rump. He had to take a few of the ribs and part of his arm and shoulder bones, to roast for a stock. The policeman sat down on the sand, chanted another rite of passage prayer and delicately performed a *Brit Milah*, slipping the penis into a small glass jar with a twist-on lid, packed with snow. The fillets and a few small bones were put into a plastic bag with chunks of dry ice to keep them fresh. Then he sawed up the rest of the boy, with a small crosscut handsaw and threw the pieces as far out into the lake as he could. The boy's head spun end over end, when the policeman grabbed it by the hair and lobbed it into the air. A soft sigh of satisfaction came from the policeman's lips, as, for a few seemingly timeless moments, he watched the moonlight catch the boy's twirling head and motionless face in a stroboscopic splendor. In a few minutes he could hear the flipping pike and catfish beginning to feed.

* * *

He picked up his board and rinsed it, as best he could, in the lake. Then the policeman swirled the hunting knife around in a patch of fresh snow, before he slipped it back into the leather sheath hanging on his side. He thought the meat stuck in the saw's teeth could someday be a problem, so he threw it way out into the lake too. It would sink into the silt and muck of the lakebed and disappear just like the boy's skull. Before he carried the board back to his car, he stirred the sand around with a stick where the boy had bled. The policeman looked down at the striations of crimson streaked through the gray sand and thought it looked like a slice of marble cake. Then the policeman dragged the plywood back up the hill to his car, opened the trunk and slid it in just as easy as he had pulled it out. He was pleased with his cleverness. The thick plastic bag holding the meat was spun, stopping after three spins. Then the top was twisted into a tight knot to make sure none of the juices would be lost. The policeman pulled the lid off of the blue and white plastic ice chest, brushed back a handful of the small irregular cubes and gingerly sat the bag of meat into a nest of ice. He then he went into the cabin. The policeman picked up the boy's clothes off the floor, put them into another plastic bag and walked out the door, being careful to pull it shut behind him. The sun had long set. He was exhausted; it had been a long day. As he was driving away the policeman stopped, looked out at the lake, and said, "Catch a little fish and a little boy pops out."

You have to understand, the policeman was a Christian soldier sent to do God's work. He was chosen. Few are chosen, but when you are, you can't refuse. The policeman knew boys, Bar Jonah said. He took his time to study them, to see if they were like the shiny spinning lure that called out to the fish. The fish that swam so freely only to be snared by latching onto that forbidden trinket being dangled in front of their pursing lips.

God gave the policeman a burden. The burden of knowing first-hand how a boy can make a man violate his God-given goodness. The policeman had to keep pictures of the boys, boys who may be vile. But the policeman would know what boys were loathsome and what their punishment should be. Some boys only need a little punishment, while others could never be saved from their sinful ways. They can only be redeemed at the feet of the Almighty. Most of the boys didn't have good mothers either. They were usually sluts, sluts that went from man to man. That was how the boys became evil. Watching their mothers corrupting good men. Usually married men. The policeman said it was good when a boy had a mom who would sacrifice everything for her son, no matter what. The son was of her flesh, of her soul.

Bar Jonah leaned over to Sherri and whispered, "The police will never find the body, because there is no body to find." It was gone. The cigarette he lit off the other never saw his lips, it just burned itself out between his fingers. Sherri was still in shock when Bar Jonah stood up and walked into his bedroom. The click of the lock as he closed the door, made her shake her head and wake up from what she was sure was a nightmare. Pam got back a bit before midnight. Sherri heard her come in but couldn't muster herself to even speak as Pam walked past the couch to her bedroom.

CHAPTER SIXTEEN

The apartment

Over the next few weeks, the stench in Bar Jonah's apartment became overwhelming. He had been defrosting meat from his freezer, making his special spaghetti sauce and chili for his friends. Every time he defrosted a package of meat in the sink, the place stunk even worse. It was foul, Sherri said. When she mentioned the smell to Pam, Pam said that she had sinus problems, so she didn't notice it so much. Sherri finally couldn't stand the filth anymore and told Pam she was going to clean the place up, when she had some time to herself.

A week or so later, before Bar Jonah left for work, Sherri told him she was going to scrub the place to get rid of the smell. He screamed at her and told her to mind her own business, saying, "I like the smell." Sherri countered, saying the place smelled like rotten meat. Bar Jonah left in a huff, putting his cigarette out in Sherri's coffee cup before he walked out the door. She ignored Bar Jonah and began by cleaning out the hallway closet. Inside she found a blue denim jacket with green plaid sleeves and a pair of black tennis shoes. There was also a plastic bag filled with a young boy's clothes, a shirt, white briefs, socks, jeans, mittens and a stocking cap. The clothes were filthy she said, like they had been rubbed in the dirt. When she pulled the clothing out of the plastic bag, white sand fell onto the floor. That night, after Bar Jonah got back, Sherri asked him where the clothes came from. He told her to mind her own business and she was never to go through his stuff again. They belonged to an old roommate, he finally said. Sherri sarcastically said the roommate must have been pretty damn small. Bar Jonah changed his story and told her they belonged to the son of a friend who used to stop by. Later in the day Sherri pulled Pam aside and told her Bar Jonah was not who she thought he was. Pam needed to be careful. Then Sherri told Pam the story of the policeman.

* * *

Pam didn't believe Sherri at first. She was mostly jealous, that Sherri seemed to know more about Bar Jonah than she'd ever did. Disgust ruled Pam's face, as Sherri went into all of the grisly details. Pam thought Sherri just did it to get under her skin and to make her think bad things about Bar Jonah. She was sure Sherri was trying to break them up. Sherri wanted Bar Jonah for herself.

The morning after Sherri found the clothes, she sat up on the burnt orange threadbare couch and wrapped a blanket around her shoulders. She looked over at Bar Jonah, sitting at the table, smoking his usual cigarette, and asked him why he was reading the school lunch menu. He snottily said he wanted to make sure the kids were getting fed a balanced diet. He was a chef; he knew about these things. After several bowls of oatmeal, he announced he would be gone for the day. A few minutes later he walked out the door. Sherri looked out the window and saw him heading toward downtown.

When Sherri began shaking the doorknob on Bar Jonah's bedroom door, it didn't take much before the brass plate vibrated away from the dead bolt enough to where she could push open the door. Bar Jonah's bedroom was disgusting. It smelled so bad Sherri thought she would gag. The rotted meat smell in the rest of the apartment was pale, compared to the reek that pervaded his bedroom like a dense fog.

As she opened the closet door, a shoe fell off the top shelf and hit her in the head. When she reached up to put the shoe back, she saw the finger of a pair of gardening gloves, poking out from a pile of yellowing briefs. Moving the underwear aside, she saw that the gloves were covered in dirt and blood. She pulled the shorts back over the gloves and returned the shoe to its perch. There was nothing more she could see without having to move too much stuff around. On the floor of the closet was an oily rope tied in a figure "8". Hanging on one of the coat hangers was a blue nylon police jacket. The jacket was covered in a thin dry cleaner bag. Pushing the clothes out of the way she saw a four by six foot piece of plywood, resting against the back wall of the closet. As best she could, Sherri tipped the plywood out and saw it was covered in triangle-shaped stab marks, that she guessed were made by the tip of a knife blade. The holes seemed to be caked in a brownish crust. She began to sweat. As Sherri was walking out of Bar Jonah's room, she glanced over and saw a gold police badge lying on top of his dresser. She pulled the door shut, making sure the lock clicked back into place.

* * *

The next day, after Bar Jonah left, Sherri showed Pam the boy's clothes in the hallway closet. Then she took Pam into Bar Jonah's bedroom and showed her the bloody gloves, rope, and board. Pam sat down on Bar Jonah's bed and began weeping and wringing her hands saying, "Oh Lordy Lordy this just can't be true." Sherri heard Bar Jonah's car, with its holey muffler, unexpectedly pull up outside the window. He was back. She grabbed Pam by the arm and pulled her, still sobbing, out of the bedroom, clicking the door lock behind them. Pam and Sherri were sitting, breathing hard, at the kitchen table when Bar Jonah opened the door and walked in. His eyes were involuntarily suspicious, his face sneering with its usual scowl, wondering what they had been saying about him. Bar Jonah went over to the blue plastic dish strainer, picked up his coffee mug and poured himself a cup of thick, hours-old coffee. Then he walked back out the door, slurping coffee over his thin dry lips, without saying a word.

After she heard him drive away, Sherri told Pam that her eyes had suddenly popped open in the middle of the night. Bar Jonah had been standing beside the couch, staring down at her while she slept. At that moment everything seemed unreal for Pam, but she was sure she heard Sherri say that she thought Bar Jonah was going to kill her. Pam later told Sherri she had a dream that night where Bar Jonah was wearing a black hood over his head.

* * *

There were certain things that Bar Jonah didn't want touched. He would get especially frantic when Sherri moved his surgical gloves, which he kept in a zip lock bag, sitting on a shelf in the kitchen. Bar Jonah always grabbed a pair of gloves and put them in his pants pocket before he left the apartment. Sherri didn't know what he did with them, except that he never had them when he came back. After she realized Bar Jonah was taking gloves with him every time he left, she began visually checking his pants pockets when he returned. This way she could see if the outline made by the gloves was still apparent in his pants. It never was.

The top of the chest of drawers was covered in small charred, scalloped furrows, where cigarettes had laid too long before burning themselves out. The third drawer down was where Bar Jonah kept his knives. Sherri said the drawer didn't have just a few knives, but was packed so full that it almost fell onto the floor when she pulled it out. Bar Jonah didn't want Sherri or Pam to bother any of his knives. They were to leave them alone. It didn't matter if they needed a knife to cut something, they

212

could ask him and he would get it for them. Sherri told Bar Jonah that his attitude about the knives was stupid. If she needed a knife she would go and get one. Bar Jonah said that would not be a good idea. The boning knife, in particular, seemed to be the cause of a lot of arguments between Sherri and Bar Jonah.

The road trip

In early October, Bar Jonah's cousin was getting married in Worcester. Tyra and Bob were scheduled to go back to Massachusetts for the wedding. In September, Tyra's brother called and said under no circumstances did any of the family want Bar Jonah there. He had been an indelible stain on the family all his life. They did not want him at the wedding. When Tyra told Bar Jonah he wasn't invited, he said he was going anyways. He didn't care. No one was going to stop him. He had things he wanted to say to his cousin that would help her in her life, plus he wanted to see all his little cousins. One of Bar Jonah's uncles called him and said he would have him forcibly removed if he showed up at the wedding. "Don't make a scene," he said. "I'm not some kid you can push around. You show up here and I'll kick your ass." On October 8, Tyra and Bob flew back for the wedding.

The morning of October 12 Bar Jonah was up early, banging stuff around in the kitchen, waking Sherri up from a sound sleep. As usual, Pam's bedroom door was closed, so she didn't hear him get up. He lit his first cigarette of the day and tossed the burnt match onto the kitchen table. Sherri watched Bar Jonah through squinted eyes, as a haze of blue smoke began to envelop him. He pulled a can of coffee out of the cabinet and scooped out eight measures into the coffee maker. Then he added six cups of water and pushed the ON button. Sherri thought it was unusual that Bar Jonah was making so much; he never made coffee for anyone but himself. He walked out of the kitchen and back down the hallway. She stretched, moaned, tossed back the soft plush throw and sat up. Sherri could hear Bar Jonah grunting in the bathroom, as she walked into the kitchen and poured a cup of coffee. A few minutes later Sherri smelled the methane odor coming from the toilet, before she saw Bar Jonah standing behind her in the kitchen. When she turned around Sherri saw his eyes, which to her looked black, as they rested uncomfortably on her face. Sherri said it felt like something stone cold overflowed from his being and expressed itself independent of his body. "What are you doing with my coffee?" he snarled. Sherri said she thought he made coffee for everyone. Bar Jonah grabbed the pot, poured the rest of the coffee into a thermos, dumped in some milk and sugar, and tightened the lid. "I am going on a road trip," he said. "I'll be back tomorrow." "Whose car are you taking?" Sherri curiously asked. "Yours hasn't been working so good." "My mom's and it's none of your business where I'm going," Bar Jonah replied. Sherri hadn't bothered to ask where he was going. Before Bar Jonah left, he pulled open the squeaky metal folding door that covered the utility closet, and dumped the coffee grounds into the trash. As he was pushing the door closed, a mouse darted through the opening and inexplicably stopped. In that instant, Bar Jonah's heavy, scuffed black boot slammed down and crushed the mouse under its waffled sole. Bar Jonah pulled the metal door open a crack more and kicked the still twitching mouse into the closet, making a thin blood streak across the floor. He closed the door, picked up his thermos, and stormed out of the apartment.

It was still dark when Bar Jonah left that morning. As he walked the neighborhood over to Tyra's place, an ashen moon hung low in the early morning sky, casting the maple trees that lined the well groomed streets in gloomy shadows against the white stucco of the houses. As Bar Jonah walked he sang the hymn, *He the Pearly Gates Will Open*, over and over again, as the cold morning air chilled his lungs.

* * *

As Bar Jonah came down 9th, he turned into the alley that ran behind Tyra's and Bob's place on 1st Avenue. He opened the garage door and unlocked her car with the key he secretly had made and now kept tucked away in his billfold. Bar Jonah backed out of the garage about 8:15 a.m. and headed down 10th Avenue towards I-15 south and on to I-90 east.

There are sections of the highways in Montana and Wyoming that are desolate. It is not unusual for drivers to find themselves to be the only car on the road. Bar Jonah liked being able to be by himself, without distractions, especially when he had things to think about.

Amanda

Amanda Dawn Gallion was fourteen years old. She was 5' 2" and weighed about 100 pounds. She had short dark brown hair. The people around Gillette, Wyoming usually mistook her for a boy when they saw her riding her bike. She was well known around town, always seeming to be in some kind of trouble with someone. On the morning of October 13, 1997 she left home for school about 7:15 a.m. It was a typical chilly fall morning in Gillette when she hopped on her bicycle and rode off. Somewhere between her house and school she disappeared. Her bicycle was found thrown along the side of the road off I-90. Amanda's social security number has never been used since she went missing.

Bar Jonah arrived in Gillette about 8 p.m. on the 12th and stayed at a small fleabag motel at the outskirts of town. He came back through Billings about 2 p.m. on the 13th and stopped at one of the antique malls. Sherri and Pam said he got home at 9 p.m. that night.

The heretic

When he walked in the door, Bar Jonah had a half-eaten donut stuck in his mouth; a restrained look of contentment played over his face. Sherri told him he looked like he was in a better mood than when he left the day before. "Did you go get some strange?" she asked. Bar Jonah stopped and gazed into Sherri's eyes, saying nothing. For a moment Sherri said it was so quiet, you could hear ice melting. He pushed the rest of the donut into his mouth and headed toward his bedroom. Bar Jonah ignored Pam, who was sitting on the couch like she didn't exist.

The evening of October 27, Sherri and Pam were sitting on the couch in the living room. Bar Jonah was sitting on a kitchen chair, smoking. The pictures of some kids he had photographed, from his car window, had just come in the mail that day, from the lab he used back east. Bar Jonah had been using the same lab for many years sending sometimes more than 100 rolls a month to be processed. He had carefully laid each photograph out on the table, using a magnifying glass to examine each child. Bar Jonah cut the heads off of the kids that he liked the best and slipped them into clear plastic baseball card sleeves. When the page sleeve was full, Bar Jonah slipped the three holes over the binder rings and went on to the next group of pictures. Sherri noticed that Bar Jonah always let his cigarette burn down to the filter, as he sat, losing himself in certain pictures. Sometimes he would take a deep breath, close his eyes, and rub his thumb gently over the image of a particular child. As Bar Jonah sat engrossed, Sherri and Pam began talking about Tarot cards. For the first time Pam told Sherri she was a Lyalorishas and a seer. Pam started talking about African Priestess rituals. Sherri interrupted Pam and told her she had learned to read the Tarot when she lived in St. Louis. But, Sherri said, she didn't learn to read the traditional way, rather, the reading she did was spiritual and based on Scripture: the universal principles of cause and effect.

Bar Jonah picked up the remaining pictures that he had not yet put into the binder and slid them back into the mailing envelope. Pam started urging Sherri to go and get her Tarot cards. Initially Sherri said no, but Pam kept insisting. Finally, Sherri got up, went to her suitcase, and found the cards lying next to her juju blessed wand that an astrologer had given her many years before. When Sherri came back out into the living room, she commented that the Tarot dated back to the Jewish Torah, long before the New Testament. Pam told Sherri she wanted to ask the cards a question about her and Bar Jonah. But Pam first wanted to know how truthful did the Tarot speak. Sherri said it was 95% for sure. You could believe in what the cards say. When he heard Sherri, Bar Jonah stood up and slammed the chair he had been sitting on against the wall. The cards were the word of the Devil and Sherri was a Devil worshipper, Bar Jonah screamed. Pam and Sherri were amazed at Bar Jonah's sudden rage. Bar Jonah told Sherri to throw her Tarot cards out the front door or he would do it for her. Pam reached over and picked up her Bible off of an end table and began reading scripture to Bar Jonah. Bar Jonah than continued the Scripture Pam was reading and finished the passages verbatim. Pam didn't know Bar Jonah knew so much of the Lord's Word by heart. After Bar Jonah finished the passage, he began reciting scripture that Jesus had shown just to him. Sherri yelled at Bar Jonah saying that *he* sounded like the Devil worshipper, and cracked, "What is this, the Gospel According to Bar Jonah?" For a few minutes there was a lull.

Pam started begging Bar Jonah to let Sherri do a reading for them. She wanted to know if they were going to be together forever. Sherri said, no, she wasn't going to do any reading. She'd go ahead and put the cards away. Bar Jonah screamed that the cards had to be thrown out. The Devil's word was not going to stay in his apartment. Sherri again tried to reason with Bar Jonah saying she would put them away and never bring them out again. Bar Jonah wouldn't stand for it. Sherri stood up and started to put the cards back into her suitcase, which was lying open beside the couch. Bar Jonah screamed again, telling Sherri the cards had to go out the door, or he was calling the cops and having her ass thrown out of his apartment for trespassing. Bar Jonah then reached out and grabbed the cards out of Sherri's hand, throwing them across the room. "The Devil will not live here," Bar Jonah screamed, as the cards went flying, seemingly in slow motion, throughout the front room. Sherri was becoming terrified of Bar Jonah. When Bar Jonah looked at Sherri through his rage, she felt glared to death. Sherri mustered up some fool's courage and retorted that he had a lot of nerve calling *her* a Devil worshipper, after what he had done. Pam, sitting on the couch, started rocking back and forth, trying to make the Bible passages she was reading out loud heard above Bar Jonah. Even though Bar Jonah was enraged and becoming more and more threatening, Pam still kept pleading with Bar Jonah to let Sherri do a reading. Bar Jonah thought Sherri had stolen Pam's mind. Pam knew how angry Bar Jonah could get. She would not have kept asking if the Devil wasn't at work inside her.

Bar Jonah came towards Sherri and put his foot on the flimsy coffee table. Pam tossed her Bible on the couch, jumped up, and grabbed Bar Jonah's shoulders, keeping him from being able to get to Sherri. Pam screamed for Sherri to go to Pam's bedroom and lock the door: she had to go *now*. Pam screamed again, "Go!" As Sherri ran back to Pam's bedroom, she heard Pam calmly repeating Bar Jonah's name over and over again just like she would invoke the name of Jesus in times of need. He wasn't responding to Pam nor was he coming down the hallway after Sherri. Back in Pam's bedroom, Sherri could hear Pam saying to Bar Jonah, "You don't want to do this, put that knife away, put it away …". That made Sherri think that Pam knew more about things that had gone on than she was saying.

* * *

It was about fifteen minutes later when Sherri heard the front door open and close. Pam called out to Sherri, telling her it was safe to come out now, Bar Jonah had left. When Sherri came back to the living room, Pam told her to get her juju wand. She wanted Sherri to create a marriage incantation before Bar Jonah came back. Pam said that even though witchcraft is irrelevant when it comes to Jesus Christ and his blood, she still wanted Sherri to summon up a marriage spell for her and Bar Jonah. Sherri looked at Pam dumbfounded.

The next morning Bar Jonah walked over and kicked the couch, telling Sherri to wake up. As Sherri was rubbing the sleep from her eyes, Bar Jonah tossed a handwritten eviction notice in her lap and told her to get out. As he was walking away, Sherri yelled out that she would leave as soon as he talked with Pam about the policeman. Bar Jonah grabbed an aerosol can that was sitting on the kitchen table, spun around, and threw it at Sherri. The can barely missed her head, instead hitting the wall and falling onto the floor. Bar Jonah looked at Sherri with a steely gaze and said, "If you don't get out now, you may not be able to. It's going to get a *lot* worse if you don't." Sherri told Bar Jonah she knew what he was capable of and would start packing up her stuff. Bar Jonah told her to hurry it up. He wanted her out of the apartment.

* * *

Sherri had sold most of what she had brought with her, so there wasn't much to pack. Right before she carried out the last load to the car she had just bought from one of Pam's church friends, Bar Jonah came up to her and asked, if she thought God ever forgave people who committed murder. Sherri told him she believed people who are killers have a price to pay. Bar Jonah nodded. As he was walking away, Bar Jonah said that after a while though it just doesn't matter.

* * *

Some of the things that she didn't care about, Sherri left at Bar Jonah's. She just wanted to get gone as quickly as she could. All she wanted to do was to get the hell out of Great Falls. But before she left the city, Sherri called Detective Bellusci. Sherri had found the card Bellusci had left in Bar Jonah's door the day Zach disappeared. Bar Jonah had tossed it in his desk drawer. Sherri found it one of the times she was prowling. Sherri wrote Bellusci's number on a yellow sticky note and walked up the block to Deaconess Hospital to use a pay phone. She spoke with Bellusci and told him she had information about the Zach Ramsay case. She thought they should talk, it was important. Detective Bellusci and Officer Redenbauch met Sherri in the parking lot behind the HiHo. Sherri sat in Bellusci's car for almost an hour, telling him and Redenbauch what Bar Jonah had told her about the policeman and the old man. She also said she thought that somehow Pam was involved. She knew more than she was saying. There was no way Pam didn't know what was going on. Sherri thought Pam liked to play crazy when she thought she was being cornered; it was her way of taking the heat off. The longer Bellusci and Redenbauch listened to Sherri, the more they thought she was crazy. They thanked her for the information as she got out of Bellusci's unmarked car. Bellusci didn't see the need to follow up on what Sherri had told him.

* * *

Once Sherri was back in Idaho, she didn't think much about Bar Jonah. He wasn't her problem anymore, and she was glad to be gone.

CHAPTER SEVENTEEN

The end of the beginning

Things started to get bad between Pam and Bar Jonah shortly after Sherri moved out. A week after Halloween, Pam told Bar Jonah she wasn't his teddy bear anymore. She had decided to break off their engagement. The day after she told him the engagement was off, Pam moved out. Bar Jonah told Tyra he threw Pam out because she and Sherri had been pressing him to have a threesome. He was taught that sex outside of marriage was a sin. Bar Jonah said he told Pam and Sherri a threesome wasn't going to happen. Pam was also accusing him of having sex with all of the women at Hardee's, from "sixteen to sixty-two." Bar Jonah said he'd had enough. He was better off without her. Pam wasn't the girl for him.

When Pam moved out, she didn't tell Bar Jonah it was mostly because she had been sleeping with a man named Ron. Pam met Ron and Lou through a friend at church several months before. Both Ron and Lou thought Pam was beautiful and secretly gave her gifts and much needed affection. However, Ron won her heart. Pam lived in a fleabag motel on 10th Avenue for a week after she moved out of Bar Jonah's. Then she moved right in with Ron. She felt safe living with Ron, especially now that Bar Jonah was beginning to follow her. He had even egged her car a couple of times, she said. At least she had someone in her life that would protect her if things got bad with Bar Jonah. Pam plodded around Great Falls with Ron for the next couple of months. There sure wasn't much else to do around that town, she would say. Pam had saved a little money and Ron took pretty good care of her too. At least for a while. But their relationship was increasingly turning bitter too. She thought Ron was getting worse than Bar Jonah had ever been, screaming things all the time, calling Pam crazy. He'd have sex with her, but it was always when he wanted it and then it'd be over real quick. Even though Bar Jonah was strange and may have killed that boy, Pam thought he had probably been the love of her life. One morning in early January 1998, Pam packed up her altar, the few clothes she had, and started driving south. She was heading to Virginia Beach. She had some family there, plus the people down south understood voodoo. She'd have friends who would respect her position as a *Lyalorishas*, and if Pam was ever going to forget Bar Jonah, she had to leave Great Falls.

Barry Flannigan

Barry always ordered the same thing at Hardee's: a flame-broiled double cheeseburger with extra cheese, a large fries, and a chocolate shake. Sometimes he would shyly ask the counter help to make his shake thin. He was driving around he would say, and it was hard to suck the thick shake up through the thin straw. If Barry were going to stay, he'd just eat his shake with a spoon, not wanting to inconvenience anyone with an extra request. When Bar Jonah watched him from the fry station, he thought Barry looked like the typical abused kid, shy, gullible, and easily manipulated. Bar Jonah knew he would let you do whatever you wanted to him; guys like Barry were all alike. Barry's face was expressionless as he sat and ate. His arms would move, seemingly without being directed, and push food into his mouth. Then he would methodically chew and chew and chew. Finally he'd pitch his head back and swallow with an audible gulp. Eating was a burden. Barry ordered the same thing all the time. It helped to prevent distractions. This way Barry could languish in his unwavering state of humiliation and feeling used. Bar Jonah liked to walk out to the counter and watch Barry's careworn eyes fall toward the table top. His fair skin, delicate face, and reddish blond hair made Barry look like he was twelve, Bar Jonah thought.

It was one of those times again when Barry didn't have a place to stay, so he slept at the local shelter, sold a few drugs, and went from store to store, pocketing whatever he needed. Barry wasn't as mysterious as he was elusive. Most everything was a deception with Barry, but nothing more than his help-lessness. Barry lured men into taking care of him with his portrayal of frailty. At times he would sit at a table in front of the counter at Hardee's and, with his head down, glance over and meet Bar Jonah's eyes, holding them for a moment and then timidly look away. Barry never ordered if Bar Jonah was tending the counter. Instead he would sit down in a far corner of the restaurant and watch Bar Jonah until someone else took over. Barry preferred to go into the restaurant during dinnertime. This was when Bar Jonah might have to help at the counter. This was when Bar Jonah couldn't get away. This was when Barry could drive him crazy.

Bar Jonah saw Barry pull up in the parking lot in his battered powder-blue car. There were bumper stickers from everywhere on the car when Barry had bought it but Barry hadn't been anywhere. A lot of cars were in the parking lot that evening and Barry was sure Bar Jonah would be busy at the counter. He walked into the restaurant and didn't see Bar Jonah. He was sure Bar Jonah would be working that night, but he was nowhere to be seen. "I'll take a flame-broiled double cheese-burger with extra cheese, a large fries, and a chocolate shake," he said to the counter help.

The pimply-faced girl put the food on a scratched, red plastic tray and pushed it toward him. Her words clicked over her braces as she repeated the order back to Barry. When his food was ready, Barry picked up the tray, walked around the corner to the back of the restaurant, and sat down. The charbroiled smell of the cheeseburger began to reach Barry's nose as he folded back the paper covering the sandwich. Barry leaned down and inhaled, taking in the aroma. When he looked up, Bar Jonah was standing right beside the table. Barry was visibly startled. He had not seen or heard Bar Jonah come up, it was as though he just materialized. Bar Jonah looked at him and asked if his food tasted okay. Barry nodded yes. There was something about being so close to Bar Jonah that made Barry so nervous he started stuffing his mouth with food. Bar Jonah sat down across from Barry and told him to meet him back at the restaurant after he got off at nine. They would go back to his apartment, Bar Jonah said. Barry nodded. Bar Jonah reached over and took some food off of Barry's tray, got up, and walked away. Barry finished eating, got back in his car, and drove around for a while. He had a couple of hours before he was going to meet Bar Jonah.

* * *

Barry decided to go to the adult bookstore on 10th Avenue. He walked in the back alley entrance and went directly into one of the private booths and closed the door. He put two dollars in quarters into a slot and pushed gay when he was prompted for what kind of movie he wanted. Barry dropped his pants and sat down on a wobbly wooden chair. He was already hard and stroking his dick, when two men sucking each other appeared on the small screen recessed into the wall of the small booth.

Barry heard someone close the door on the booth beside his. He waited a few minutes when a hard dick appeared through the glory hole in the wall. Barry leaned over and wrapped his lips around the dick. The dick began to fuck Barry's mouth.

224

Barry strained his eyes to watch the action on the small screen, while the dick fucked his mouth. In a few minutes, the dick began to move faster. There were no moans or sighs, other than what was playing on the video, when the dick suddenly filled Barry's mouth with cum. Barry pulled his mouth off of the dick, wiped his chin clean with the sleeve of his shirt while still stroking his penis with the other. Barry started jerking himself faster as he began to think of Bar Jonah. In a few seconds Barry threw his head back and moaned quietly as he felt his hand become sticky with his cum. He rubbed the cum off of his hand onto the wall of the booth, pulled his pants up and left for Hardee's.

* * *

It was a little before nine when Bar Jonah saw Barry drive up. Barry stayed in his car smoking a cigarette and drinking the cup of coffee he had picked up on the way. Not long after Barry arrived, Bar Jonah untied the drawstrings around his waist and started working the top loop of the apron over his head. As always, the neckpiece got caught on his double chin while he was trying to shimmy it over the back of his head. He tossed the greasy apron on top of some frozen meat, put a cigarette in his mouth, lighting it before he walked out the door.

Barry's car leaned noticeably further to one side, when Bar Jonah opened the door and climbed in. Bar Jonah looked at him and told him to turn right out of Hardee's, his place was just a few blocks down the street on the left, he said. Barry noticed how Bar Jonah smelled of old grease and crotch rot. Barry didn't mind. That night he wouldn't have to stay at the shelter, plus he might be able to pick up a few things laying around Bar Jonah's apartment that he could turn over for some extra cash. At the stop light at 10th Street and 26th Avenue, Barry coyly leaned over to Bar Jonah and told him he had never done anything like this before, he was a virgin. Bar Jonah said nothing.

As soon as Barry turned left onto 26th, he immediately made another turn into Bar Jonah's parking lot.

* * *

The smell almost knocked Barry over when Bar Jonah opened the door to his apartment. He had *never* smelled anything like that before. Barry told Bar Jonah his apartment reeked of rotted deer. He wanted to know if Bar Jonah was a hunter. Bar Jonah said no. Then he smiled and told Barry he found the odor refreshing. He walked toward the bedroom, ordering Barry to follow him. When they got to the bedroom, Bar Jonah took his clothes off and climbed into bed. Barry tripped over one of the half-dozen trash bags, filled with empty tin cans, that were stacked beside Bar Jonah's bed. His eyes were drawn to the deep cut crevice on Bar Jonah's right leg. Barry was also shocked when he saw how small Bar Jonah's dick was.

Barry took his clothes off and climbed into bed with Bar Jonah. Bar Jonah reached under the bed and grabbed a piece of orange rope. He rolled over and straddled Barry's chest, pinning him onto the bed. Barry tried to push him off, but Bar Jonah weighed more than 300 pounds; he couldn't budge him. Bar Jonah grabbed Barry by the hair, lifted his head up and slipped the rope around his neck. Barry protested. Bar Jonah told him to shut up; he wasn't going to kill him. He said he was going to make him pass out right when he came. He'd like it. He was an expert. Bar Jonah pressed his full weight against Barry's chest while tightening the rope around his neck. The pressure on Barry's chest was terrible. When he exhaled, Bar Jonah's weight prevented him from then inhaling. Barry was sure he was going to suffocate. Then Bar Jonah began lifting himself slightly off of Barry's chest, allowing him to take a short breath. Barry was beginning to panic, trying to suck in as much air as he could. When Bar Jonah raised himself up off of Barry's chest, he tightened the rope causing him to momentarily black out. Bar Jonah now had a rhythm going, waking

Barry up and then, making him black out again. Bar Jonah was reaching around with his other hand stroking Barry's dick up and down. Finally, Bar Jonah lifted himself off of Barry's chest allowing him to take in a deep breath. Bar Jonah wanted Barry to come, jerking his dick insistently. Right as Barry came, Bar Jonah pulled hard on the rope and slammed his fat ass into Barry's chest causing him to pass out again.

* * *

Barry knew he wasn't dead when he began to wake up and feel air easily filling his lungs. His chest hurt and his neck burned from the rope, but he had never experienced anything like that before. When Barry opened his eyes he saw Bar Jonah sitting beside him on the bed. Bar Jonah quickly reached over, clutched Barry's hair in his hand and shoved his dick into Barry's mouth. Bar Jonah's dick was so small Barry had to roll his tongue around to find it; he also almost gagged from the smell of Bar Jonah's crotch. With both hands, Bar Jonah held Barry's mouth tight against his dick coming almost immediately. After Bar Jonah came, he pulled Barry's mouth off of his dick and pushed him back onto the pillow. Bar Jonah leaned over and got a cigarette from the night stand. He slipped it between his lips and took a long drag, as the flame from the lighter cast a loutish shadow of Bar Jonah's head against the dark ceiling. He offered Barry a cigarette. Barry said, no, he couldn't smoke yet. He was still too stuporous.

* * *

Bar Jonah laid his head on his pillow and stared at the ceiling. He drew the smoke through his cigarette, sucking it far down into his lungs. As his chest began to deflate, a furtive veil of smoke curled out of his nose, rolling over his mustache, rising upward, mottling the light in his street lamp-lit bedroom. He snuffed out the cigarette against the wall and flipped the butt through the air, hearing it softly bounce off the thin bent metal blinds. Bar Jonah tucked his arms down to his side, cupping the undersides of his substantial belly with his hands to keep it from rolling away from him. For a brief moment he likened his huge abdomen to a sailor on the deck of a ship without a tether, being tossed hither and yon by a rough sea. Bar Jonah then abandoned himself to feeling intoxicated under the influence of the reverie of his domination.

Bar Jonah told Barry he could stay the night. In fact, he wanted him to move in. For a moment, Barry thought he was dreaming. Could he really have a warm bed to sleep in for the rest of the winter? Barry finally fell sound asleep waking several times in the night to Bar Jonah's loud, wet, snoring. The next morning Barry rolled over and asked Bar Jonah if he really had asked him to move in. He may have misunderstood him in his state of erotic bliss. Bar Jonah said yes. Even in his delight at having a warm place to stay, Barry was nervous about Bar Jonah. He had never had sex like that but he also never had anyone completely take control of him. Once they had got in bed, there was nothing Barry could have done to stop Bar Jonah. He did what he wanted to do. And for a moment, he had thought Bar Jonah was going to kill him. Barry had no other place else to go; he told Bar Jonah he would stay. Through sleepy eyes, Barry saw Bar Jonah step behind his closet door. The bright flame of a match was at once replaced by the breathing orange glow of Bar Jonah's cigarette. A brief second later, dense cerulean smoke and the smell of sulfur filled the bedroom. Barry turned over and went back to sleep.

When Barry got up, he found that Bar Jonah had already left. There was a note on the kitchen counter, next to the coffee pot, "See ya later my friend, please lock the door when you leave—Have a nice day—Hope you had a better night—a virgin—Hah."

* * *

Bar Jonah got Barry a job at Hardee's in late spring of 1998. Everyone knew they lived together, but one of the shift managers said they didn't give a shit. Bar Jonah got tired of always being asked to work extra shifts. He had been at Hardee's three years and had seniority; he demanded respect. Bar Jonah told Barry he was sick and tired of them being bothered on their days off by the phone calls telling them to come into work. By September, he'd had enough. Bar Jonah sat down and wrote a letter to the manager:

Attention, Hardee's managers, & supervisors: You will not! I repeat, you will not call Barry & my residence. We never gave you our telephone number nor do we want you to have our telephone number. If we get anymore phone calls from any of you for any reason, we will view this as harassment and take legal action. We are getting sick and tired of your harassing phone calls and threats of being capped, if we don't come in and so on. If these phone calls or verbal threats continue we will take further actions with the courts and/or other law enforcement agencies.

Sincerely,
Nathan Bar-Jonah.,
P. S. Do not call us again for any reason

CHAPTER EIGHTEEN

Lori Big Leggins

On Christmas Day, 1998 Lori Big Leggins, her children, Roland Johnston, and Stormy Ackerman and her husband Gerald moved into the small two-bedroom apartment above Bar Jonah's. Lori's sister, Tanya Big Leggins, was also living with the family. Tanya's son, Stanley, was planning on moving down from the Fort Peck reservation over in far northeast Montana, after school was out. Lori was five feet tall and weighed over 350 pounds. She walked sway back, seemingly being pulled along by a massive belly that dragged against the top of her knobby knees. Lori's deep-set eyes offset a broad nose that lay flattened against a slightly scalloped, Pekinese face framed in long, coal-black hair. Her kids always seemed to be getting into something. Even though her husband lived with them, the boys were always starving for a man's attention. They pretty much ran all over the neighborhood. Everyone around the area knew them. They were polite boys, the neighbors would say, but their parents sure didn't play much close attention to what they did. Rarely a day went by, in good weather, when one of the boys didn't almost get run over from darting in and out of traffic on 10th Avenue. There wasn't much she could do, Lori would gigglingly say. They just ran wild. One of the first things

Lori noticed when they moved into the apartment was the smell. They looked all over the place but they couldn't figure out where it was coming from. Lori had even said something about it to the manager when they first looked at the apartment. He assured her he would take care of it. The carpet probably just needed to be shampooed.

* * *

Lori thought the blimpy-looking man who lived in the apartment below them was nice when he offered to hold the stairwell door open for her when she was moving in. He told her he was on his way over to his mother's to have Christmas dinner. She was fixing a big Christmas ham with sweet potatoes. He'd be back later if she needed any help, he said. Lori noticed right off how her new neighbor didn't get upset when her youngest boy, Stormy, ran around the corner of the building and slammed right into him. The man just reached down and put his arm around her boy's shoulder. He sure was strong, Lori thought, seeing how Stormy couldn't do anything but squirm, until the man took his arm from around him. Then he told Lori to sit her box down and wait just a minute. It was Christmas day and he wanted to get something for her kid. Lori told the man that the boy who ran into him wasn't her only kid; she had another one upstairs. The man said he would get a little something for him too. He turned around, slipped his key into his front door lock and turned the doorknob. As the door began to open, the stink that Lori had been smelling upstairs, rolled out of the man's apartment like it was alive. A hint of the untameable odor even hung in the air after a wind gust twisted its way through the breezeway. When the man came back out, Lori said his place sure did smell bad. All the men she's grown up around were hunters. She knew that smell, just like something was dead in there. The man told her he had just butchered a deer and then handed her a small toy car for each of her kids. He was an antique dealer, he said, who specialized in toys for boys. He laughingly said that he was just an overgrown boy himself. As he walked away, the man reached out to shake her hand and said "Merry Christmas," adding that he was looking forward to getting to know her boys.

* * *

Lori had never been able to get the kids much because money was always tight. Even though Gerald had gotten a job at the refinery, they were still on public assistance and just barely scraping by. After they paid the bills and set aside money for cigarettes, beer, and Keno there wasn't very much left over for the boys. Lori noticed that the skinny blond-headed fellow, who lived with the fat man, didn't seem to like her boys. Mostly he wouldn't even speak to them, just mainly ignored them when he saw them. In fact, Lori wondered if he might even be a queer. He struck Lori as being real selfish and wanting her new friend all to himself. The flit acted like he was jealous of how much Lori and her boys liked Bar Jonah and how good he was to them.

* * *

Lori and Gerald never seemed to be at home. Lori liked to smoke and drink the free beer while she played Keno, at one of the local casinos until all hours of the morning. She always smelled of sweat and cigarette smoke when she did get home. Her husband worked late at the refinery monitoring stack temperatures and didn't have much to do with her or the boys. His pride was in his means to provide a regular paycheck. Bar Jonah told Lori he had seen that she was usually out late. He'd be happy to watch the kids for her anytime. Even though he'd always wanted them, Bar Jonah never had any kids of his own and it would make him feel good to help her out. The boys could even stay overnight if she got stuck. It was no bother; he'd always find a way to make room. All she had to do was call the boys and tell them to go on downstairs. He was always at home at night, because he didn't have to work the late shift at Hardee's anymore since he'd been promoted to manager. The antique toy business was mostly on the weekends. The boys could feel like his place was theirs too. Bar Jonah also told Lori he was also involved in undercover police work but he wasn't allowed to talk about it. The best part was that Lori didn't even have to pay him. Being with her boys was payment enough, he said, they were a lot of fun, especially little rambunctious Stormy.

Roland, the older boy, always seemed to have some kind of problem he needed to talk to Bar Jonah about. He was getting to that age where he needed the advice of a man. Bar Jonah was quickly becoming his best friend. Roland could talk to Bar Jonah about anything.

All of Lori's kids were pretty slow and in the special classes at school. But Bar Jonah said he never once made them feel like "retards". In fact he said he thought they were real smart. Stormy though was a lot more messed up than Roland. The kid was just crazy-acting at times. Bar Jonah told Barry that he thought Lori was really the dumbest of the bunch though. But, she was nice and let Bar Jonah spend as much time with the boys as he wanted. Lori thought Bar Jonah was the best neighbor she'd ever had.

Roland, Stormy, and Stanley

The boys loved to sit on the couch and eat potato chips and hot dogs with Bar Jonah while they watched videos. Bar Jonah liked to show the boys the movie, *Alive* over and over again. He said it was one of his favorites. Bar Jonah told the boys that it was a true story about the Uruguayan soccer team, whose plane had crashed in the Andes Mountains, way far away, down in South America. Then when there wasn't any food left, the survivors had to eat the unlucky ones who had died in the crash, just to stay alive. The boys and Bar Jonah would all pile on the couch together, sitting on top of each other, always playing around, pushing into each other. Having fun. Sometimes when Bar Jonah and Roland were talking, they would eat a few bags of chips just themselves. Bar Jonah listened attentively as Roland tried to make sense of getting older. One day he secretly confided to Roland that he was a US marshal who worked undercover as an antique dealer. Sometimes Bar Jonah got called away by headquarters to go on secret assignments. Roland was impressed and told Bar Jonah that he could trust him to keep his true identity a secret. Even though it was against the rules, Bar Jonah even pinned his badge on Roland's tee shirt and let him wear it around the apartment. Sometimes, Roland got to wear Bar Jonah's US marshal's cap too. But, like everything else they did together, Roland was not allowed to tell anyone. Bar Jonah wanted to protect Roland. He didn't want him to get in trouble for impersonating a lawman.

* * *

Bar Jonah was always kidding Roland about his fat roly-poly belly that hung out over his black sweat pants. Roland would laugh, raise his shirt and squeeze the fat rolls between his fingers. Bar Jonah liked to bet Roland a hotdog that he had a bigger belly. He'd raise his shirt, push out on his massive stomach and yell for Roland to look. Roland would laugh when he saw Bar Jonah being so silly. Sometimes Bar Jonah liked to take pictures of the kids to add to his photo albums. Bar Jonah was a professional photographer and had been part of his camera club when he was in high school. Roland could be a professional too, Bar Jonah said. Especially when Bar Jonah saw the picture Roland had taken of him, sitting on the couch, making a funny face with his fingers in his ears. Roland had even captured Bar Jonah sticking his tongue out. That was something only a *real* photographer could do. Roland liked that he got Bar Jonah's United States Marshal tee shirt in the picture too. Right after Roland took the picture of Bar Jonah in his US marshal shirt, Stormy came running into the living room. Bar Jonah grabbed Stormy, picked him up, and sat down on the love seat, tucking Stormy under his left arm, yelling to Roland to take their picture. Stormy's face was covered in chocolate and his blue shirt and shorts were wet and dirty. Bar Jonah joked that Stormy looked like an ice cream cone that had been dipped in chocolate. Roland turned around when he heard Bar Jonah yell, lifted the camera to his left eye and snapped the picture. Boy, did he get a good shot, Bar Jonah said. Two great pictures on one roll of film, that was something a lot of professionals couldn't even do. Roland felt Bar Jonah was so nice to him that he was becoming the dad he never had.

* * *

Barry didn't like the boys hanging around so much. He thought they were a pain in the ass. Stormy was out of control, Barry would complain. He was always running through the apartment, screaming you stink, you stink, and knocking the knick-knacks over. It really pissed Barry off when Stormy used the couch as a trampoline, springing high in the air and landing, most of the time, in Bar Jonah's recliner. Bar Jonah didn't mind though. Sometimes he would catch Stormy in mid-jump, swing him around, fall down on the couch, pull up Stormy's sleeveless, blue cartoon shirt, rub his belly, and tickle his ribs. At times, Stormy would become hysterical when Bar Jonah tickled him. But Bar Jonah wouldn't stop, all the while telling Stormy how much fun they were having.

Stormy always made a mess when Bar Jonah gave him a candy bar, smearing chocolate all over his mouth. Bar Jonah thought it was so funny. He would laugh and laugh and laugh at Stormy. Then Bar Jonah would grab Stormy as he darted by, hold him down, and lick his face clean. Sometimes Stormy's arms and legs would get scuffed and bruised, but that was just part of the fun. One time, Lori saw Bar Jonah hold Stormy down and lick the chocolate off of his lips. She laughed and said it was the only time she had ever seen Stormy's face not smudged with food. Sometimes Roland would get pissed when Bar Jonah pinched Stormy's butt. He'd yell for Bar Jonah to leave his little brother alone and make Stormy go back upstairs with him. Stormy would yell and scream while Roland was carrying him up the flight of stairs. Pretty soon Bar Jonah was knocking at their door, holding a couple of just heated-up hot dogs rubbed just right with ketchup, ready to play again. Roland always forgave Bar Jonah when he kidded around with Stormy. Barry would yell at Bar Jonah and tell him he needed to stop that kind of shit. Bar Jonah would tell Barry to mind his own fucking business. It was his place, Bar Jonah would say. Even though Barry paid Bar Jonah a $100 out of each check, he was still a guest. Bar Jonah said he could go just as quickly as he came. It was still cold outside and Barry didn't want to be stuck out on the streets again. He thought it was best if he kept his mouth shut.

* * *

Lori was always hitting Bar Jonah up for some extra cash to pay her rent. Bar Jonah complained but most of the time he found some way to get her the money she asked for. Lori had met Bob a couple of times when he came over to visit Bar Jonah. She told Bar Jonah that Bob looked like a smacked ass and that he probably still had the first nickel he ever made. He just had that cheapskate kind of look about him. Sometimes when Bob brought Tyra over, Bar Jonah would hit up Bob for some money for Lori in front of Tyra. Bob always said no. Tyra's head would follow her eyes to the ground when she heard Bob tell Bar Jonah that he didn't have any money: she knew he was lying. Tyra always made sure that Bob noticed her disappointment at his stinginess. Bob frustratedly would pull out his billfold and grudgingly give Bar Jonah however much he said he wanted. Tyra's eyes brightened when she lifted her head back up, letting her pleasure be known with Bob's generous change

237

of heart. When they got back to her place, Tyra never failed to walk into her bedroom, open one of her dresser drawers, move her unmentionables aside and count out the exact amount of money Bob had given to Bar Jonah. Tyra always folded the money in half, before she slipped it into Bob's out reaching hand. Lori would wait until after Bob and Tyra left, before she told Bar Jonah that the landlord was on her again about not paying the rent. There wudn't enough money for food either. Bar Jonah would put his hand into his pants pocket, pull out the money that Bob had given him and hand it to Lori, saying he was sure glad that he could help her out. Lori always thanked Bar Jonah and tucked the money into the pocket of her stretchy pants.

Not with my kids either

Kerri Winn, her son Tyler, and her husband Martin lived in the apartment right next to Bar Jonah. She had seen the boys coming and going out of Bar Jonah's place at all hours of the day and night. Kerri had also heard the yelling and screaming through the thin drywall, since they had moved in just a few weeks before. It was weighing on her mind.

Just as the sun was beginning to go in for the night, eight-year-old Tyler came running home. He told his mother that he wanted the fat man next door to leave him alone. He kept rolling a ball to Tyler, asking him if he wanted to come into his apartment and play. Martin, who was a slightly built man with thick glasses and thin lips, went outside and found Bar Jonah standing in the breezeway holding the small blue ball. Martin asked Bar Jonah why he was trying to get his step-son into his apartment. Bar Jonah said he just wanted to play with him. Martin told him he was a grown man and too fucking old to go around trying to play with kids. Bar Jonah took a step forward and shoved his chest into Martin's, pushing him into the brick wall. Bar Jonah's eyes bore into Martin's.

He needed to mind his own fucking business, Bar Jonah threateningly said.

Martin's well-toned arm lithely negotiated its way around Bar Jonah's belly shoal like an eel. His steel like thumb snapped hard into the plexus of Bar Jonah's throat, pushing him against the rust stained brick wall. When Martin leaned close to Bar Jonah's face, he could smell the effluvium of stale cigarette smoke on his breath. In a quiet, controlled voice, Martin said, "One time, one warning, you ever go near my kid again, I'll kill you." Bar Jonah kept his arms down at his sides, making no threatening moves and muttered that he was just trying to be a good neighbor. Martin shoved Bar Jonah with his thumb, turned around, and walked away.

When he got back to their apartment Martin told Kerri what had happened. Kerri knew Martin didn't make idle threats. He'd been a sergeant in the Army Rangers; Bar Jonah wouldn't stand a chance if Martin went after him. After they talked, Kerri and Martin decided it was best to find another place to live. Kerri had no concerns about Martin being able to protect Tyler; if he was there. But neither of them could watch Tyler all of the time. It was best to get him out of harm's way.

Two weeks later, when Kerri was loading the last box onto the moving truck, she saw Lori drive up. Kerri had tried to catch Lori at home since Martin had had it out with Bar Jonah. But she was never there. A bedraggled Gerald answered the door one of the times Kerri had tried to find Lori. Kerri tried to talk to Gerald but he said he was tired from working so late and Kerri should talk with Lori. Then he had closed the door, leaving Kerri standing on the well-scuffed burlap WELCOME mat.

Kerri walked up to Lori as she was getting out of the car and started telling her about Bar Jonah trying to get Tyler to come into his apartment. Lori waved her hands up and down and told Kerri that Bar Jonah was a good man. He babysat for her kids all the time. Kerri, and especially her husband, should keep their nose out of other people's business. Lori said Bar Jonah had told her how Martin had threatened to kill him, just for being nice to his kid. Martin sounded like a lunatic who could fly off of the handle and hurt somebody. Lori said she was glad they were moving out. Kerri told Lori she thought Bar Jonah was a child molester and Lori shouldn't be letting her kids around him. Lori turned around and grabbed the case of beer off the front seat that she had bought at the drive-through on the way home. She leaned back, rested the beer box on top of her belly and walked, shifting from side-to-side, toward the stairwell. Lori pressed the case of beer against the side of the apartment building with her stomach, turned the handle on the storm door and swung it open with her foot, catching it with her right butt cheek as it began to spring back close. Lori then raised her right hand high in the air and extended her middle finger toward Kerri, before she made her way up the stairs.

The hunted

After school, the kids always stopped over at Bar Jonah's for a snack. Bar Jonah never failed to have hot dogs and chips ready to feed their hungry bellies. The school lunches barely offered enough food for growing boys, he would say. Stormy always had dried sleep dust caked in the corners of his tired eyes when he walked in Bar Jonah's front door. After a couple of hot dogs, a plateful of chips and some pop, Stormy's eyes would start to get heavy and his head would begin to nod. Bar Jonah would say he thought it would be a good idea if they took a nap together. After hot dogs he was tired too. He'd pick Stormy up, kick the debris in the hallway aside, and carry him into his bedroom, lay Stormy down in bed and tuck him under the covers. Bar Jonah rarely had anything on when the boys came over except his underwear. "We're all guys," he'd say, so he didn't have much to take off when he and Stormy crawled into his comfy bed. Bar Jonah always held Stormy close against him to make him feel safe.

After school was out in June, Tanya's boy, Stanley came down from the reservation to live upstairs with the rest of the clan. Stanley was a little older than Stormy and never stopped talking. Lori said he could rattle on forever and a day and still end up not saying a thing. He sure liked to be around people too. Ne'er missing a chance to corner someone and tell them what was on his mind. Like Roland and Stormy, Stanley was in special classes too.

* * *

In the beginning, Stanley didn't come down to visit Bar Jonah as much as Roland and Stormy. But once Roland convinced Stanley about how much fun and good food they always had at Bar Jonah's, Stanley started coming down all of the time too; sometimes even more than Stormy. Stanley liked to laugh and jump on top of Bar Jonah, Roland, and Stormy when they got into a great big huddle on the couch. He'd lie in wait until they all looked like a lump, where you couldn't tell one from the other, then take a running start, spring high in the air and land smack dab right on top of the bunch of them. "Just like popping the cherry on top of a banana split," Bar Jonah would say, as he'd pull an arm out of the clump, reach up and pull Stanley down into the thicket. Stanley was the boy that Bar Jonah would later try to hang.

It wasn't long after Stanley started coming down to play that Bar Jonah sat down on the couch beside him, reached out one day, and got him in a headlock. Then Bar Jonah rolled his hand into a fist and began grinding away on top of Stanley's head with his knuckles. Roland started laughing and told Bar Jonah to keep on giving Stanley a Dutch rub. Bar Jonah was laughing too. They were being so silly. Stanley tried to pull his head out of the crook of Bar Jonah arm, yelling that Bar Jonah was hurting him. Bar Jonah rubbed harder. Roland thought it was so

241

funny that he had tears running down his face. Stanley twisted his body around and swung his right leg up in the air, catching Bar Jonah in the face with his knee. Bar Jonah opened up the buckle of his arm and let Stanley out of the headlock. Stanley, trying not to cry, reached up with his hand and began rubbing the top of his bruised head. Then Stanley felt Bar Jonah's hands encircle his throat and begin to squeeze, while shaking his head back and forth. Roland screamed at Bar Jonah to leave Stanley alone. Bar Jonah continued to squeeze Stanley's neck. Stanley's face was starting to turn blue and red marks from Bar Jonah's hands were beginning to come up around Stanley's neck. Roland jumped up from where he was sitting, went over, and started trying to pull Bar Jonah's hands from around Stanley's neck. Bar Jonah's eyes were glazed over. Then Roland screamed again for Bar Jonah to stop choking Stanley. Bar Jonah suddenly released his hands from around Stanley's neck and shoved him back into the corner of the couch. Bar Jonah said he'd had enough of the brats, as he stormed down the hallway toward his bedroom.

Roland pulled on Stanley's arm and said they had to get out of Bar Jonah's apartment and go back upstairs. Roland lifted Stanley to his feet and helped him make his way out of the apartment and up the stairs. It so happened that Gerald was at home. When he saw how red and swollen Stanley's neck was, he asked what the hell had happened. Roland told Gerald what Bar Jonah had done to his cousin. Gerald stormed out the door and down the stairs, saying out loud that he had told Lori to keep the boys away from that queer but she wouldn't listen. When Gerald got to the bottom of the stairs, he rolled up his hand into a fist and punched Bar Jonah's door. "Come out here and try to grab my neck, you fucking freak," he screamed.

* * *

After Roland and Stanley ran out of the apartment, Bar Jonah came out of his bedroom. He went to the refrigerator and took

242

out a new package of bologna, sat down on the couch and started eating slice after slice. Bar Jonah never made a sound as he listened to Gerald bruising his knuckles on his front door. Just as Bar Jonah folded the last piece of bologna into a triangle and pushed it into his mouth, Gerald gave up. Bar Jonah could hear Gerald's heavy boots slamming down on the hard rubber slip guards, barely tacked to the stairs, as he stomped back up to his apartment.

Later that evening, Lori got a talking to from Gerald about not letting the boys go back downstairs. Stanley must have done something *really* bad, Lori told Gerald. Bar Jonah wouldn't have tried to hurt him otherwise. Plus the marks on Stanley's neck would go away in a couple of days. Lori told Gerald she didn't want him to hurt Bar Jonah. He was her friend and he took good care of the boys. She'd be sure and talk to Tanya about Stanley behaving himself when he was down there at Bar Jonah's. Lori did tell Gerald she'd talk to Bar Jonah about choking the boys. If there was a problem, he should come and talk to her first.

Not with my boy you don't

Bar Jonah had called Doc right after the boys had moved upstairs and told him about his good fortune. A few weeks later, Bar Jonah told Doc that the boys came to visit him all the time. They even stayed overnight. Doc anxiously joked that it must be making Bar Jonah's *jouissance* throb like a plucked bass string. Bar Jonah could hear the jealously in Doc's voice, especially when Doc slyly asked if their complexion was dark like Negro boys. Doc especially liked Negro boys, he said. Bar Jonah deliberately didn't answer, instead laughing, saying that he sure was spending a lot of money on hot dogs and potato chips. Doc graciously offered to help Bar Jonah babysit sometime. Doc didn't think he would feel threatened by Bar Jonah if the boys were there too, so he offered his house for a big slumber party. They could all have fun together. Bar Jonah retorted, "No way! These are my kids." Doc admired Bar Jonah's relentless dedication to loving boys more than any man he had ever met. However, Bar Jonah's selfishness seemed uncalled for. These boys were not like Zach. They weren't "keepers." They were but mere playthings to be enjoyed and then discarded. Certainly they were not worthy of being made a fuss over.

* * *

Bar Jonah saw himself as a pedophile among pedophiles. Even though Bar Jonah let Doc believe that he had much to teach him, Bar Jonah just played Doc along. Bar Jonah was pleased that he had been able to introduce a man of Doc's age to so many new pleasures. Doc hadn't known much about the delicacies of special game meat, until he met Bar Jonah. Bar Jonah taught Doc how to fillet and cure exotic meats. There is nothing better if you cut the meat right off of the bone yourself, Bar Jonah liked to counsel. Doc said Bar Jonah made the best chili and spaghetti sauce that he'd ever tasted. But, Bar Jonah was selfish with his meat too, not letting Doc have as much as he'd like; it seemed like Bar Jonah was always running low. Doc would be the first to get some fresh meat just as soon as Bar Jonah could get some more.

* * *

Bar Jonah also taught Doc how to go out and set up situations in public places, where they could feel the tiny breath of a frantic child warming their cheeks until his lost mommy could be found.

Bar Jonah and Doc would regularly drive around for hours, going from store to store, until they discovered a little boy, separated from his mother, standing alone in a deserted aisle. There were always misplaced children waiting to be found, especially in toy stores. Bar Jonah and Doc were never disappointed.

It always happened the same way. The boy would be standing alone, frantically turning his head from side to side, his tender young sniffly nose red and raw. Bubbly tears would be rolling down his puffy cheeks, ripe for the reassurance that he was safe, until his mommy came to find him. Bar Jonah also taught Doc how to more convincingly look worried and concerned, as they tightly carried the child from aisle to aisle, playfully peaking around each corner; "No, there didn't seem to be a lost mommy down that way. Let's try another aisle, okay," Bar Jonah would hushedly murmur into the child's ear.

Their mothers were so thankful to see the two kindly men, one old and looking frail, securely comforting their distressed and frightened child, who had suddenly disappeared from their sight. How had he gotten away so fast, the stray parent would almost always ask. To those ensconced in their desperation, Bar Jonah's avid attention to their children was soothing to their misery. But to some observers, who did not live in a world of emotional welfare, Bar Jonah's and Doc's charades were seen as menacing. On those rare occasions when he was confronted, Bar Jonah's face would suddenly acquire the somber immobility of a dead man. Then he would become incensed with indignation and silent rage, turn his back, and walk away with the child still clutched tightly against his chest, daring the concerned observer to come after him.

Bar Jonah and Doc were as careful as could be at selecting just the right kind of boy. It took a lot of practice for Bar Jonah and Doc to be able to develop their collective sense of selection.

Doc said they had to look and act a certain way or else someone would call the law on them. He always insisted on wearing a dark blue suit with a tie when they went hunting. There had to be a tie. In Montana, almost no one wears suits and ties. When someone was seen in a suit and a tie, they were immediately thought to be respectable. Probably a doctor or lawyer, Doc would advise. Doc also insisted that even though Bar

Jonah didn't own a suit, he *had* to wear a tie. Two men walking around in ties screamed respectability. Doc regularly tried to make Bar Jonah put out his cigarette before he went into the stores. He was rarely successful. Even though it was illegal to smoke in stores, Bar Jonah would intemperately go into a building with a lighted cigarette precariously balanced on his lower lip. One time Doc said he was flabbergasted when a security guard in the local store approached Bar Jonah and told him to put out his cigarette. Bar Jonah pulled out his US marshal's badge, that he had mounted on a piece of hard black leather, from his pocket and told the security guard to mind his own fucking business before he arrested him. The security guard told Bar Jonah he didn't care who he was, he wasn't allowed to smoke in the mall. Bar Jonah grabbed the security guard by the arm, spun him around, and pushed him up against the wall. Assume the position, Bar Jonah said. The guard did as he was told, as Doc stood in disbelief. Bar Jonah sweep kicked the guard's feet apart, while pressing his hand into the small of the guard's back. All the while Bar Jonah continued to puff on his cigarette and blow smoke in the direction of the guard's face. Bar Jonah called the security guard a rent-a-cop and told him that if he'd apologize, he wouldn't press charges against him for interfering with a real lawman in the performance of his duty. With Bar Jonah pressing him into the wall, the guard turned his head around and sheepishly said he was sorry, he didn't mean to be disrespectful, and most certainly not to interfere. The guard told Bar Jonah he had hopes of going to the police academy someday and the last thing he needed on his record was an interfering charge. Bar Jonah said he understood and wouldn't cause any problems for him. But Bar Jonah said the security guard had to understand that when a peace officer flashes a badge, it means you are to do what the fuck you are told; especially a Fed. Bar Jonah took the guard by the back of the shirt collar, pulled him away from the wall, and spun him around. Doc was amazed at how adroitly Bar Jonah whirled the guard around like a toy top. Bar Jonah then reached out and extended his hand. He hoped to see the security guard in the line of duty. It's hard to find good men who think for themselves. The security guard, grateful the US marshal wasn't going to press charges, eagerly shook Bar Jonah's hand, thanking him profusely. Doc, who was laughing hysterically, said that even he could not believe Bar Jonah's audacity.

After the confrontation with the security guard, Doc told Bar Jonah that if he hoped to live a long life outside of the eyes of the law he had to become, what Doc called, more stylish. Bar Jonah always seemed to get what he wanted, but he was crude and unsophisticated in the way he got it, Doc would continuously complain. He had lived to be a very old man. Yes there were many bouts with the law, but always for relatively short stretches. Jail was unavoidable; it was just part of spending your life being dedicated to loving boys. But one had to keep the time inside to a minimum, because the time on the outside with those so in need of affection was what mattered. The time outside was the time one could spend offering boys the love they deserved. So few understood.

Doc said Bar Jonah had the keenest ability to charm boys that he had ever seen. Bar Jonah told Doc that he had been honing his sense of finding boys since he was a youngster. He was able to let the boys see that his love for them was not a sham. When a boy feels that a man is being a sham, he will recognize it and feel an aversion to the love being offered. Doc liked to call the boys he and Bar Jonah found, their *muzhiks* or boys who had almost no breeding and who, like a dry barren field, needed to be tilled and cultivated. These were little Dickens's urchins who, in their own delightful ways, were begging to be rescued and loved by a Fagan. But Doc, laughing through his Truman Capote snort, would announce that he was not an impostor like Fagan. He truly loved boys. But boys could only be loved for a short time. It was always temporary, as they were always just on loan, Doc would emphasize, because they always got older. And when they did, they lost their delightfulness and became demanding. And when they became demanding, they just had to be turned back out onto the streets.

* * *

One of Doc's gravest concerns was that after Bar Jonah had discovered a boy who was ripe with the possibility of receiving tender affection, he would at some point always turn violent and try to choke the youngster. Sometimes in Doc's lucid moments, he would ask himself if he was wrong about Bar Jonah. Did he really love boys the same way Doc did, or was there something more beastly about Bar Jonah? Doc said that he would never try to hurt a boy unless the boy tried to hurt him first. Then of course, it may be unavoidable.

Doc never let his doubts about Bar Jonah linger for long. Like flashes of light, Doc would push the thoughts out of his mind just as quickly as they would appear. He always came back to all of the special things that Bar Jonah had done for him. Doc deeply appreciated Bar Jonah for showing him how to "taffy-up" his world. With Doc becoming so old, it took more for Doc not to become bored. Bar Jonah had brought a new sense of vitality and excitement into Doc's life. Doc's deepest fear was not going to jail, but of dying and disappearing as though he had never existed.

On those occasions when Doc saw Bar Jonah lose his composure, Doc feared that if Bar Jonah weren't more careful, he would end up spending the rest of his life in prison, or worse. Bar Jonah assured Doc that the only way he could end up behind bars again was if he made a mistake and left something behind. And now he had learned to *never* leave anything behind. Besides, Bar Jonah said, he wasn't eighteen any longer. After he got out of Bridgewater in 1991, he had beaten every rap the cops had accused him of. He wasn't about to go back inside. But, when the tribulations of life did come his way, he turned to Christ to get him through. He and Christ had so much in common. They had both suffered so much.

Even though Doc was in awe of Bar Jonah's keen sense of finding lonely boys, Doc always hedged his admiration with caution, especially after Zach. And, because of Zach, Doc's admiration for Bar Jonah was clouded by a deep resentment. Zach had been the one special boy that Doc thought he might keep for a long time. Zach was still so young when Doc brought him along and into his life. And, Doc was so old.

Doc told Bar Jonah that Zach had awakened a love in him that he had not felt since he was a young man. Zach reminded Doc of another boy he had known more than fifty years before. Like that boy, Zach stirred the embers of his heart. But Doc's love for the boy of so long ago was unrequited. Doc's favorite book was *Der Tod in Venedig*, Death in Venice. Like the book's main character, Gustav von Aschenbach, Doc began to fret about the way his body was betraying him. In those private moments, when Doc looked into the mirror, he would see a decaying carcass. Doc thought his face looked like a chocolate chip cookie, warm just out of the oven. Just a few moments before in the oven light, the cookies were proud and upright, then, in the blink of an eye, they had collapsed and fallen. In an attempt to become more attractive and youthful, Doc began to wear outlandishly loud, colorful clothes, thinking that somehow, they made him more desirable. However, others would say they made him look like a pathetic nitwit. Like Tadzio, Aschenbach's own unrequited love interest, the lost boy of many years ago left Doc deeply wounded. When Doc would remember the words of the lost boy, his worst doubts about himself were confirmed and a cruel pain rose up in his heart. Then, Doc would collapse and cry hysterically. The first time Doc cried in front of Bar Jonah was when he told him that Zach was the balm that had soothed the wound from so long ago.

Doc thought he might have died before he lost interest in Zach. Two weeks before Zach vanished, Doc told Bar Jonah that he was thinking about taking Zach away. Doc had enough money saved up and Canada was just a couple of hours up the road. Doc and Zach could pack a few things in the car and make it look like they were just going up to Canada for the weekend; a special time away for a grandfather and grandson. There couldn't be suitcases and boxes in the car or a nosey border guard might become suspicious and ask questions that Doc would prefer not to have to answer. A couple of days before Doc lost Zach, he told Bar Jonah he was beginning to pack up a few of his dolls to take up to Canada with him. He couldn't take many, just a few of the special ones. Right before they were going to pull out Doc was going to open the back door of his house and turn his sixty cats loose on the neighborhood. His precious felines had served as his constant hedge against hopeless despair for so many years; it was time to give them their freedom. But unlike Doc's Tadzio of long ago, Doc knew his love for Zach was requited.

Doc said that Zach so wanted to go to Canada with him. They would probably be leaving in a few days. Zach was excited about the adventures that he and Doc were going to have; about starting his new life with Doc. Doc confided in Bar Jonah that it wouldn't be long 'til they'd be ready to go.

NOTES

Adams, D., personal communication, July, 2009.

Bar Jonah, N., personal communication, January, 2002–May, 2002.

Beljan, P., personal communication, January, 2002–May, 2002.

Bellusci, W., personal communication, June, 2009.

Brown, R., personal communication, April, 2002.

Brown, T., personal communication, April, 2002.

Cameron, J., personal communication, April, 2009–December, 2011.

Flaherty, P., personal communication, July, 2009.

Patterson, R., personal communication, June, 2009–August, 2009.

Gustovich, D., personal communication, August, 2009.

Hipskind, G., personal communication, June, 2009.

Howard, R., personal communication, May, 2009–June, 2010.

Howard, S., personal communication, October, 2009.

Kimmerle, D., personal communication, August, 2009.

Light, B., personal communication, April, 2009–12 June, 2012.

Metzger, M., personal communication, July, 2009.

Perkins, M., personal communication, August, 2010–November, 2011.

Richardson, M., personal communication, August, 2009.

Scott, L., personal communication, July, 2009.

Spamer, B., personal communication, August, 2010–June, 2012.

Theisen, T., personal communication, April, 2009–December, 2012.

Wilson, J., personal communication, June, 2009.

All trial related material is taken verbatim from trial transcripts or court related material in the public domain.

All poetry by Bar Jonah is a matter of the public record.

REFERENCES

Belkin, D. (2000). Cops Seek Other Child Victims in Cannibal Case/ City Horrified by Alleged Cannibal Case/Boy, 5, May Have Been Served to Neighbors. *Boston Globe*, December 31, p. 1. Available at: www.sfgate.com/news/article/Cops-Seek-Other-Child-Victims-in-Cannibal-Case-2718264.php#ixzz2HD9zrJLl.

Ceci, S., & Bruck, M. (1993). Child Witnesses: Translating Research into Policy. *Social Policy Report, 7*(3), Fall.

Dracula Has Risen from The Grave (1968). Dir. Freddie Francis. Perf. Christopher Lee, Rupert Davies. Hammer Film Productions.

Great Falls Tribune (1991). Letter testifying to the miracles of Jesus Christ. November.

Hamblen, S. (1954). *This Ole House*, released by EMI on the His Master's Voice label as catalogue numbers B 10761 and 7M 269.

Interview with Bar Jonah, Missing Children International Ministry, July 2005.

In the Name of Jesus All Things Are Possible (1749). Charles Wesley, Hymns and Sacred Poems, Volume II. http://www.hymntime.com/tch/htm/a/l/l/allthings.htm.

The Texas Chain Saw Massacre (1974). Dir. Tobe Hooper. Perf. Marilyn Burns, Edwin Neal. Vortex Films.

ABOUT THE AUTHOR

John C. Espy, PhD, LCSW, has been practicing psychotherapy and psychoanalysis for the past thirty-five years. He was supervised by R. D. Laing for many years and conducted a weekly supervision group with Sheldon Kopp. He has worked extensively in the area of primitive and psychotic personalities and has interviewed more than twenty serial murderers and pedophiles in the United States and Europe as part of his research on the manifestation of malignant projective-identification. His current practice primarily focuses on clinical and forensic consultation and long-term treatment. He was previously a neurotoxicologist with NASA and has taught at numerous universities throughout the United States. Dr. Espy is also a long-standing member of the *American Academy of Psychotherapists*, the *American Association for Psychoanalysis in Clinical Social Work*, and northwestern United States group moderator for the *International Neuropsychoanalysis Society*.